REHEATED CABBAGE

Reheated Cabbage

Tales of Chemical Degeneration

IRVINE WELSH

JONATHAN CAPE
LONDON

Published by Jonathan Cape 2009

2 4 6 8 10 9 7 5 3 1

First published in Great Britain in 2009 by
Jonathan Cape
Random House, 20 Vauxhall Bridge Road,
London SW1V 2SA

www.rbooks.co.uk

Addresses for companies within The Random House Group Limited
can be found at: www.randomhouse.co.uk/offices.htm

The Random House Group Limited Reg. No. 954009

A CIP catalogue record for this book is available from the British Library

ISBN 9780224080545
ISBN 9780224080552 (tpbk edition)

The Random House Group Limited supports The Forest Stewardship
Council (FSC), the leading international forest certification organisation.
All our titles that are printed on Greenpeace approved FSC certified paper
carry the FSC logo. Our paper procurement policy can be
found at www.rbooks.co.uk/environment

Typeset by Palimpsest Book Production Limited
Grangemouth, Stirlingshire

Printed and bound in Great Britain by
CPI Mackays, Chatham, Kent ME5 8TD

To Kris Needs

CONTENTS

ACKNOWLEDGEMENTS

Only one of these stories, 'I Am Miami', is new, in the sense of it not having been published before. Versions of the other stories have appeared in various publications over the years, most of which are now out of print in their original format – usually one of those toe-curling Scotsploitation or drugsploitation anthologies that prevailed in the nineties, for which I have to assume at least some culpability. Sorry about that.

My thanks go to the following: Harry Ritchie for 'A Fault on the Line' in *New Scottish Writing* (1997); Nick Hornby for 'Catholic Guilt' in *Speaking with the Angel* (2000); Richard Thomas for 'Elspeth's Boyfriend' in *Vox 'n' Roll: Fiction for the 21st Century* (2000); Kevin Williamson for 'Kissing and Making Up' in *Rebel Inc.* (1994) and 'The Rosewell Incident' in *Children of Albion Rovers* (1996); Richard Benson and Craig McLean, formerly of *The Face,* for running the serialised 'The State of the Party', and to Sarah Champion who subsequently published the entire story in *Disco Biscuits* (1997); Toni Davidson for 'Victor Spoils' in *Intoxication* (1998).

Thanks to Robin Robertson for encouraging me to review these stories and get this collection into print.

In late January, 2009, Janice Welsh and Kelly Docherty, two of the most loving and vivacious women I've known, died sudden, untimely deaths within a few days of each other. For me and many, many others, Edinburgh will never be quite the same again.

A Fault on the Line

As far as it went wi me it wis aw her ain fuckin fault. The cunts at the hoaspital basically agreed wi ays n aw, no that they said sae much, bit ah could tell they did inside. Ye ken how it is wi they cunts, they cannae jist come oot and say what's oan thir fuckin mind like that. Professional fuckin etiquette or whatever the fuck they call it. Well, seein as ah'm no a fuckin doaktir then, eh! Ah'd last aboot five fuckin minutes wi they cunts, me. Ah'll gie yis fuckin bedside manner, ya cunts.

Bit it wis her ain fault because she kent that ah wanted tae stey in fir the fitba this Sunday; they hud the Hibs–Herts game live oan Setanta. She goes, — Lit's take the bairns doon tae that pub it Kingsknowe, the one ye kin sit ootside ay.

— Cannae, eh, ah sais tae ur, — fitba's oan it two. Hibs fuckin Herts.

— Wi dinnae huv tae stey long, Malky, she sais, — it's a rerr day. It wid be nice fir the bairns.

So ah thinks tae masel, mibbe no too bad an idea but. Ah mean, ah hud ma bevvy in the fridge fir the game, bit a few scoops beforehand would set ays up nicely fir the kick-oaf. So ah sais, — Aye, awright then, but wir no steyin oot long, mind, the fitba's oan at two so wuv goat tae be back by then. So ah'm thinkin, lit hur git hur ain wey n it'll keep her fuckin trap shut for a bit.

So wi gits oot, n it wis a rare day n aw. Wi heads along tae the fuckin pub n wi starts gittin a few bevvies sunk back: her

3

oan the Smirnoff Ices n me oan the pints ay Stella. The bairns ur happy enough wi thair juice n crisps, even though ah hud tae batter him for pillin her hair whin the cheeky wee cunt thought ah wisnae lookin. Eh goat a shock awright whin ah gave um a fuckin wrap acroass the jaw. Ah sais, — Aye, n dinnae fuckin well burst oot greetin like a wee lassie, Jason, or yill fuckin well git another yin!

Anywey, ah've goat an eye oan the fuckin cloak, fir the fitba likes, but she's flingin thum back like fuck n whin ah tells ur it's time tae drink up n move, she starts giein ays fuckin grief. — Kin we no jist stey fir one mair? she's gaun, n ah'm gaun, — Awright, bit jist a fuckin quick yin, mind, then wi fuckin well Johnny Cash.

So ah fling back ma pint but she's fuckin well strugglin. That's her aw ower: thinks she kin fuckin well take a peeve, but she cannae handle it when it comes tae the fuckin big time. Ah jist tells her, — C'moan, we need tae fuckin nash. So ah nod tae the bairns n thir comin doon the road wi me, n she's laggin behind, the fuckin fat cow thit she is. That wis the main reason that it wis her fault; too fuckin well fat, the doaktir said it; he fuckin well telt the cunt, fuck knows how many times, eh. Ah'm shoutin, — C'moan!

Course, aw she kin dae is tae gie ays that fuckin look which gits ma fuckin goat.

— Git movin, n dinnae well pit that fuckin face oan, ah tells the cunt.

So wi gits intae Kingsknowe Station n ah goes, — Wi kin cut through here. She turns roond n starts walkin doon the platform tae thon overheid bridge. Ah goes, — C'moan tae fuck, ya radge, n jumps straight doon oantae the tracks, ken? She starts makin a fuckin exhibition ay hersel: gaun oan aboot the train comin, n ah should be able tae see that cause ay the people at the platform. — Aye, bit you're forgettin something,

4

ah goes, — ah used tae work for the railways. This wis before me n wee Tam Devlin goat the boot. The bevvy, ken? The cunts git as stroppy as fuck aboot that. Even a couple ay pints, that's you fuckin well snookered. N ah wisnae the fuckin worse, bit it wis scapegoatin, as the cunt fae the union pit it. No thit that did much fuckin good but, eh no.

— Bit it's comin! she sais. — Thir aw waitin oan it! Ah deeks at the fuckin cloak at the station n goes, — It's no due fir another five minutes yit! Moan tae fuck! Ah take wee Claire n lifts her doon oantae the track, n we go over n ah lift her up ontae the platform at the other side. The wee man, that wee cunt Jason, he's ower like a shot n she finally waddles oaf the fuckin platform doon oantae the track. Fuckin embarrassment that fat cunt.

So ah've goat wee Claire lifted oantae the platform, then ah hears this tinny noise and the track under ma feet starts tae vibrate. It sounds like one ay they InterCity non-stoapin joabs. Ah jist fuckin tipples: these cunts've been diverted tae here cause ay that flood damage oan the other line. Ah minded readin aboot that shite in the *News*. So ah'm up sharpish and ah'm sayin tae this fat cunt: — Gie's yir fuckin hand!

Well, ah grabs her mitt, bit the fuckin speed oan this InterCity joab, ah mean these cunts seem like thir gaunny rip the whole fuckin station apart the speed they go through it at, an wi her bein that fuckin hefty, well, ah managed tae sort ay half git her up oan the platform and she's screamin aboot the bairns and ah'm sayin the fuckin bairns ur awright, fuckin move, but the fuckin train comes along and it fuckin well hits her, n ah jist feels this force, pillin her, wrenchin her right ootay ma fuckin grip.

Well, ah fuckin well jist aboot shat masel, ah'm fuckin well tellin yis. Ah wis expectin her tae be in fuckin Aberdeen or somewhere like that, ken, bit she's only a few feet away fae ays

further doon the platform n she's lookin up at ays n shoutin,
— You, ya fuckin stupit cunt, at me, in front ay every cunt in
the station, eh. So ah'm tellin her tae shut her fuckin mooth
or she'll git ma fuckin boot right in it and tae git up oaf her
fat erse n git a fuckin bend oan n wee Claire's laughin n ah
looks at Jason and he's jist standin thaire frozen tae the fuckin
spot, eh, so ah'm aboot tae lamp the wee cunt whin ah look
doon at her n ah realise that she's goat nae fuckin legs; it's like
the fuckin train hud jist clean whipped thum oaf, n she's tryin
tae come taewards ays crawlin along the fuckin platform, pillin
hersel wi her flabby airms and thaire's this trail ay blood comin
fae her.

The radgest thing aboot it aw is that ah looks doon the
platform n ah sees the fuckin legs, jist sort ay severed fae her
boady. At the thigh, likes, eh, the baith ay thum. So ah shouts
at the wee cunt: — Jason! Dinnae jist fuckin stand thaire, pick
up yir ma's legs! Git a hud ay thum! Ah wis thinkin thit ye
could git thum tae the hoaspital n git thum stitched back oan.
The wee bastard jist starts greetin, right oot ay fuckin control.
Some cunt's shoutin tae git an ambulance, n she's lyin on the
groond cursin n ahm thinkin aboot the fuckin fitba, kick-oaf
in ten minutes' time. Bit then ah gits tae thinking thit the
ambulance'll maist likely huv tae go past oor bit oan its wey
up tae the hoaspital n ah could bail oot n catch up wi her
back up thaire, eftir the game, likes. So ah starts gaun, — Too
right, mate. A fuckin ambulance then, eh.

Wee Claire's went ower tae her ma's legs n she's picked thum
up, gathered thum in her airms and she's running taewards ays,
n ah lits that sneaky wee cunt Jason huv it, right acroas the
fuckin jaw, n eh fuckin well felt that yin cause that stoaps ehs
greetin right away. — You fuckin well should've goat they legs,
ya daft wee cunt, fuckin leavin it up tae yir wee sister! She's
only a bairn! How auld ur ye? Nine! Fuckin well act it!

This auld cunt's doon at her side hudin her hand and sayin, — Yir awright, it'll be fine, the ambulance is on its wey, try tae be still, n aw that shite. Another guy says tae me, — My God, this is terrible. Ah jist goes, — Fuckin well surein it is, probably missed the first two goals, eh. This nondy cunt comes up tae ays n sais, — I know you must be under terrible stress but it'll be okay. She's hanging in there. Try to comfort the children. Ah jist goes, — Aye, right ye are.

So ah sais tae the bairns, jist as the ambulance comes, — Yir ma's gaun tae the hoaspital fir a bit, bit thir's nowt wrong wi her.

— She's loast her legs, wee Claire goes.

— Aye, ah ken that, bit thaire's nowt wrong wi her, no really. Ah mean, aye, fir anybody else, anybody normal, likesay you or me, it wid be bad tae huv nae legs. Bit no fir yir ma cause she's that fat she widnae be able tae git roond oan her legs that much longer anywey, ken?

— Will Ma die? Jason asks.

— Ah dinnae ken. Ah'm no a fuckin doaktir, um ah? Dinnae ask such daft questions, Jason. What a laddie for fuckin questions! See, if she does, n ah'm no sayin thit she will, but see if she does, jist sayin, right? Jist supposin thit she wis tae die, n this is jist sayin, mind . . .

— Like pretend, wee Claire goes. Mair brains thin her fuckin ma, that yin.

— That's right, hen, jist pretend. So if she wis tae die, n mind, wir only jist sayin, it's up tae youse tae be good n no tae gie ays a hard time, cause ye ken what ah'm like when ah start gittin a hard time. Ah'm no sayin thit ah'm wrong n ah'm no sayin thit ah'm right; aw ah'm sayin is dinnae youse be giein ays a hard time at a time like this. Or yis git this, right? ah goes, clenchin ma mitt n shakin it at the wee cunts.

So by the time the ambulance boys manage tae lug her intae

the fuckin van, wi her fuckin weight, it'll be fuckin half-time. Ah takes the legs oaf the bairn n goes tae lob them in the back wi her, but this ambulance boy takes them n wraps them in polythene n sticks thum stump doon intae a bucket ay ice. We gets in the back wi her n the boy thit's drivin's waistin nae time. Wir near oor bit n ah sais, — Ah'll jist bail oot it the roundabout ahead, mate.

— Eh? the boy goes.

— Jist lit ays oaf here, ah sais.

— Wir no stoapin here, mate, we're no stoapin until we git tae the hoaspital. Nae time tae lose. You'll need tae register your wife and look after the kids here.

— Aye, right, ah goes, but ah wis still thinkin ahead. — Is thaire a telly oan the wards, mate? Bound tae be bit, eh?

This cunt jist looks at ays aw funny like n then goes, — Aye, thaire's a telly.

A fuckin wide cunt. Anywey, she's goat that oxygen mask ower her face n the guy's gaun oan tae her aboot tryin no tae talk n ah'm thinkin: some fuckin chance, ah've been tryin tae git her no tae talk fir fuckin years, eh. Hearin her n aw: gaun oan tae me like it's ma fuckin fault. It wis her wantin mair fuckin drink as usual, pished-up cow. Ah telt her, if ye spent as much time lookin eftir the fuckin bairns as ye did oan the fuckin pish, then they might no be so far behind at the school, especially that wee cunt Jason. Ah turns tae him n goes, — Aye, n dinnae think thit you're jist gaunny doss oaf the school, jist because yir fuckin ma might be in dock fir a few weeks. You'd better fuckin well shape up, son, ah'm tellin ye.

Sometimes ah think tae masel that ah'm giein the wee cunt too much ay a hard time. Bit then ah go: naw, cause ah goat it aw, the very fuckin same treatment fae ma auld man n it did me nae fuckin herm at aw. Cruel tae be kind, like they say.

N ah'm livin proof thit it's the best wey. Ah mean, ye nivir see me in any fuckin bother wi the polis, no since way back. Learned ma fuckin lesson: ah keep ma nose clean n ah gie they cunts a wide berth. Aw ah ask ootay life is a few bevvies, the fitba n the occasional ride.

That makes ays think bit: what's it gaunny be like ridin her if she's no goat any fuckin legs . . . ? So we gits up the casualty n this doaktir cunt's gaun oan aboot me bein in shock n ah'm thinkin aboot the fitba n if these cunts've scored awready ah'll be in fuckin shock awright. Ah turns tae the boy n goes, — Hi, mate, ken me n her, ken like whin wir thegither?

Cunt wisnae gittin ma drift.

— Ken in bed, likes? The cunt nods. — See, if she's no goat any fuckin legs, will ah still be able tae cowp it, likes?

— Sorry? this cunt goes.

Thick as fuck. A fuckin doaktir this is n aw. Thought ye hud tae huv fuckin brains tae dae that joab. — Ah'm talkin aboot oor sex life, ah tell um.

— Well, assuming your wife survives, your sex life should be normal, the cunt says, lookin at ays like ah wis some kind ay radge.

— Well, ah goes, — that's a bit ay fuckin good news, cause it wisnae fuckin well normal before! No unless ye call a ride every three fuckin months or something like that normal, n that's no what ah'd fuckin well call normal.

So thaire ah wis, tryin tae watch the fuckin game oan the waitin-room telly. Nae bevvy or nowt, n aw they radges hasslin ays wi forms n questions n the fuckin bairns playin up, gaun oan aboot is she awright, n when ur wi gaun hame n aw that shite. Ah fuckin well warned the wee cunts, see whin ah git youse hame, ah telt them.

Tell yis one thing fir nowt though: whin she's oot ay that hoaspital, see, if she cannae dae things aroond the hoose, ah'm fuckin offski. Too fuckin right, ya cunt. Lookin eftir ah fat cunt wi nae fuckin legs! That will be fuckin shinin bright! It wis her ain fault as well, the fuckin fat cunt. Fuckin things up fir me like that. No thit the game wis anything tae write hame aboot, mind you, another fuckin nil–nil draw bit, eh.

Catholic Guilt
(You Know You Love It)

It was a steaming, muggy day. The heat baked you slowly. My eyes were fuckin streaming from the pollutants in the air, carried around on the pollen. Nippy tears for souvenirs. Fuckin London. I used to like the sun and the heat. Now it was taking everything, sucking out my vital juices. Just as well something was. The lassies in this weather, the wey they dress. Fuckin torture, man, pure fuckin torture.

I'd been helping my mate Andy Barrow knock two rooms into one at his place over in Hackney and my throat was dry from graft and plaster dust. I'd come over a bit faint, probably because I'd hammered it a bit on the piss the last couple of nights. I decided to call it an early day. By the time I'd got back to Tufnell Park and up to my second-floor flat I felt better and in the mood to go out again. Nobody was home though; Selina and Yvette, they were both out. No note, and in this case no note is really a note which says: GIRLS' NIGHT OUT. FUCK OFF.

But Charlie had left me a message on the machine. He was as high as a kite. — Joe, she's had it. A girl. I'm down at the Lamb and Flag. Be there till about six. Come down if you get this in time. And get a fucking mobile, you tight Jock cunt.

Mobile my hole. I fuckin hate mobile phones. And the cunts that use them. The ugly intrusiveness of the strange voice: everywhere pushing their business in your face. The last time

I was in Covent Garden on a brutal comedown all those fuckin tossers were standing in the street talking to themselves. The yuppies are now emulating the jakeys; drinking outside in the street and blethering shite to themselves, or, rather, into those small, nearly invisible microphones connected to their mobiles.

But I didnae need too much persuasion tae head down there, no with this fuckin thirst on me. I nip out sharpish, breathless in the heat after a few yards, feeling the grime and fumes of the city insinuating itself intae me. By the time I get down to the tube station I'm sweating like the cheese on yesterday's pizza. Thankfully it's cooler doon here, at least it is until you get on that fuckin train. There's a couple of queers sitting opposite me; the camp, lisping type, their voices burrowing into my skull. I clock two sets of those dead, inhuman, Boy Scout eyes; a lot of poofters seem to have them. Bet ye these cunts have got mobile phones.

Makes me think back to a couple of months ago when Charlie and I were over at the Brewers in Clapham, in that fairy pub by the park. We went in, only because we were in the area and it was open late. It was a mistake. The poncing and flouncing around, the shrill, shrieking queer voices disgusted me. I felt a sickness build in my gut and slowly force its way into my throat, constricting it, making it hard for me to breathe normally. I grimaced at Charlie and we finished our drinks and left.

We walked over the Common in silent shame and embarrassment, the weakness of our curiosity and laziness oppressing us. Then I saw one of *them* coming towards us. I clocked a twist of that diseased mouth, fuck knows what that's had in it, and it was pouting at *me*. Those sick, semi-apologetic queer eyes seemed to look right into my soul and interfered with my essence.

That cunt, looking at me.

At me!

I just fuckin well lashed out. The pressure of my body behind the shot told me it was a good one. My knuckle ripped against queer teeth as the fag staggered back, holding his mouth. As I inspected the damage on my hand, relieved that the skin hadn't drawn blood and merged with plague-ridden essence of pansy, Charlie flew in, no questions asked, smacking the cunt a beauty on the side of his face and knocking him over. The poof fell heavily onto the concrete path.

Charlie's a good mate, you can always rely on that cunt tae provide backup, no that I needed it here, but I suppose that what ah'm sayin is that he likes to get involved. Takes an interest. Ye appreciate that in a cunt. We stuck the boot into the decked pansy. Groaning, gurgling noises escaped from his burst faggot mouth. I wanted to obliterate the twisted puppet features of the fairy, and all I could do was boot and boot at his face until Charlie pulled me away.

Charlie's eyes were wide and wired, and his mouth was turned down. — Enough, Joe, where's yer fucking head at? he reprimanded me.

I glanced down at the battered, moaning beast on the deck. He was well done. So aye, fair enough, I'd lost it awright, but I didnae like poofs. I told Charlie that, as we headed off across the park, swiftly into the dusky night, leaving that thing lying whining back there.

— Nah, I don't see it that way, he telt us, buzzing with adrenalin. — If every other geezer was a queer, it'd be an ideal world for me. No competition: I'd ave me pick orf all the skirt, wouldn't I?

Glancing furtively aroond, I felt we'd got away undetected. Darkness was falling and the Common seemed still deserted. My heartbeat was settling down. — Look at the fairy on the groond back thaire, I thumbed behind me as the night air cooled and soothed me. — Your bird's expecting a kid. Ye want some pervert like that teaching your kid in the classroom? Ye want that faggot brainwashing him that what *he* does is fucking normal?

— Come on, mate, you belted the geezer so I was in with ya, but I'm a live-and-let-live-type of cunt myself.

What Charlie didnae understand was the politics ay the situation; how those cunts were taking over everything. — Naw, but listen tae this, I tried to explain tae him. — Up in Scotland they want tae get rid of that Section 28 law, the only thing that stops fuckin queers like that interfering with kids.

— That's a load of old bollocks, Charlie said, shaking his head. — They didn't have no Section fucking nothing when I was at school, nor me old man, nor his old man. We didn't need it. Nobody can teach you who you want to fucking well shag. It's there or it ain't.

— What d'ye mean? I asked him.

— Well, you know you don't want to shag blokes, not unless you're a bit like that in the first place, he said, looking at me for a second or two, then grinning.

— What's that meant tae mean?

— Well, you Jocks might be different cause you wear fucking skirts, he laughed. He saw ah wisnae joking so he punched me lightly on the shoulder. — C'mon, Joe, I'm only pulling your leg, you uptight, narky cunt, he said. — We was out of order but we got a fucking result. Let's move on.

I mind that I wisnae that chuffed about this. There's certain things that ye dinnae joke about, even if ye are mates. I decided it was nothing though, and that I was just being a bit paranoid in case somebody might have seen us stomp the queer. Charlie was a great mate, a good old boy; we wound each other up a bit for a laugh, but that was as far as it went. Charlie was a fuckin sound cunt. So we did move on; to a late nightspot that he knew, and we thought no more about it.

It all comes back to me during this tube ride though. Just looking over at the nauseating pansies across fae me. Ughhh. My guts flip over as one of them gives me what seems to be a sly smile. I look away and try to control my breathing. My fingers dig into the upholstery of the seat. The two fairies get off at Covent Garden, which is ma fuckin stop. I let them go ahead and into the lift, which will take us up to street level. It's mobbed, and just being in such close vicinity of those arse bandits would make my skin crawl, so I elect to hold on for the next lift. As it is, I'm feeling sick enough when I get out and head for the Lamb and Flag.

I move up to the bar and Charlie's talking into his mobile phone. Twat. Seems to be with this lassie, who looks a bit familiar. He hasn't seen me come in. — A little girl. Four twenty this morning. Five pounds eleven. Both fine. Lily . . . He clocks me and breaks into a broad grin. I squeeze his shoulder and he nods over at the bird, who I instantly take to be his sister. — This is Lucy.

Lucy smiles at me, cocking her head to the side, presenting her cheek for a greeting kiss, which I'm happy to deliver. My first impression is that she's fuckin fit. Her hair is long and dark brown, and she has a pair of shades pushed up on top of her head. She wears blue jeans and a light blue top. My second impression (which should be contradictory) is that she looks like Charlie.

I knew Charlie had a twin sister, but I'd never met her before. Now she was standing with us at the bar and it was disconcerting. The thing was that she really *did* look like him. I could never, ever imagine a woman looking like Charlie. But she looked like him. A much slimmer, female, infinitely prettier version, but otherwise just like Charlie.

She smiles at me and gives me a sizing-up look. I suck in my beer gut. — You're the famous Joe, I take it? Her voice is high, a wee bit nasal, but a softer version of Charlie's south London twang. Charlie's south London accent is *so* south London that when I first met him I thought that he just had to be a posh cunt, trying it on.

— Aye. So you're Lucy then, I state in obvious approval, looking over towards Charlie, who's still blabbering into the mobby, then back to his sister. — Is everything okay?

— Yeah, a little girl. Four twenty this morning. Five pounds eleven.

— Is Melissa okay?

— Yeah, she had to work pretty hard, but at least Charlie was there. He went away during the contractions and –

Charlie's off the wobbly and we're hugging and he's gesturing for drinks as he takes up the tale. He looks happy, exhausted and a bit bewildered. — I was there, Joe! I just went out for a coffee, then I came back up and I heard them say, 'The head's coming,' so I thought I'd better get in there sharpish. Next thing I knew it was in me arms!

Lucy looks at him disapprovingly; her thick, black eyebrows are just like his. — *It* is a *she*. Lily, remember?

—Yeah, we're calling her Lily – Charlie's mobile rings again. He raises his eyebrows and shrugs. — Hi, Dave . . . Yeah, a little girl . . . Four twenty this morning . . . Five pounds eleven . . . Lily . . . Probably the Roses . . . I'll call yer in an hour . . . Cheers.

Just as he went to draw breath, the phone rang again.

— It's funny how we've never met, Lucy says, — because Charlie's always talking about you.

I think about this. — Yeah, he'd asked me to be best man at the wedding but my old man was pretty ill at the time and ah had tae go back up the road. Ah think it was better though, one of ehs mates fae the manor daein it, somebody that knew the family n that.

The old man pulled through okay. No that he was keen to see me in any case. He never forgave me for no going to our Angela's communion. Couldnae tell him but, couldnae tell him it was because of that priest cunt. No now. Too much water under the bridge. But that cunt'll get his one day.

— I dunno, might have been nice to have seen you in a kilt, she giggles. Laughter makes her face dance. I realise that she's a little drunk and emotional but she's actively flirting with me. Her resemblance to Charlie makes this unnerving, but strangely exciting. The thing is, I mind that cunt casting aspersions, just after we'd battered that poof on the Common. I'm now wondering how he'd feel if his sister and me got it on.

As Lucy and I chat to each other, I can sense Charlie picking up the vibe. He's still talking on the phone, but it's charged with urgency now; he's trying to end the conversations asap so he can work out what's going with us. I'll show that cunt. Casting aspersions. English bastard.

— Nigel . . . you heard. Good news travels fast. Four twenty this morning . . . A little girl . . . Five eleven . . . Both doing well . . . Lily . . . The Roses . . . Probably nine but I'll phone you in an hour. Bye, Nige.

I catch the barman's attention and signal for three Beck's and three Smirnoff mules. Charlie raises a brow. — Steady on, Joe, it's going to be a long night. We're going down the Roses tonight, to wet the baby's head.

— Sound by me.

Lucy pulls on my arm and says, — Me n Joe's started already.

I'm thinking that Charlie's done a good PR job on me cause I've as good as pulled his sister without saying a fuckin word. By the look on the poor cunt's face he thinks so as well; thinks he's done *too* good a job. — Yeah, well, I got to get back, he whines, get some things sorted out for Mel and the baby coming home tomorrow. I'll see you two later on down the Roses. Try not to get too sozzled.

— Awright, Dad, I say in a deadpan manner, and Lucy laughs, maybe a bit too loudly. Charlie smiles and says, — Tell ya wot, Joe, I could tell she was Millwall. She came out kicking!

I think about this for a second. — Call her Milly instead of Lily.

Charlie pushes down his bottom lip, raises his brow and rubs his jaw as if he's actively considering this. Lucy pushes him in his chest. — Don't you dare! Then she turns to me and says, — You're as bad as he is, you are, encouraging him! She's quite loud for a quiet pub and a few people turn round, but nobody's bothered, they know we're just enjoying a harmless high. I'm right into her now. I fancy her. I like the way she moved that one extra wee step forward into my space. I like the way she leans into you when she talks, the way her eyes dart about, how her hands move when she gets excited. Okay, it is an emotional time, but she's a banger, game as fuck, you can tell. I'm liking her more and more, and seeing less and less of Charlie in her as the drink takes effect. I like that mole on her chin; it's no a mole, it's a fuckin beauty spot, and her long, luxuriant, dark brown hair. Aye, she'll dae awright.

— See ya, Charlie goes. He gives me a bear hug, then breaks it and kisses and hugs Lucy. As he departs, the mobile goes off. — Mark! Hello! . . . A little girl . . . Four twenty . . . Sorry, Mark, you're breaking up a bit, mate, wait till I get outside . . .

Lucy and I leisurely finish our drinks before deciding to move on. We're off around the West End and go down Old Compton Street and, as usual, the place is teeming with arse bandits. Everywhere you look. I'm disgusted, but I say nowt to her. It's almost obligatory for a bird in London to have a fag mate these days. A loyal accessory for when the real man in her life fucks off. Cheaper than a dog and you don't have to feed it or take it for walks. Mind you, you don't have to listen to an Alsatian lisping and bleating doon the phone that its Border collie partner sucked off a strange Rottweiler in the local park.

Dirty fuckin . . .

I get up off the stool and have to sit down again for a bit cause I feel faint. My heartbeat's racing and there's a pain in my chest. I'll have to take things easier; drinking heavily in this heat always fucks me.

— You okay, Joe? Lucy asks.

— Never better, I smile, composing myself. But I'm thinking about how I had to sit down for a bit earlier today, over at Andy's. I picked up the sledgehammer and was itching to let fly at his wall. Then I felt this kind of spasm in my chest and I honestly thought I was going to pass out. I sat down for a bit and I was fine. Just been caning it a bit lately. That's what being single again does for you.

I get up and I'm a bit edgy in the next pub, but I concentrate on Lucy, blacking out all the queer goings-on around us. We have another couple of beers, then decide to go for a pizza at Pizza Express to soak up some of the booze. — It's weird that we haven't met before, you being one of Charlie's closest mates – Lucy considers.

— And you being his twin, I interject. — Tell ye what though, you're a lot better looking than him.

— So are you, she says, with a cool, evaluating stare. We look at each other across the table for a couple of seconds. Lucy's quite a skinny lassie, but she's got a bust on her. That never fails to impress, that one: substantial tits on a skinny bird. Never ceases to cause me to take a deep breath of admiration. She takes her shades from her head and sweeps her hair back out of her eyes in that Sloaney gesture which, for all its camp, let's face it, never fails to get the hormones racing. No that she's a posh bird or nowt like that, she's just a salt-of-the-earth type, like her brother.

Charlie's sister.

— I think that's what's called an awkward silence, I smile.

— I don't want to go to Lewisham, Lucy says to me with a toothy grin, as she stoops forward in the chair. She's sitting on her hands, to stop them flying about, I think. She's quite expressive that way – they were fairly swooping around in that last pub.

But aye, fuck south London the now. — Nah, I'm no that bothered either. I'm enjoying it with just the pair of us, to be honest.

Then she says to me, — You don't say very much but when you do it's really sweet.

I think of the smashed poof in the park and clench my teeth in a smile. Sweet talk. — You're sweet, I tell her.

Sweet talk.

— Where do you stay? she quizzes, raising her eyebrows.

— Tufnell Park, I tell her. I should say more, but there isnae any point. She's doing fine for the both of us, and I sense that I can only talk myself out of a shag right now, and I'm no about tae dae that. Not with the way my sex life's been lately.

It's a bummer sharing a gaff with two fit birds and no going oot wi anybody. Everybody says, lucky bastard, but it's sheer torture. But I find that the more you say that you're not shagging either of them, the less inclined people are to believe you. I feel like that *Man About the House* cunt.

Aye, ah could dae wi a ride.

So could she, by the sound ay things. — Let's get a cab, Lucy urges.

In the taxi I kiss her on the lips. In my celibate paranoia I'm expecting them to be cold and tight, like I've misread the signs, but they're open, warm and lush, and before I know it we're eating each other's faces. The snatches of conversation when we come up for air reveal that we're both in the process of getting over other people. We urgently rap out those monologues, both knowing that if we weren't so close to Charlie we wouldn't have bothered, but in the circumstances it seems only manners to be up to speed with each other's recent history. But whether we're really over our exes or not, it's nae bother: rebound rides are better than okay if celibacy is the only alternative.

I remember with satisfaction and relief that I recently visited the launderette and washed a new duvet, which I've got on my bed. So when we get back to mines I'm delighted that Selina and Yvette are both still out and I don't have to go through tiresome introductions. We shoot straight through to the bedroom and I'm fucking one of my best mate's twin sister. I'm on top of her and she's chewing her bottom lip, like . . . like Charlie when we were in Ibiza last year. We'd pulled these two lassies from York and we were riding them back in the room, and I looked over and saw Charlie biting his lower lip in concentration. Her eyes, her brows, so like his.

It's putting me off, I can feel myself going a bit soft.

I pull out and gasp, — From behind now.

She turns over, but she doesn't get up on her knees, just lies flat and smiles wickedly. I wonder for a second whether or not she wants it up her arse. I'm not into that. She looks good though, and I am rock hard again, the troubling Charlie associations all gone from my nut. All I can see is that long hair, slender body and peach of an arse, spread out before me. I struggle to push in to her fanny, trying to keep some of my weight on my arms as I thrust into her.

It's going in though, and soon we're fucking away again for all we're worth. Lucy gives the odd appreciative groan, without making a big fuss. I like that. I'm looking at a spot on the headboard to avoid getting too turned on and blowing early, it's been a while and I . . .

I'm feeling . . .

WHOOSH . . .

PHOAH . . .

OH . . .

OOOOHHH . . .

No . . .

I think I've blown it there for a bit, the room seems to darken and spin, but I come to my senses and we're still at it.

The strange thing is that I'm suddenly aware that her dimensions seem to have changed. Her body is like it's rounder and fuller. And she's quiet now, it's as if she's passed out.

And . . . there's somebody in the bed next to us!

It's Melissa! Charlie's wife, and she's asleep. I look at Lucy, but it *isn't* Lucy. It's Charlie: I am . . . I am . . . I am fucking Charlie up his arse . . .

I AM FUCK –

A spasm of horror shoots through me, the rigidness going from my erection to my body. My cock instantly goes limp, as God's my witness, and I pull out, sweating and trembling.

I realise, to my further shock, that I'm not at home any more. I am in Charlie's flat.

WHAT THE FUCK IS THIS . . . ?

I slide out of the bed. I look around. Charlie and Melissa seem to be in a deep sleep. There's no sign of Lucy. I can't find my clothes, all my gear has gone. Where the fuck is this? How the fuck did I get here?

I grab a smelly old Millwall top with *South London Press* on it and a pair of jogging trousers that lie in a heap on a laundry basket. Charlie likes to run, he's a fitness fanatic. I look at him back there, still dozing, out for the count.

I pull on the clothes and go through to the front room. This is Charlie and Melissa's place alright. I can't think straight, but I know I have to get out of there fast. I promptly leave the flat and I run like fuck through the streets of Bermondsey until I get to London Bridge. I head to the tube station but I realise that I have no money. So I trot over London Bridge towards the city.

My head is buzzing with the obvious questions. What the fuck has happened? How did I get to south London? To Charlie's bed? To Char – it's obvious that my drink was spiked in some way, but who the fuck set me up? I can't remember!

I CANNAE FUCKIN REMEMBER!

I'M NO AN ARSE BANDIT!

That fuckin Lucy. She's a weirdo. But no her brother, surely no. Me and Charlie . . . I can't believe it.

I can't . . .

But the strangest thing is that just when I ought to be fuckin suicidal, I am, in spite of myself, settling into this weird calmness. I feel tranquil, but strangely ethereal; somehow disassociated from the rest of the city. Although I'm still at a loss to work out what has happened, it all seems secondary, because I am cocooned in this floaty bubble of bliss. I must be daydreaming, as I cross the road at the Bishopsgate, because I don't see a cyclist come careering into me . . .

FUCKIN . . .

WHOOSH . . .

Then there's a flash and a ringing in my ears and miraculously I am standing at Camden Lock. There is absolutely no sense of any impact having taken place with the boy on the bike. Something is up here, but I'm not bothered. That is the thing. I feel fine, I don't care. I head up Kentish Town Road, towards Tufnell Park.

The door of my flat is locked and I have no keys. The girls

might be in. I go to rap at the door, and bang – a whoosh of air in my ears and I am standing inside the living room. Yvette is ironing, while watching the television. Selina is sitting on the couch, skinning up a joint.

— I could handle some of that, I say. — You're no gaunny believe the night I've had . . .

They ignore me. I speak again. No reaction. I walk in front of them. No recognition.

They can't see or hear me!

I go to touch Selina, to see if I can elicit some response, but then I pull my hand away. It might break the spell. There is something exciting, something empowering, about this invisibility.

But there is something wrong with the pair of them. They seem in as much shock as I am. It must have been some night they've had as well. Aye, girls: we pay for our fun.

— I still can't believe it, Yvette says. — A bad heart. Nobody knew he had a bad heart. How can something like that not be picked up?

— Nobody knew he had *any* heart, Selina snorts. Then she shrugs, as if in guilt. — That's not fair . . . but . . .

Yvette looks sharply at her. — You fucking cold cow, she hisses in anger.

— Sorry, I . . . Selina starts, before slapping her forehead in confusion. — Oh fuck, I'm going to take a shower, she suddenly decides and leaves the room.

I opt to follow her into the bathroom, to watch her take her clothes off. Yes. I'm going to enjoy this invisibility lark. Just as she starts to undress . . .

WHOOSH . . .

I'm not in the bathroom any more. I am pumping away . . . yes . . . ye-es . . . I'm fucking somebody . . . they're starting to come into focus . . .

It must be Lucy, it was all some fuckin daft hallucination, some acid flashback or the like, it was all . . .

But no . . .

NO!

I am on top of my mate Ian Calder, shagging him up his arse. He is unconscious, and I am giving him one. I can see we are on the couch in his house back in Leith. I am back up in Scotland, shagging one of my oldest pals up his fuckin hole, like I'm some kind of queer rapist!

OH NO, MY GOD . . . NO IN FUCKIN SCOT-LAND . . .

I feel as if I'm going to throw up all over him. I withdraw, as Ian starts to make those delirious sounds, like he's having a bad dream. There is blood on my cock. I pull up the bottoms on my tracksuit and run out the house into the street.

I am in Edinburgh, but nobody can see me. I am going mad as I run screaming, up Leith Walk, down Princes Street, trying to avoid people. But as I pick up speed on the corner of Castle Street I collide with this old woman and a Zimmer frame . . .

Then . . .

WHOOSH . . .

I am in a prison cell, but I am fuckin well shagging this guy up his arse. He lies unconscious on the bed underneath me.

OH FOR FUCK SAKE . . .

It's my old buddy Murdo. He's inside for dealing coke.

YUK . . .

I pull out and jump down from the top bunk. I am sick, but in dry, racking coughs, holding myself against the cell wall. Nothing will come up. I look about as Murdo comes to, his face twisted in pain and confusion. He turns round, touches his arse, sees the shit and blood on his fingers and starts screaming. He jumps down, and I start to shout, crippled with fear: — I can explain, mate . . . it's no what it seems . . .

But Murdo ignores me and moves over to his sleeping cell mate in the lower bunk, launching into a savage attack on the poor cunt. His fist thrashes into the startled jailbird's face. — YOU, AH KEN YOU! YOU DID SOMETHING TAE ME! AH KEN YOU! YA DIRTY FUCKIN SICK BUFTIE BASTARD! YA FUCKIN BEAST!

— AAGGHH! IT'S HOOSEBREKIN AH'M IN FIR – the boy protests through his shock.

WHOOSHHH . . . The guy's screams fade as I am . . .

I am standing in a chapel of rest, at the back of the hall. The crematorium; Warriston, or Monktonhall, or the Eastern. I dinnae ken, but they are all there; my ma n dad, my brother Alan and my wee sister Angela. In front of the coffin. And I know, straight away, just who is inside that coffin.

I am at my ain fuckin funeral.

I'm screaming at them: what is this, what's happening to me?

But again, nobody can hear me. No, that's no quite right. There's one fucker who seems to be able to; this fat old boy with white hair, who's wearing a dark blue suit. He gives me the thumbs up. The old cunt seems to have a glow about him, with shards of incandescent light emanating from him.

I move across to him, completely invisible to the rest of the congregation, just as he seems to be. — You . . . you can hear me. You ken the Hampden Roar here. What the fuck is this?

The old guy just smiles and points at the coffin at the front of the mourners. — Nearly late for yir ain fuckin funeral thaire, mate, he laughs.

— But how? What happened tae me?

— Aye, ye died when you were on the job with your mate's sister. Congenital heart problem you didn't even know about.

Fuck me. I wis mair ill than I thought. — But . . . who are you?

— Well, the old boy grins, — I'm what you'd call an angel. I'm here to assist you in your passage over to the other side. He coughs, raising his hand to his face, stifling a laugh. — Pardon the pun, he chuckles. — I've had all sorts of names in different cultures. It might help you tae think of me as one of the ones I'm least fond of: St Peter.

The confirmation ay my death induces in me a bizarre elation, and no small relief. — So I'm deid! Thank fuck for that! It means I never shagged my mates up the arse. Ye hud me worried for a bit there!

The old angel cunt shakes his heid slowly and grimly. — You're not over to the other side yet.

— What d'ye mean?

— You're a restless spirit, wandering the Earth.

— How come?

— Punishment. This is your penance.

I'm no having this. — Punishment? Me? What the fuck have ah done wrong? I ask the bastard.

The auld guy smiles like a double-glazing salesman who's about tae tell me there's nowt they can dae aboot their crappy installation. — Well, Joe, the truth is that you're not a bad guy, but you have been a bit misogynistic and homophobic. So your punishment is to make you walk the Earth as a homosexual ghost buggering your old mates and acquaintances.

— No way! No way am ah gaunny dae that! You cannae fuckin well make me . . . I say, lamely tailing off as I realise that the sick old bastard has been doing exactly that.

— Aye, this is your punishment for being a queer basher, the angel gadge smiles again. — I'm going to watch and laugh at you being crippled with guilt. Not only am I going to make you do it, Joe, I'm going to make you *keep* doing it until you enjoy it.

— No way. You must be fuckin joking. I'll never enjoy that.

I point at myself. — Never! You cunt . . . I spring at the bastard, ready to throttle him, but in another swish of sound and flash of light he's gone.

I sit at a vacant seat at the back of the chapel, my head in my hands. I look around at the congregation. Lucy has come up for it, she's sitting quite close to me. That's nice of her. Must've been a fuckin shock for her. One minute you've a stiffer inside ye, the next it's just a stiff. Charlie's there too, he's with Ian and Murdo at the back of the hall.

They are all standing up.

Then I see him. That dirty old cunt of a priest.

Father Brannigan. Him, putting me to rest! That filthy, evil auld cunt!

I'm looking over at my parents, screaming silently at them for this appalling betrayal. I mind of me saying to them, I dinnae want tae be an altar boy any mair, Ma, and my mother being so disappointed. My old man never gave a fuck. Let the laddie dae what eh wants, he said. But when I didnae come tae our Angela's communion and I couldnae tell them why . . .

Aw fuck . . . that dirty old cunt touching me, and worse, making me do things to him . . .

I never would, never *could* say. Never. Never even thought about it. I always vowed he'd fuckin well get it one day. Now he's here, he's sending me off, his pious lies ringing throughout this chapel.

— Joseph Hutchinson was a kind, sensitive, young Christian man, taken untimely from us. But, through our grief and loss, we should not fail to remember that God has a plan, no matter how obscure this may seem to we mortals. Joseph, who once served at the altar of this very house of the Lord, would have understood this divine truth more than most of us . . .

I want to roar the truth at them all, to tell them what that dirty old cunt did tae me . . .

WHOOSHHHH . . .

Then I'm on auld Brannigan and he's screaming under my weight; his old skinny, smelly bones, crushed under my bulk. I'm giving it to the dirty old cunt; pummelling him right up his arse and he's screaming. I'm snarling in demented rage: — You cannae tell anybody, or God will punish you for being a sinner, and I'm fucking him and fucking him harder and harder. He's screeching beyond agony and bang! . . . his heart stops, I feel it stop as his last breath escapes him. Brannigan's body judders underneath me and his eyes roll towards heaven. I feel his essence rise up through his body and through mine, planting a thought into my psyche that says YOU CUNT as he floats away, a soundless cry coming from his spirit like a balloon farts out air as it flies into space.

I'm sobbing and crying to myself, saying over and over again in my self-disgust, — When will it be over? When will this nightmare end?

— WHOOSH . . .

And then I'm with my best mate Andy Sweeney; we grew up together, did almost everything together. He was always more popular than me – better looking, brighter, good job – but he was my best mate. As I said, we did everything together – well, almost everything. But now I'm on top of him and I'm shagging the arse off him . . . and it's horrible. — WHEN, I'm screaming, — WHEN WILL THIS FUCKIN NIGHTMARE END?

And he's in the room with us, the auld St Peter boy from the funeral. He's just sitting in the armchair watching us in a studied, detached manner. — When you start to enjoy it, when you cease to feel the guilt, that's when it'll end, he tells me coldly.

So there I am shagging my best mate up his arse. God, am I feeling disgusted and crippled with revulsion, loathing and guilt . . .

. . . feeling sick and ugly, in constant torture as I am compelled to pump away like a rancid fuck machine from hell, feeling like my soul is being ripped apart . . .

. . . going to a place beyond fear, humiliation and torture, and hating it, loathing it, detesting it so fuckin much . . . a pain so great and pervasive that I'll never, ever grow to feel anything other than this sheer horror . . .

. . . or so I keep telling that daft cunt of an angel.

Elspeth's Boyfriend

Thaire's some cunts thit ye hit it oaf wi, n some cunts thit ye dinnae. Take Elspeth's boyfriend fir example; a right fuckin case-in-point, that yin. Ah mean, ah'd nivir even met the cunt until Christmas Day, but aw wi'd goat fi the auld lady leadin up tae it wis 'Greg this' n 'Greg that' n 'eh's an awfay nice laddie'.

So that gits ye thinkin tae yirself, right away: aw aye?

Christmas, eh. Some cunts lap it but tae me it's a load ay shite. Too commercialised. It's usually just the faimlay for us. But ah've fuckin moved in wi ma burd Kate, oor first festive season thegither. We hud a big row aboot it n aw; mind you, ye eywis dae at Christmas. Wouldnae be a fuckin Christmas withoot every cunt gittin oan each other's nerves.

As ye kin fuckin guess, she's moanin thit wir gaun tae muh ma's instead ay hers. The thing is thit ma brar Joe n ehs wife Sandra n thair two wee bairns n ma sister Elspeth wid be thaire. Tradition n that. That's what ah telt Kate, ah eywis go tae ma auld girl's at Christmas. That cow ah used tae be wi, that June, she's takin the bairns tae *her* auld lady's. No thit it bothers me, but it means thit muh ma'll no see thum at Christmas. That's June but; fill ay fuckin spite.

Ye cannae fuckin win wi burds at Christmas. Aye, Kate wis aw humpty n aw. She goes, well, you go tae your ma's n ah'll go tae ma faimly's. Ah sais tae her, dinnae start gittin fuckin wide, wir gaun tae muh ma's n that's that. Dinnae try n snub ma auld girl.

So that wis that settled. Nearer the time ah gits oantae the auld lady, askin her when she wants us roond. She gies ays aw this, 'Oh lit me see, when did Elspeth say thit her n Greg wir gaunny come roond again . . . ?'

Well, ye git the fuckin picture. By the time it's Christmas Day, me n Joe've hud wir fuckin fill ay Elspeth's boyfriend, this fuckin Greg cunt or whatever they call um. Ah'd been oot oan the pish aw Christmas Eve wi some ay the boys, n Joe wis in the same boat, ye could see it fae the cunt's eyes, he wis fucked n aw. Aye, it goat fuckin well messy that night. Lines ay charlie racked up every five minutes; boatils n boatils ah champagne bein guzzled. That tae me's what Christmas is aw aboot, jist littin yirsel go. Specially the champagne; ah love that stuff, could quaff it till the cows come hame. Must be the aristocrat n ays. Blue fuckin blood.

Ye suffer the next day but, no half ye fuckin dinnae.

So that Christmas mornin, me n hur huv this big argumint again. Ma heid is fuckin nippin, n ma sinuses feel like some cunt's went n poured a load ay concrete intae them. Tryin tae git ready tae go roond tae muh ma's hoose, n feelin like that, she asks ays, — What dae ye think ah should wear the day, Frank?

Ah jist looks at her n goes: — Clathes.

That shuts ur fuckin mooth fir ah bit.

Then ah sais, — How the fuck should ah ken?

She looks at ays n goes, — Well, should ah git aw dressed up?

— Wear whit ye fuckin like, ah telt ur, — ah'm no gittin aw trussed up like a fuckin turkey jist tae sit peevin n watchin the telly roond at muh ma's. Levi's, Ben Sherman n Stone Island cardy, that'll dae fir me.

So that seems tae satisfy hur, n she pits oan this sports gear. Casual but quite smart, ken?

Aye, ah kin tell a mile away thit she's taken the fuckin strop, but. Ah jist think, well, if she wants tae be aw antisocial this Christmas, that's fuckin well up tae her.

Wi heads doon the road n gits tae the auld girl's. Joe n that wis awready thaire.

— Aye aye, Franco, that Sandra goes tae me.

— Aye, ah goes. Nivir saw eye tae eye wi her. Too much ah a mooth oan it. Dinnae ken how oor Joe kin be daein wi that. His choice but. Widnae fuckin well be mine anywey. At least her n Kate git oan, n that's a good thing, cause it keeps the bairns oaf Joe's back n lits us git a peeve in peace. Ah gits a can ay Rid Stripe open. Ah'm gaunny git fuckin well hammered; it's what Christmas is aw aboot.

Wi firin intae the lagers awright. Wir jist sittin thaire, thinkin through oor hangovers, 'if this cunt Greg or whatever ye call the boy, if eh starts gittin wide, eh's gaunny git a fuckin bat in mooth, Christmas or nae fuckin Christmas.'

Eftir a bit the door goes, n it's Elspeth. This tall, dark-heided cunt wi a side partin comes in behind her. Eh's aw done up tae the nines in a smart coat n suit – ye kin tell that this cunt really fancies ehsel. What goat me wis the side partin. Ken how some things jist git oan yir fuckin nerves fir nae reason? Bit then what *really* wound ays up wis thit eh wis cairryin a bunch ay flooirs. Flooirs, oan fuckin Christmas Day! — For you, Val, eh goes tae the auld girl, giein her a wee peck oan the cheek. Then the cunt comes up tae me n goes, — You must be Frank, n eh pits ehs hand oot.

Ah'm thinkin, aye, who the fuck wants tae ken, likes, but ah lit it go, cause ah didnae want tae cause a scene. Jist didnae take tae this smarmy poof at aw but, ye ken how it is wi some people? Try as ye might, ye jist cannae fuckin well take tae thum.

But ah bites the bullet n shakes the cunt's hand, thinkin, Christmas n that, the season ay goodwill.

— Good tae meet ye finally, eh sais. — Elspeth talks about ye a lot. In very glowing terms, I should add, the cunt goes.

Ah feel like asking the cunt what the fuck eh's oan aboot, is eh tryin tae git wide or what, but eh's turned away n eh's ower tae Joe. — And you must be Joe, eh goes.

— Aye, sais Joe, shakin ehs hand, but no gittin up oot the chair. — So you're oor Elspeth's felly then, aye?

— I certainly am, eh smiles, at her, n ah catch um giein her hand a squeeze. She's lookin aw that daft wey at um, like she's nivir been oot wi a gadge before.

— Love's young dream, that Sandra goes, cooin away, like one ay they big fat fuckin pigeons thit the auld man used tae keep. Ah mind ay wringin a couple ay the cunts' necks eftir eh'd battered ays once. The best thing tae dae wi they cunts, though, is tae set thum oan fire. It's barry watchin thum tryin tae take oaf, whin thir blazin away n screamin in agony. Ah'll gie yis fuckin cooin, ya cunts.

Sometimes ah used tae jist go doon tae the loft oan ehs allotment and burn a couple ay the bastards thaire, or git yin n nail it tae the hut. Jist tae see the expression oan the auld fucker's face when eh came hame, aw pished n upset. Blamed every cunt n aw; vandals, gyppos, neighbours, publicans. Wanted tae kill half ay fuckin Leith. Ah'd be sittin thair in the chair opposite, lookin aw innocent, jist gaun, — Ohhh . . . which one wis it they goat this time, Dad? N he'd be fuckin well jist aboot in tears. The cunt wid smash up the hoose in a fit ay rage, before hittin the boozer again. Come tae think ay it, it wis probably me that drove the cunt tae drink! Him n ehs fuckin daft pigeons.

That fuckin Sandra. Nivir mind the fuckin turkey, stick that fat cunt in the oven n wi'll be feedin half ay fuckin Leith through until next Christmas. Ah dinnae ken aboot stuffin it but, ah'll no be volunteerin fir they fuckin duties anywey. Nae fuckin chance!

So this big, bloated rooster's right up tae Elspeth's boy. — Ah'm Sandra, Joe's wife, she sais tae this Greg, aw that flirty, slutty wey.

This cunt goes up and kisses her twice, once oan each cheek, like some fuckin weirdo. Ah dinnae hud wi that, kissin a woman ye dinnae ken, in somebody's hoose. At Christmas, at a fuckin faimlay gatherin. Aye, ah'm watchin Kate, thinkin thit if eh does that tae her, eh's fuckin well gittin the nut rammed oan um. Fuckin smarmy poof.

But she sees me lookin at her, n she kens how tae behave. Goat her well fuckin trained. Aye, *she* kens no tae show ays up. Must huv a word wi Joe aboot that Sandra, embarrassin um like that. Ah ken that big cow; a leopard nivir fuckin well changes its spoats, right enough. Used tae call her the 32 bus, back in the day. That wis cause every cunt rode her roond the schemes. Still, it's no fir me tae say. So Kate pits her hand oot for him tae shake, n keeps her eyes doon, away fae his. — Ah'm Kate, she mumbles.

Handled that yin well. Aye, mibbe the message aboot eggin boys oan is startin tae git through. Jist as fuckin well, fir her sake. The wey ah see it is thit whin a lassie's wi somebody, she's no meant tae be giein other boys the come-on aw the time. Ye cannae trust a fuckin cow like that, n yuv goat tae huv trust in a relationship.

This Greg looks aw surprised, n gies a wee smile. Somethin creepy aboot that bastard. Ken how some cunts jist set yir fuckin teeth oan edge? The fucker reminds ays ay that cunt ay an insurance man thit used tae come roond oor bit whin wi wir bairns. Eh'd eywis gie us these sweeties; really crap yins like dolly mixtures, aw that cheap shite. Aye, ye could tell he wis a fuckin right oily cunt underneath it aw. Ah eywis took the sweeties oaf the cunt, but. Too fuckin right ah did. Nivir liked that fucker though.

The auld girl's been in the kitchen aw mornin, workin oan the meal. Her face is aw rid. She likes tae make a big effort fir Christmis. Widnae be me anywey. Fuck slavin ower a hoat stove oan Christmas Day. Ye cannae work oot what's gaun oan in some cunts' heids but. Now she's tryin tae organise every cunt; makin a big fuss aboot us aw openin oor presents under the tree. Ah'm no bothered wi aw that shite. Whae cares aboot fuckin presents? As far as clathes n aw that goes, ah've goat the money tae git what the fuck ah want. Ye like tae git what you want tae wear, no what some other cunt wants tae gie ye. Ay gied the burd two hundred quid fir clathes, n muh ma the same. Then ah gied Joe a hundred tae git somethin fir the bairns, n fifty bar tae oor Elspeth for whatever she wanted. The only presents ah goat wis fir ma ain bairns. That wis only because ah kent thit if ah gied June the money tae git thum somethin, like a fuckin PlayStation or a bike, they'd end up wi some plastic shite fae Ali's Cave. Aye, the rest wid go oan fuckin snout fir her. So that wis aw. The rest ay thum, it wis jist: here's yir fuckin Christmis present offay me, jist git what the fuck ye want.

It's the best fuckin wey. Aw that fuss aboot wrappin fuckin presents up? Ah couldnae be daein wi that. Fuck wrappin presents.

Rap some cunt's fuckin jaw.

Ah'm lookin ower at that Kate. Two hundred fuckin bar fir clathes ah gied her, n she comes intae muh ma's dressed like a fuckin frump, showin ays up. Oor Elspeth's made an effort, she's goat a nice black perty dress oan, aw fir that smarmy Greg cunt n aw. Even that fuckin cow Sandra hus. Mingin auld fuckin hen done up as spring chicken, mind, but at least shi's fuckin well tried. Kate but; a fuckin jaikey on Christmis Day! In muh ma's hoose n aw!

Thir aw makin a big fuckin fuss aboot presents. It's 'ooh, this is lovely' n 'oooh, it's jist what ah eywis wanted'. Then thir aw at me tae open mine, so ah jist thinks, might as well, keep the cunts happy. If it fuckin well means that much tae thum. Ah gits a blue pastel-coloured Ben Sherman oaffay Kate, n a yellaw Ben Sherman offay Joe n Sandra. In ma auld girl's parcel thaire's another Ben Sherman, a black, broon n light blue striped yin. Ah think ah must've asked fir Ben Shermans offay every cunt; mind you, ye cannae go wrong wi shirts. Thaire's one left, marked oan the gift tag: *To Francis, from Elspeth and Greg. Merry Christmas.*

It feels like another fuckin Ben Sherman, but whin ah rips it open it's a sweater wi the new club crest oan it.

— That's nice, muh mother sais. Elspeth goes, — Aye, it's the new yin. It's goat the original Harp crest, wi the ship for Leith, n the castle fir Edinburgh. Thir smilin at ays, n it gits right oan ma fuckin tits. Tryin tae take the fuckin pish here. Tae me, whin ye buy some cunt official club merchandise, it's like you sayin tae thum thit ye think thir a fuckin wanker. Ah widnae be seen deid wearin that shite. That's fir fuckin wee bairn n fuckin dippit cunts, that. — Ta, ah goes, but through gritted teeth, ken?

Ah'm thinkin, that's gaun right in the bucket whin ah git hame, tell ye that fir nowt.

Ye kin understand it if it wis Elspeth thit made the mistake. Ah mean, that's birds fir ye. But if that Greg cunt wis in oan buyin it, it means thit eh wis tryin tae take the pish. Ah'm fuckin well fumin at that disrespect, so tae stoap masel fae sayin somethin ah shouldnae, ah go ben the scullery tae git another can fae the fridge. Then ah'm thinkin thit that Greg's such a big fuckin lassie ehsel, he probably disnae huv a fuckin clue either.

Ma heid's still nippin n ah swallay a couple ay extra-strength Anadin wi a moothfae ay beer. Whin ah gits back ah sees this fuckin Greg cunt's playin away wi Joe's bairns, oan the fuckin flair wi aw thair toys. Meant tae be the fuckin bairns' new toys, no fir some big pansy tae ponce aroond wi. Ah pills Joe aside n back intae the kitchen, n goes — Ye want tae watch that cunt aroond the bairns. Touch ay the fuckin Gary Glitters thaire, ah'll tell ye that fir nowt.

— Ye reckon? Joe sais, pittin ehs heid roond the door tae check it oot.

— Defo. Ye ken how fuckin plausible they cunts kin be. That's the thing. Ah'd lay ye even money thit that cunt's oan the stoats' register. Ye kin spot the type a mile away.

Muh ma sees us n comes ben. — What are you two oan aboot, standin here in the kitchen drinkin like fishes?! Git oot thaire n try n be social, it's meant tae be Christmas!

— Right, Ma, ah goes, lookin at Joe. That Greg cunt might huv brainwashed her, that's wimmin fir ye, no goat much brains tae fuckin wash in the first place, bit Joe n me huv been aroond long enough tae see right through a cunt like that.

Best keepin the auld lady fuckin sweet but, or shi'll huv a coupon oan her aw day. So wi gits back through wi the rest ay thum n ah sits doon n picks up the *Radio Times*. Ah starts tae circle aw the programmes wir gaunny watch. The wey ah see it is thit some cunt's goat tae decide, tae stoap every fucker fae squabblin, so it might as well be me. That's what ah like best aboot Christmas, jist sittin back wi a few cans n watchin a good film.

Ya beauty! James Bond's oan. *Doctor No*, n it's jist aboot tae fuckin well start.

Sean Connery, the best fuckin Bond. Ye dinnae want some fuckin poncey English cunt, no fir James Bond.

Mind you, no thit ah really agree wi huvin some cunt fae Tolcross as Bond. Thaire's cunts fae Leith thit could've done that joab jist as well as Connery. Auld Davie Robb, drinks in the Marksman, he must be aboot ages wi Connery. A fuckin hard cunt in ehs day, everybody'll tell ye that. Intae everythin, he wis. Cunts like that could've been good Bonds, if they'd goat the fuckin trainin, likes.

— Wir no watchin *Doctor No*, muh ma sais, — Come on, Francis!

— Ah'd awready picked it but, Ma, ah tells her.

She's standin thaire, wi her airms aw folded, the fuckin billy ay the wash-hoose, like she wants ays tae gie her the remote. Nae chance ay that. Sometimes ah think thit muh ma forgets thit this is as much ma hoose as it is hers. Ah might no huv steyed here fir years, bit this wis the hoose thit ah grew up in, so ye still eywis think ay it as your hoose. Ah think she sometimes firgets that. — Yuv seen it loads ay times! she moans.

— The wee yins might want tae watch the cartoon videos they goat fir Christmas!

— *Toy Story 2* . . . one ay the bairns goes. That wee Philip, a sneaky wee bastard, that yin. Takes eftir ehs ma.

Some cunts are that fuckin clueless thit ye huv tae explain everything. — Naw, cause that's the whole point ay gittin a fuckin video, ah goes tae thum, — thit ye kin watch it any time ye like. Ye cannae watch the Bond film any time ye like. Ye either watch it or ye dinnae, n yuv goat tae watch a Bond film at Christmas. Joe? Ah turns tae ma brar.

— Ah'm no bothered, Joe goes.

Sandra looks acroas at him, then at me, then at Kate. Ye jist ken that big cow's gaunny say somethin cause she goes aw that huffy, puffed-up wey. — So wi huv tae watch what Frank wants again, ah take it. Fine, she goes, aw sarcastic.

— Dinnae fuckin start, Joe goes, pointin at her.

— Ah'm jist sayin what yir ma's sayin, thit the bairns —

Joe cuts her oaf. — Ah sais dinnae fuckin start. Eh lowers ehs voice. — Ah've telt ye.

She sits bristlin away on the fuckin couch, bit she's no lookin at anybody n she's no sayin nowt.

Joe looks at me, n shakes ehs heid.

It wis aboot time eh wis gittin her telt.

Muh ma looks ower at Greg n Elspeth. They've been sittin oan thair ain; jist whisperin away, n laughin tae thumselves in the corner, aw antisocial. Meant tae be a fuckin faimlay Christmas wir huvin here. If the cunts wanted tae dae that, they could fuckin well dae it ootside. — What dae youse two want tae watch? muh ma asks thum.

They look at each other like thir no bothered, and this smarmy cunt, this Greg poof goes, — Well, ah'm with Frank. Ah think it would be a good laugh tae watch the Bond movie. Then the cunt goes in this posh voice, — Ah, Mr Bond, I've been expecting you . . . n muh ma laughs n ah even sees a wee smile oan the corner ay Joe's lips.

Of course, the bairns are aw laughin now, n every cunt suddenly thinks it's aw a fuckin great idea tae watch the Bond movie, now thit this fuckin Greg wanker's intae it.

Ruined ma fuckin enjoyment ay the film.

These cunts; that two, that Greg n Elspeth; thuv been whisperin tae each other aw the wey through the fuckin picture anyway. Eftir makin aw that fuss aboot it, that cunt wisnae even watchin the film, right. At the end ay it, the pair ay thum git up n stand in front ay the telly. Ah'm jist aboot tae tell thum tae sit the fuck doon cause ah want tae change channels tae see that fuckin *Snowman* cartoon, fir the sake ay the bairns, ken, n thir blockin the signal fae the remote.

— We've got a little announcement to make, this Greg cunt goes, and Elspeth moves close tae um and they hud hands. Muh ma's lookin aw excited. It's like she's waitin fir the last fuckin number oan her caird doon at the Mecca. The Greg cunt coughs. — It's difficult tae know how to say this, but, well, yesterday, I asked Elspeth if she would do me the great honour of becoming my wife, and I'm delighted tae say that she said yes.

Ma auld girl stands up, aw delirious, n stretches her airms oot like that Al Jolson cunt, aw ready tae burst intae song. But it's tears she bursts intae, n she's sayin how beautiful it is; her wee lassie n she cannae believe it, n aw that crap. What a fuckin fuss tae make ower nowt. It's like some cunt hud slipped an ecky intae her sherry. Ah widnae pit it past yon Greg. Sly-lookin gadge, ken? Aye, Sandra n Kate are aw excited n Joe's wee yin says, kin she be a bridesmaid? and they say, aye, of course ye kin, n aw that shite. Ah couldnae fuckin believe ma ears. Gittin mairried! Oor Elspeth n this fuckin nonce cunt in the suit!

Her heid's in the clouds. That's Elspeth but, eywis thinkin thit she's better thin any cunt else. Spoiled rotten by bein the youngest, n the only lassie, that's what it wis. Nivir hud it rough, no like me n Joe. Thinks thit she kin jist suit ehrsel. Some cunt should tell her: it disnae fuckin well work that wey, no in the real world.

So ah'm fuckin well sittin thaire, ma nut poundin, n thair aw shriekin away as she pills oot a ring n sticks it oan her finger, showin it oaf. — It's beautiful, muh ma goes.

— Very nice, that Sandra sais. — Did eh git doon oan the bended? Bet eh did, she goes, lookin at that Greg, then glancin doon at ma brar like eh's nowt.

Fuckin Elspeth but. Ah dinnae ken what she's playin at. Ah mind ay that last boy she wis gaun oot wi, he wis a good cunt.

Keith, the boy's name wis. He hud a big motor n aw, and a no bad flat. They pit the perr fucker away though, jist fir dealin a wee bit ay bugle. It's fuckin well oot ay order, cause jist aboot every cunt's at that game these days. Ye cannae really class charlie as drugs, no in ma book. Ah mean, it's no like it's schemies fuckin killin thirsels wi smack. What it is, is a designer accessory fir the modern fuckin age. That's the problem wi this fuckin country though; too many cunts livin in the Dark Ages, no prepared tae move wi the times.

This Greg cunt vanishes for a bit, then eh comes back wi a huge boatil ay champagne n some glesses. The wey that Sandra's lookin at the boatil, ye'd think it wis a fuckin vibrator thit she wis gaunny stick up her fanny. So fuckin pretty boy pops the cork n it flies acroas the room, hittin the ceilin. Ah'm ower n checkin tae see if it's left a mark whaire it hit the paintwork, n if it hus, that cunt kin pey fir muh ma tae git her fuckin ceilin redone. Lucky fir him it husnae. Eh pours the drink intae the glesses. Joe takes a gless fae the cunt, but ah wave um away. — Dinnae like that stuff. That's crap, ah tell the boy.

— Stickin tae the beer, aye, eh goes.

— Aye, ah sais.

— Come on, son, it's a special occasion, yir sister's engagement, muh ma goes.

— Disnae bother me, ah dinnae like they fizzy bubbles, they git up ma nose, ah tell her, lookin ower at the Greg poof, wi ehs fuckin side partin n ehs suit n crew-neck shirt withoot a tie. Ah wanted tae tell her that *he* gits up ma fuckin nose, but ah kept quiet, Christmas n that.

Aye, it's no fir me tae say nowt, but ah'll run a check oan this cunt. Somethin fuckin right iffy aboot that radge. Eh looks the type ay cunt that's no too sure aboot whether tae catch the one or the six, if ye ken what ah mean. Probably one ay they fuckin bent shots that shag the young poofs up the Calton Hill. In the fuckin closet, n usin oor Elspeth as cover.

See, if that cunt gies her Aids, eh's fuckin well deid.

Well, that fuckin loudmoothed hoor Sandra goes, raisin her gless in a toast, — Tae Elspeth n Greg!

— Elspeth n Greg, every cunt sais.

Ah'm sayin nowt, but ah never take ma eyes oaf that cunt. Aye, pal, ah'm fuckin well wide fir you. Every cunt else's makin a big fuss, n even Joe shakes the boy's hand. Ah'm shakin nae cunt's hand, that's a fuckin cert.

— Well, ah'd best git the dinner served up, the auld lady sais. — This hus been the happiest Christmas I've hud in years. See, if yir faither wis here . . . she bubbles at Elspeth.

If oor faither wis here eh'd huv fuckin well done what eh eywis did – drunk us oot ay hoose n hame n made a fuckin exhibition ay ehsel.

This cunt Greg puts ehs hand oan muh ma's wrist n slides ehs other airm around oor Elspeth's waist. — Ah was just sayin tae Els last night, Val, it's my one big regret that I was never able tae meet John.

What's that cunt sayin aboot ma fuckin auld man? He didnae ken ma fuckin auld man! This fuckin cunt thinks eh kin jist come in here n take ower everything, jist cause eh caught oor Elspeth at a vulnerable time. Jist cause she wis oan the rebound so tae speak, wi that fuckin perr Keith boy gittin sent doon. Ah've seen smarmy cunts like this Greg before, seen thum in action. Eywis oan the lookoot fir some lassie tae take a len ay.

Naw, she's makin a big mistake n she hus tae be telt.

So wir sittin doon at the table tae oor dinner, n the auld lady's only went n arranged it soas thit ah'm sittin next tae this fuckin smarmy, side-partin child molester. Ah'm gled now thit that fuckin June took oor bairns tae her hoor ay a ma's hoose.

— So what line ay work are ye in, mate? Joe asks the Greg boy.

Elspeth butts in before the cunt kin speak. — Greg works fir the council.

— Huv a word wi the cunts aboot that council tax, fuckin well oot ay order, ah goes. Muh ma n Joe n Sandra nod away, agreein wi that, n ah've fuckin well goat the cunt thaire. The council's a fuckin waste ay money as far as ah kin see. They could shut the whole fuckin loat doon the morn n nae cunt wid notice any fuckin difference.

Elspeth gits aw snooty. — That's no Greg's department. He's in planning. A Principal Officer, she says, aw fill ay it.

So it's planning were gittin now, is it? Aye, n ye ken what that cunt's fuckin well plannin awright; plannin tae git ehs fuckin feet under the table. Well, no in this hoose eh's no.

Sittin thaire, drinkin ehs wine, chompin intae that dinner like eh's tae the fuckin manor born. The crawlin cunt goes, — You've really pulled oot aw the stops here, Val. Delicious. Cooked tae a treat.

Ah'm sittin next tae um, ragin, n ah swallays a moothfae ay grub. Thaire's somethin, a wee bone or the likes, stickin a bit in ma throat. Ah takes a sip ay wine.

— Ah'd like tae propose a wee toast, the Greg cunt goes, raisin ehs gless. — Tae family.

Ah tries tae cough up, but it's stuck fast. Ah cannae git any air, ma fuckin nostrils are aw blocked up wi that charlie fae last night . . . ma sinuses are packed solid wi crap . . .

Fuckin hell.

— Uncle Frank's no well, the wee boy says.

— Ye awright, Francis son? Somethin no gaun doon? muh ma goes. — Eh's gaun red . . .

Ah waves the cunts away, n ah stands up. That daft cow Sandra's tryin tae gie me a bit ay breed. — Force this doon, force it doon . . . she goes . . . but ah'm fuckin well chokin anywey, n she's fuckin tryin tae kill me . . .

Ah pushes her aside, n ah'm gaspin n chokin, n ma heid's spinnin n ah see the horror in thair faces roond the table. Ah cough, n this sick comes up n catches in ma fuckin throat n flies back doon, aw hoat n burnin, right back intae ma fuckin lungs . . .

YA CUNT

AH'M FUCKIN CHOKIN . . .

Ah'm grabbin the table, n bangin oan it, then grabbin at ma throat . . .

AW YA FUCKER . . .

Ah feels this bang oan the toap ay ma back; one dunt, then another, n ah feels somethin loosen n it aw comes up, that fuckin blockage is away n ah kin breathe . . .

Sweet fuckin air . . . ah kin breathe . . .

— Awright, Franco? Joe asks.

Ah nods.

— Well done, Greg, ye saved the day thaire, eh goes.

— Ye certainly did, that Sandra says.

Ah'm gittin ma puff back, tryin tae work oot what happened. Ah turns tae this Greg. — Some cunt battered ays oan the back thaire. Wis that you?

— Aye, ah think ye swallowed the wishbone, eh goes.

Ah smacks the nut oantae the cunt, n eh faws back, hudin ehs face. Thaire's screams fae the women n the bairns n Joe's ower n eh's goat a grip ay ma airm. — What ur ye fuckin daein, Franco? The boy helped ye! Eh saved yir fuckin life!

Fuckin baws tae aw that; ah brushes ehs hand oaf. — Eh battered ays oan the back in muh ma's hoose! Nae cunt lays thair hands oan me! In muh ma's hoose, oan Christmas Day! That'll be fuckin right!

Muh ma's screamin, callin ays an animal, n oor Elspeth's daein her nut. — That's it, that's us finished, she goes, lookin at me, shakin her heid. — We're gaun, she sais tae muh ma.

— Aw dinnae, please, hen, no the day! muh ma pleads.

— Sorry, Mum, we are off. She points at me. — He's ruined everything. Eh'll be happy now. Good. We'll leave yis to it. Merry fucking Christmas.

This Greg cunt's goat ehs heid up, wi a serviette oan ehs nose, tryin tae stem the blood. A bit ay it's goat oantae ehs shirt though. — It's awright, it's awright, eh laughs, tryin tae calm thum aw doon. — It wis nothing! Frank's hud a bad fright, eh's in shock, eh didnae ken what eh wis daein . . . it's nae bother, ah'm fine . . . it looks worse than it is . . .

Ah mind ays thinkin, ah'll gie ye a loat worse thin that, ya cunt. Ah sits doon, n ah'm still gittin ma breath back. Thir aw arguin like fuck. Elspeth's greetin n he's tryin tae calm her.

— It's awright, eh didnae mean it, darlin, let's just stay for a bit. For Val's sake, eh's gaun.

— You dinnae ken um! Eh hus tae spoil everything, she sobs. It's aw a big excuse fir her tae go aw greetin-faced n spoiled, as usual.

Joe n Sandra ur sortin oot muh ma n the bairns. She's moanin aw that usual shite aboot whaire did she go wrong n aw that. It's me thit fuckin well went wrong, comin here oan Christmas Day.

Ah jist heaps some mair sprouts oantae ma plate, n fills up ma gless. Ah feel like sayin tae thum, if yis are gaunny eat yir Christmas dinner, fuckin well sit doon n eat it. If yis urnae, git the fuck away n gie me peace tae finish mine.

Aye, mibbe ah should've cooled it, n goat a hud ay the cunt ootside, instead ay littin fly like that in muh ma's hoose. That cunt wis too wide fir ehs ain good, but. Far too wide. Awright, eh did try n help, but eh gie'd ma back a fuckin right dunt. Nae need fir that. N ah suppose thit what it aw boils doon tae is thit thaire's jist some cunts ye cannae take tae. Ye fuckin try, but ye ken deep doon thit yir nivir gaunny see eye tae eye, n that's that.

Kissing and Making Up

At the bus stop a paunchy gadge with a sweaty curry-and-lager-fart erse surreptitiously tweaks the head of his cock through the material of his sport-and-leisurewear trousers in response to the presence of several children who are hanging around outside the school gates by the newsagent's.

The guy reeks of stale sweat and his fleshy features hang slack and heavy, like saturated boiled chicken waiting to be scraped from the bone. It was a long day's night drinking yesterday. This boy's got the horn in a big way. He's positively alpine. A trip to the go-go's is certainly called for here. So he heads for the Bermuda Triangle of Tolcross where he's just one of the pubic lice that crawl into the bar in search of the big black bush. Outside the first pub he approaches, he notes with approval the sign on the blackboard: TANYA, 2:00.

Yeaaahhhsss, he thinks, the hoor wi the Caesarean scar is on. The gadge cannae take his eyes of that scar, that and the bruises on her arms and thighs which he knows has been inflicted by her dealer boyfriend. Seeker they call him, and nobody knows why. He often watches with furtive glances, Seeker's treatment of her, and he approves. Seeker knows how to control these slags. He knows how to hurt them. He fucks all those freaky junkie hoors and pays them in smack. That's a real man. He wishes he knew Seeker's secret. He could never master the hoors in that way. The nearest he came was with Julie, her with the two kids. She was feart. You could tell she was. Her last felly used to have heavy hands. Fast hands too. Always ready to let fly if the slag crossed him. He'd prepared her well. Once a slag got used to that sort of discipline she wanted it all her life. *Needed* it all her life. And the best part was kissing and making up. Always the best part.

But she left him too. Suddenly discovered a bit of bottle. Called his bluff. Those fuckin dykes at that fuckin refuge. Getting the polis involved in what was essentially a fuckin domestic dispute. That was what he told the polisman, a domestic dispute. The polisman was obviously sympathetic. He gave a look as if to say: sorry, mate, my hands are tied. Court fuckin order next. Scotland Yard, from coming within a mile of the fuckin slag. How's that supposed tae work with him in the next stair?

But that Julie. He'll fuck her again, polis or nae polis. Only he'll fuck her good next time. The thought makes him hard in his shellsuit troosers. He anticipates Tanya coming on.

He looks across at Seeker, sitting still with a gin and tonic in front of him. He flashes the odd coffin-plate smile at acquaintances. The smile is like a photographer's flash bulb, it explodes then is instantly gone leaving his face set in hard neutrality. A younger guy in a ponytail and a pretty, but haggard and bewildered-looking young woman join Seeker. The young guy shakes Seeker's hand and with a leery smile introduces the woman and Seeker theatrically kisses her hand and she smiles like a rabbit in the glare of headlights.

Then a cheer goes up and Tanya is on, gyrating on a raised platform in a flimsy two-piece which has gone through the washing machine ten times too many to be seen in public. Bronchitic old guys with half-pints stare intensely, imprinting Tanya's image on their tired minds, collecting wanking material for tonight's swift one of the wrist between the foostie sheets of a frozen flat.

The pub smells of nicotine and vomit. Someone puked over the carpet last night. They hadn't bothered cleaning it, just rearranged one of the tables to partially conceal it. Our boy looks at Tanya's bored face, studies where the acne has left her with scar tissue, that same acne that probably once made her grateful for male attention in spite of her streamlined curves, as if she was doing them all a big favour when it came to opening her legs. Then there's the scar. Phoah, that fuckin scar. He wonders where the brat is that caused that scar. At Tanya's – not that Tanya is her real name though it's possible – or at Tanya's ma's hoose or in care. Foster-parents. Like his wee laddie. Pit up for adoption. That was the stupid slag of a mother of his's fault of course. Incapable, they said. Incapable of looking eftir a bairn. Well, these social work cunts dinnae always ken what's best, and whae can say that *they're* capable of looking eftir bairns?

This thought fails to comfort him because although Tanya's on and the music has pumped up, it's that fuckin ravey shite and that nigger pish, what aboot country n western, that was his kind ay music, 'Stand by your Man' n that, but anywey Tanya's giein it big licks and she's closer to him and he can see that scar above her cheap, washed-out knickers, that thin scar just above the start of that bush, and his chest seems to be caving in and the blood is leaving his head and the smoky air is getting strangely thin and he sees his own hand going out and his index finger gently touching the scar and Tanya snaps away and shouts, — Fuck off! and there's a wee roar and she turns back into the dance.

Now our boy's a wee bit worried because you dinnae touch Seeker's women in that way. No fuckin chance of that. But Seeker flashes over a smile at him and say what you like aboot that cunt Seeker, he kens how to control these hoors and he's no a bad cunt, yuv goat tae gie the cunt that, he's alright, and our boy nods back at Seeker and we're all in this together, man. Our boy, Seeker, they ken each other's faces, they ken that each other are both alright, really sound cunts as a matter of fact. No mates perhaps, but sort of mates-in-waiting, guys who would lap each other up if they kent each other and may get tae sometime. Aye. Too right.

Tanya finishes her set and eftir a few more pints our boy makes an exit. He'll cut round the back of the pub, down the side lane and across the gap site to get his bus back hame. But he's aware of someone else in the side lane with him and he turns and it's Seeker; Seeker's in the side lane and he nods and says, — Awright, mate?

Our shellsuit-bottomed boy is about to say, — Aye, sound, and maybe wi a wee apology tae Seeker for pittin his finger on the boy's goods, ah mean, respect is called for, when Seeker's crash helmet smashes into his cheek. Our boy staggers against the wall, and turns to meet the second blow from the helmet which knocks two teeth out and slackens a further two. As he keels over, Seeker's boot comes down with force on his testicles, then into his head.

It's over. Twenty-two seconds.

Seeker retires to the bar, the business sorted out. He has not spoken another word to our boy. Awright, mate, is all he said. This in itself, he feels, was a little too much.

Our man in the shellsuit troosers stays down for a bit, then staggers to his feet. Supported by a wall he throws up some lager-vomit and dazedly makes his way across the site towards the bus stop. Angry our man certainly is. But it's no Seeker he's angry with; he understands Seeker, he would do the same in that position. He kens Seeker. It's that cunt, her with the scar that he hates; all these fuckin troublemaking bastards.

Her and that fuckin Julie slag. Well, he'll pay that fuckin hoor a visit, and sort the cunt out for good.

Maybe they'll kiss and make up again; the best part, eywis the best part. Or maybe this time there'll be nothing left ay the hoor tae kiss and make up wi.

The Rosewell Incident

For Kenny, Craig and Woody

I

Another convoy of travellers hustled along through the busy traffic which clogged the city's arteries, rolling onto the slip road off the congested bypass and snaking painstakingly towards the mobbed field which rumbled with the buzz of small competing sound systems.

From the disused railway bridge overhead, a sweating PC Trevor Drysdale kept a watchful eye on the scene. Drawing a wheezy breath of the baked, mucky air, Drysdale wiped his brow and gazed heavenwards at ragged clouds which failed to block out the sun's leery heat.

Out of the range of Drysdale's vision and earshot, in a stinking enclave underneath the concrete bypass, the local young team were also filling their lungs with the chemicals the traffic spewed out, to complement the ones they voluntarily ingested.

Despite the heat, Jimmy Mulgrew felt himself shudder. It was the bevvy and the drugs, he reasoned. It always kept a part of you from being warm. That, and lack of sleep. He embarked on another flinching spasm, more severe than the last, as Clint Phillips, standing over a prostrate Semo, brought the heavy hammer crashing down on the side of the boy's strong, square jaw. The jaw was concealed by a pillow, wrapped around his head and secured with tape, leaving only his eyes, nose and mouth visible. Even with this protection, Semo's head still jolted to the side under the impact of Clint's blow.

Jimmy looked across at Dunky Milne, who raised his brows and shimmied his shoulders. He took a step forward and wondered whether or not he should intervene. Semo was his best mate. But no, Clint was staying cool and checking on him. — Awright, Semo? Is it away? Is that it broke, aye?

Semo looked up at Clint, registered his ugly smile. Even wasted on a temazepam capsule and some super lager, Semo could still feel the pain in his jaw. He moved it around. It was sore, but still intact. — It isnae broke yit, he drawled, his spittle dribbling into the pillow.

Clint bristled, taking on a prizefighter's gait. He turned and shrugged to Jimmy and Dunks, who looked back neutrally at him. There was something moving uneasily in Jimmy's chest, and he wanted to say 'that's enough' but nothing came out as Clint crashed the hammer with vicious force into the side of Semo's head.

On impact, Semo's head jerked again, but then the boy staggered to his feet. An old man walking a chunky black Labrador dog looked startled as he turned the corner and came upon them. The young team's stares burned him and he violently pulled the pissing, whining beast along the road as it tried to urinate on one of the concrete support pillars. The man disappeared around the other bend that led up from the slip road to the old village, before he had the chance to witness the youth with the pillow taped around his head tear the hammer from the other boy's grasp and smash him full in his unprotected face with it.

— FUCKEN RADGE! Semo roared, as Clint's cheekbone shattered and part of his top row of teeth were scattered in a sickening splintering sound which gave Jimmy a nauseous but uplifting feeling. Jimmy didn't really like

Clint, basically because Clint worked in the garage and Shelley hung around there, but he also wasn't enthusiastic about this scam.

Clint was holding his face in his hands, looking up at Semo and screaming like a demented hyena, spitting blood and teeth. He turned to Jimmy and Dunks in tearful appeal. — It wisnae meant tae be me! he bleated. — It wis meant tae be that cunt! He hud the fuckin jelly! He hud the pillay!

Semo looked completely away with it. He wasn't letting go of the hammer, nor was he removing his rapacious gaze from Clint.

— It's done now but, eh? Jimmy shouted. — Moan, lit's goan see the polis! He winked at Semo, who let the hammer rest by his side.

— Fuck youse! Clint whined. — Ah'm gaun hame!

— Come back tae mines, Jimmy said.

Clint was in no position to refuse, allowing himself to be led back to Jimmy's house. They went upstairs to his bedroom, and listened to some tapes. Clint managed to swallow two jellies and passed out on Jimmy's floor. Jimmy went downstairs for a bin liner and put it under Clint's head, to stop the blood from getting everywhere.

Jimmy started to relax when he heard his father turning up the volume on the telly's handset downstairs, compelling him to increase the output from his Bass Generator tape. The telly volume nudged up an increment; Jimmy corresponded. It was a familiar ritual. He smiled at Dunky and gave the thumbs up, and they opened a tube of Airfix. Clint was out for the count, and Semo was also asleep. Jimmy tenderly cut the tape and let the pillow flap back, enabling his friend's head to rest natur-ally on it. Semo's jaw was badly swollen, but his injuries were minor in comparison to the mess Clint's coupon was in. Letting a couple of drops of the nippy, burning liquid drip onto his tongue, Jimmy felt himself satisfyingly struggle for breath as the vapour filled his lungs.

2

Shelley Thomson had six toes. When she was wee her father told her that she was an alien from outer space and that she was found abandoned by her parents when a UFO dumped her in a field outside Rosewell. The truth, however, was that it was her father who had abandoned Shelley. When she was six years old, he simply did not come home one day from work. Her mother, Lillian, refused to tell Shelley whether she knew anything at all about her dad's disappearance.

As a result, Shelley somewhat idealised the memory of her father, and this was particularly the case when her adolescent battles with Lillian hit a particularly discordant pitch. Growing up into a dreamy, speculative fifteen-year-old, Shelley had developed a fascination for UFOs.

When she realised that she was pregnant after missing two periods and then scoring positive twice on different Boots home-testing kits, Shelley claimed that the father was a seven-foot alien who came to her in the night and took her semi-conscious to a place which may or may not have been a spacecraft and lay on top of her. She told her friend Sarah that there was the 'feeling of doing it' without any genital interaction.

— Aw aye? Sarah scoffed. — What was eh like? Brad Pitt? Liam Gallagher?

Sarah tried not to show that she was impressed that her friend did not allow herself that kind of indulgence. Instead,

Shelley described the alien in classical terms: a long, thin hairless body, large slanted eyes, etc. Impressed though she was, Sarah was far from convinced.

— Aye, right, Shelley, she disdained. — It's Alan Devlin's fae the garage, eh?

— Nuhp!

Alan Devlin was an attendant at the local garage at the bottom of the slip road which led onto the bypass. He had an easy, engaging manner with young girls from the local school, whose grounds backed onto the filling station. Clint Phillips, Alan's bashful seventeen-year-old YT, would wait nervously outside and keep watch while the senior attendant indulged himself in the back shop with the local youngsters, Shelley and Sarah being among those he numbered in his schoolie harem. Clint longed for a piece of the action but was too shy in himself, due mainly to his bad spots, and therefore too un-exotic to the girls, and Devlin would tease him mercilessly about it. Many times Clint wished that Mr Marshall, the garage manager, who was never there, would come by and surprise them, but he never did. Marshall was an alcoholic and always on the piss in one of the local pubs come lunchtime. Clint nonetheless liked to infer that he'd fucked Shelley; this annoyed the fuck out of his mate Jimmy Mulgrew, who had the hots for her in a big way.

Alan Devlin came from the city and had been involved with a gang of football casuals known as the Capital City Service in his teens, but gave up when his older brother Mikey mysteriously vanished one evening, never to return. Mikey Devlin had been a top boy. In the five years since the disappearance of his idolised big brother, Alan Devlin had re-evaluated life. The gig was basically fucked, you were here one minute and gone the next. The point was to take what you can get. For Alan, this meant shagging as many birds as possible. His success with young girls was based on charm, persistence, and an ability to tap into their obsessions. Shelley had allowed him to fuck her after hearing this story. As her father had vanished, she felt a bond to Alan Devlin. Previously, this tall, thin schoolgirl had only let him touch her small, pubescent breasts, often as he and Sarah had full intercourse.

Shelley, and for that matter Sarah, always vowed never to visit Alan in the garage again. They were drawn out of boredom, however, and unfailingly mesmerised by the older lad's easy flattery. Before they knew it, Alan's hands would be all over one, or both, of them.

3

The shanty town of travellers had spilled from the old municipal travelling people's site onto the toxic wasteland alongside it. The settlement was growing daily. Millennium fever: these wee cunts were crazy for it, thought PC Trevor Drysdale. They weren't real travelling people, they were just cheeky bastards out for bother. As if he didn't have enough of that from the local youths. There had been a fight outside the chip shop last night. Again. Drysdale knew who the troublemakers were, with their drugs and smart-arse behaviour. Later this week he was up before the promotion board. There was still time to get the kind of result that could swing it. Had he not scored brownie points with his firm, but sensitive dealings with the travellers? Sergeant Drysdale. It sounded good. That new suit from Moss Bros. It fitted like a glove. Cowan, the chairman of the promotion board, was a stickler for appearances. Brother Cowan was also known to him from the Craft. The job was as good as his.

Drysdale walked down the path to the edge of the reservoir. Beer cans, wine bottles, crisp packets, glue tubes. That was the problem with working-class youth today; economically excluded, politically disenfranchised and full of strange drugs. It was a bad combination. All these wee cunts wanted to do was to party into the next century and see what this cultural watershed brought. If the answer was 'the same old shite', as it surely would be, Drysdale morosely reflected, then the wee fuckers would just shrug and party on into the next one.

Trevor Drysdale was realistic enough to know that there had never been a golden age of a 'clip round the earhole' in enforcing the law in these parts. Yet he did remember the realpolitik equivalent of social control, 'the kicking in the cells'. The old school of rough-and-ready Scottish youth respected that great institution of law enforcement, the slippery steps. Now, though, most of them were too full of drugs to feel the kicking or even remember they'd received it. After a few jellies, that kind of damage went with the territory. Yes, such an activity could still be therapeutic for the individual officer, but as a method of enforcing the law it was worse than useless.

What a place, Drysdale mused, letting his gaze sweep over the reservoir down across the city's topography and back up to the Pentland Hills. It had changed here alright. Even as conditioned to its incremental development as he was, sometimes the nastiness of the arbitrary, incongruent nature of the locale jarred with him. Old villages, shoebox modern housing developments, barren fields, scabby, moribund farms and industrial estates, leisure and shopping complexes, motorways, slip roads and that rancid piece of brown, derelict wasteland they bizarrely called the Green Belt. That terminology seemed like yet another calculated insult perpetuated on the locals by the authorities.

But if there was one thing that concerned him more than the gloom which had solidified the place like a gel, it was this new wave of optimism. Millennium fever. In other words, another excuse for young cunts to go shagging and drugging while the rest of us have to work away in a state of loathing and fear, he reflected with rancour, feeling his ulcer bite. It had to be stopped. There were thousands of them now, crowded onto that strip of land.

Drysdale looked down from the steep bank by the water. He could see that makeshift village of lost souls expanding, getting closer and closer to his own Barratt estate. Thank fuck for the slip road that divided them. It was surely now time for the government to declare a national emergency; take off the kid gloves. But no; the sly fuckers were holding off, crossing their fingers for a few drug-related deaths. Then they'd whip up hysteria among a supposed moral majority and bring in some more repressive measures. It had to be worth a few percentage points in the polls and party conference season, and an election itself, were coming up soon. There would be a round of 'get tough' speeches followed by a few witch-hunts. Drysdale had heard it all before, but to hear it more loudly would at least mean that they hadn't given up. Let's get some fucking blood spilled here, he ruefully willed, dispatching a rusty can into the dank water with a crisp volley.

4

The young team's plan had been an inadvertent success. The next morning Clint Phillips woke up on Jimmy Mulgrew's floor in agony, and they had been forced to take him to the hospital, where he was X-rayed, examined and admitted. Jimmy considered it a bonus that Clint, rather than Semo, had been hospitalised, although with Clint not at the garage shop, they would have to watch what they nicked with that big Alan Devlin cunt around.

Anyway, Clint would be out in a day or so, then they could go round to the small police substation, and register the crime with the polisman Drysdale, blaming a group of the travellers for the assault.

5

The Cyrastorian pushed his long fingers against his temples. He could feel himself steadily moving from the centre of the Will, out into the peripheral zones of its influence. Sometimes Gezra, the Elder, felt that he had been wrong to pursue this line of work beyond his allotted span. It was as if he could feel the very chill of deep space insinuating itself into his flesh and bone, through the translucent aura of the Will, which protected him and all his world's sons and daughters.

In the darkness of his craft, illuminated only by the images which panned up of the observed planet, the Appropriate Behaviour Compliance Elder for this sector pondered as to the likely destiny of the rogue youth's ship. Earth seemed almost too obvious. After all, their specimen had been from that world. Specimen. Gezra smiled across his thin lips; he would have to stop using such a pejorative, demeaning term. After all, the Earthman had been inducted, electing to stay a part of Cyrastorian culture, rather than return home with a memory wipe, and this in return for strangely modest rewards. There was little to be gained in attempting to understand the primitive psyche of the Earth creature.

The Appropriate Behaviour Compliance Elder reluctantly decided that he needed to use external technology to locate the renegade youths. This prospect filled the Elder with distaste. Cyrastorian philosophy was based around the dismantling and demobilising of external technology, and the ruthless promotion of the Will, those individual and collective psychic powers, by which his race had developed and advanced their civilisation from their own decrepit, post-industrial age, now several millennia past.

As with Earth humanoids, the early history of Cyrastor had been dominated by a procession of prophets, evangelists, messiahs, sages and seers who had contrived to convince both themselves and their followers that they were privy to the secrets of the universe. Some achieved little more than ridicule in their own lifetime, others would have an influence on generations.

The remorseless rise of science and technology conspired to undermine the great religions as the basis of truth, without ever reducing the humility, wonder and reverence experienced by all intelligent life forms as they contemplated this immense, amazing universe. Yet as Cyrastorian technology itself advanced and opened up what seemed like a vast expanse but would retrospectively only be regarded as a corner of their civilisation, it simultaneously threw up more mysteries than it had the capacity to resolve. This was always the way with knowledge, but of greater concern to the Cyrastorians was their culture's inbuilt tendency to gear all such technology towards the consumption of resources without being able to eliminate poverty, inequality, disease and the wasted potential of its citizens.

At the very height of their technological advancement, this

pragmatic and idealistic people faced up to their spiritual crisis. A body known as the Foundation was established by the Principal Elders. Its brief was to promote spiritual enlightenment, and to liberate the Cyrastorian potentialities of the mind from its hitherto supposed physiological limitations. Centuries of meditation resulted in the creation of the Will, a collective pool of psychic energy that every Cyrastorian could draw upon, and, by the very act of living and thinking, contributed to in accordance with the levels of their personal training and their ability to learn. As the Will had all but eradicated cultural and social differences, this proved to be very similar in all Cyrastorian citizens.

It had previously been somewhat hilarious for Gezra to fritter away leisure moments watching primitive cultures like Earth continue down their blind alley of external technology development. Now however, many of the renegade Cyrastorian youth were moved by at least the idea of this visceral touch, feel and taste nonsense. Primitivists, they sought physical types of interaction for its own thrilling sensation, and often with races who were little more than savages. Gezra knew, however, that the renegade leader, the Younger called Tazak, had, for all his rhetoric about the cult of physicality, extremely developed psychic powers, and would sense any Elder attempts at the detection of his presence through the exercise of the Will.

6

The young team were sitting drinking cheap wine by the reservoir. Jimmy remembered that, only a few years ago, they had fished for perch and pike in its waters. Glue had taken over.

It wasn't really that it was less boring, more that being glued up was like the excitement of a catch spread over the whole day. There was an aroused sense of wasted purpose and at the same time a comfort in the oblivion it produced. Of course, they all knew that it was going nowhere. While intoxication provided a multitude of misadventures, tales of which could, under certain conditions, get you through periods of mind-crushing straightness, it too often only led to greater frustration and anxiety.

But fuck it though. Jimmy yawned and stretched, feeling the pleasurable unravelling of his limbs, you always tended to follow the line of least resistance. What else was there? Jimmy thought of his parents, now split up, their quaint notions of 'respect', hued from an era of full employment and half-decent wages, floundering on the remorseless, depressive nothingness around them. He couldn't respect them, nor could he respect society. He couldn't even respect himself, only band together with his pals to enforce others to respect him, in a way which became more limited and proscribed every day. You just had to stick together with your mates, and make sure there was a clear tunnel ahead and hope for a better world if and when you emerged into the light.

Maybe the travellers had the right idea, Jimmy thought. Perhaps movement was the key. Why the fuck had the sad cunts come here though? The stretches of wasteland, between the Barratt schemes, industrial estates and flyovers, had become home to people from all over Britain and even further afield. All those fucked-up cunts, talking about a 'force' that had brought them here. Here! For fuck sakes. Anyway, to fuck with all those cunts, Clint was out tomorrow. They'd register the crime with Drysdale and then take the criminal injuries compensation wankers to the cleaners. Easy.

Jimmy swigged back half a bottle of Hooch lemonade. They

had graduated to beer and spirits, their current favourite tipple being a few Hooches, super lager and fortified wine with capsules of temazepam if available. Their mate Carl had almost drowned the other week, falling asleep by the side of the reservoir, only for it rise in the evening. When the others, who had staggered back into town, had realised he was absent and gone back to find him, it was nearly over his mouth and nostrils.

Looking up at the ugly, hollow sky, Jimmy wondered if there was anything out there. This was one of the top places in Britain for UFO sightings, and every six months or so, scientists and journalists and UFO spotters would be hanging about the town. It was always in shitey redneck places like this where there was fuck all to do that people saw those things, he reflected bitterly, lobbing an empty bottle into the reservoir. Why the fuck would aliens come here? He'd been talking to that dippit wee Shelley too much, her that was getting fucked by that Alan Devlin cunt, the city boy from the garage. He resented the city boy, not just for fucking a girl he had sexual designs on (after all, he had sexual designs on almost any girl), but because Devlin had threatened to baseball-bat him after he'd caught Jimmy stealing some crisps.

It had to be said, though, that Shelley was pure class. Jimmy knew that from the time at the chippy when he had offered to buy her chips; she had asked for curry sauce on them. It was these wee touches that marked out the top manto from the park-and-ride brigade. But this aliens baws, though, it got on his nerves. That was how that Alan Devlin was riding her, getting her head messed up with all that shite.

Glue had always been Jimmy's drug of choice. He loved the stunning rush of the vapour, the way it stuck to his lungs, catching his breath. He knew that it meant he possibly wouldn't live long, but every auld cunt in the town seemed as miserable as fuck so there seemed to him to be no real virtue in longevity. It was quality of life that counted and he considered that you were better being cunted than on a fuckin training scheme for a pittance with some red-faced tossbag shouting at you and then paying you off after two years to make way for the next dippit cunt. If any cunt couldn't see that, then, as far as Jimmy was concerned, they didn't have a fuckin brain. — The logic is inescapable, he sniggered to himself.

— What you sayin, ya daft cunt? Semo laughed.

— Nowt, Jimmy smiled, dropping some Airfix model glue on his tongue, enjoying the nip and sensation of asphyxiation. Then, when air filled his lungs, he savoured the spinning in his head. As the throbbing in his temples receded, he squirted the rest into an empty crisp packet and went for it.

— Pass it ower, Jimmy ya cunt, Semo moaned, guzzling a can of super lager and wincing. It tasted foul. You were better starting on the hooch until you got cunted enough no tae taste the lager, he decided. It wisnae too bad cauld, but warm . . . fuck it.

Jimmy reluctantly passed the bag to Semo. For a brief second he felt that the ground was going to rise up and smack him in the chin, but he weathered that storm and rubbed his eyes in an attempt to restore some vision.

Dunky was chewing on something or other. — Mind when we used tae fish here? Good times, he mused.

— Borin as fuck but, eh? Semo said, then, with a sudden abruptness which caused Jimmy to start inside, asked him: — Hi, you rode that Shelley yit, Jimmy? Yuv been sniffin roond it enough.

— Mibbe ah huv, mibbe ah huvnae, Jimmy smiled. In his fantasy they were going out together. He liked the way people were starting to associate them. He played his desire like a poker hand, flirting with his friends about his feelings for her, in a strangely deeper way than he ever did with her.

— Some cunt wis sayin she's up the kite, Dunky said.

— Fuck off, Jimmy snapped.

— Jist gaun by what ah fuckin heard, Dunky replied, unconcerned. He rolled over, feeling the blazing sun bite into his face.

— Dinnae fuckin spread aroond stories, right, Jimmy dug in. He knew it was that cunt Clint, with his big mouth. He could see Clint's huge, loose, slavering gob, just before Semo had shut it so deliciously with that hammer. He could see Alan Devlin, shouting at him to put they fuckin crisps back. He could see, in his mind's eye, the smiles Devlin got from the girls, including Shelley, and how powerless they seemed to be to do anything but giggle with a sexy nervousness under his patter. Jimmy had tried Devlin's style, but it never hit the mark, not in the same way. He felt like a little girl secretly putting on her mother's dress.

— Aye, right, Dunky scoffed.

Dunky wasn't really making an issue of it, but Jimmy was. He stood up and jumped on top of his friend, pinning him to the ground. He grabbed a handful of Dunky's red hair and twisted. — Ah sais dinnae fuckin spread roond stories! Right?

In the background Jimmy could hear the encouraging wheeze of Semo's low, mirthless laugh. Jimmy and Semo, always Jimmy and Semo. Just like it was always Dunky and Clint. Semo's hammer had been symbolic, it had changed the balance of power between the four of them. This was in case Dunks forgot exactly what that blow had meant. — Ah sais right?! Jimmy growled.

— Right! Right! Dunky squealed as Jimmy relaxed his grip and rolled off him. — Fuckin radge, he moaned, dusting himself down.

Semo sniggered uncontrollably. — Ah'd ride her, he said.

— Ah'd ride her mate n aw. That Sarah. That would be awright, eh, Jimmy? You wi that Shelley n me wi that Sarah.

Jimmy allowed himself a smile. Semo was his best mate. The concept was not without appeal.

7

Shelley was reading *Smash Hits* while her mother was making the tea. Liam out of Oasis was a shag, she considered. Abby Ford and her pals at the school were always going on about Oasis. Abby Ford always seemed to have the money for clothes and records. That was why all the laddies at the school were hanging around her. Shelley had to concede that she liked the way Abby wore her hair. She would let hers grow. She'd been daft to get that crop, but it had annoyed her mother. Abby was okay, although Sarah didn't like her. Shelley and Abby had chatted a bit. Maybe her and Sarah would become pals with Abby Ford, Louise Moncur, Shona Robertson and that crowd. They were alright. Shelley wished that she could get the money for good clothes.

But Liam out of Oasis. Mmm-hmm. Better even than Damon or Robbie or Jarvis. Looking deeply into Liam's eyes, in that picture, Shelley fancied that she could see a bit of his soul in them. It was as if he was staring only at her. Shelley Thomson convulsed appreciatively that only she could crack this secret code in these eyes, and feel this bond between them. It would be great if Liam could meet her, possibly when Oasis played Loch Lomond. He would see what a great pair they would make, and that they were really meant to be together! Love at first sight! She didn't know whether she would keep the baby

or get rid of it. That would of course be up to Liam as well;
he would have to be consulted. It was only fair. Would he want
to bring up someone else's child as his own, an alien as well?
If he loved her, and she could tell, by the way he looked at
her, that he truly did, then it would present no problem. It
would be brilliant if Sarah married Noel. That would make
them sisters-in-law. How good would that be?

— Shelley, tea, her mother said briskly. Shelley put down
the copy of *Smash Hits* and went up to the table. The image
of Liam's soulful, brooding eyes still burned and she imagined
him touching her breast and felt a fluttering current of electricity in her stomach. She sat down to oven chips, sausages
and beans, eating in brisk, economical movements. Shelley ate
like a horse, and even though she was pregnant (she didn't
know for how long, having had very little morning sickness),
she was as thin as a rake. She was crazy for chips, she loved
the ones at the chippy, especially with the curry sauce. Her
ma's chips – small, crinkly and ungenerous – they never really
cut it.

She was different from her mum, she smugly reflected. Her
mother, who just needed to look at a McCain's oven chip for
another few not-quite imperceptible fat cells to cluster around
her stomach and under her chin. Shelley saw this as a defect
in her mother's character. Her mother looked haggard. And
bloated. Was it possible to look both at the same time? Too
right, Shelley thought, looking up at Lillian staring out of the
window from behind the net curtains, a fearful expression on
her face. She always seemed to be thinking about something
ominous. Shelley had to keep in with her, though. Her mum
liked Oasis as well. There was the possibility, slight, but nonetheless real, that they would go to Loch Lomond together. Her
mum once joked that she fancied Noel. A joke, but it had
been tasteless and it had cut Shelley to the quick. Imagine if

her mum got off with Noel! Married him! Ugh! It would spoil things between her and Liam if that were to come to pass. No way. Noel would have more taste than that.

There wasn't enough food; she'd be hungry again soon. Tonight she'd go down to the chippy. Jimmy Mulgrew would be there. He was okay, but she didn't fancy him. He was too real, too here. Too Rosewell. He was awkward. Jimmy never knew the right things to say, like Alan Devlin at the garage did, or like Liam would. Okay, so Liam was from somewhere just like Rosewell really, but he had moved on, had shown that he had what it took to become a star. But she'd go to the chippy anyway, and then get home for *The X-Files*.

8

Jimmy and Semo were hanging around on the corner outside the chippy. The pubs were ready to close in half an hour. Jimmy wanted some chips but he and Semo had been barred by Vincent, the proprietor, for previous acts of minor theft and vandalism. Jimmy's heart rose when he saw Shelley and Sarah walking towards them. Shelley gave him a coy smile and Jimmy felt something move inside of him. He wanted to tell her how he felt, but what could he say? Here, in front of Semo and Sarah? What could he say to this tall, slender beauty who kept him awake at nights and who had been responsible for his sheets becoming as stiff as a board since she had flowered in the last few months and had got a number one like that Sinead O'Connor lassie? This called for genuine courtship, not darkened gropes down the quarry with the likes of Abby Ford and Louise Moncur whom he and Semo had christened

'The Reservoir Dogs'. But how could he ask her out? Where could they go? The pictures? The botanics? Where did you take lassies on proper dates?

Inspired by the shining moon overhead, which illuminated the obelisk of the office block above the garage, Jimmy moved towards her. — Eh, Shelley, goan git ays some chips, ah'll gie ye the money likes. Vincent's only went n barred us, eh.

— Awright then, Shelley said, taking the money from him.

— Mind n git curry sauce oan thum, Shel, he smiled, chuffed at her not registering negatively to his referring to her in that more intimate and informal way.

They watched the girls move into the chip shop. — Two fuckin wee rides but, eh? Semo observed, parting his dry lips with a darting tongue and rubbing at the swelling on his jaw. — Ah'd shag thum baith, he hissed, then he grabbed Jimmy and gave him a theatrical pelvic hump.

Inside the chip shop Sarah turned to Shelley. — They're fuckin daft! Supposed tae be sixteen! They wouldnae ken what tae dae wi a real woman! The girls sniggered at the image of the boys through the shop window as they jostled and rucked with each other in nervous excitement.

9

The craft was many millions of light years from the Earth, and many millions more from its native solar system. Its occupants could witness, through the technology the Cyrastorian youth so professed to enjoy, images of the planet in great clarity. They knew that it was almost as effective as the pictures they could see through the Will, but this was easier and lazier. It gave the

Cyrastorian Youngers and their solitary Earth friend time to enjoy a fag.

— Been a few fuckin changes wi the boys since ah wis last oan Earth, the ex-Hibs casual Mikey Devlin said to Tazak, the Cyrastorian youth's leader, as the monitor on the ship panned the East Stand at Easter Road.

— Ah kin bet, mate, the tall, gangling Tazak replied, puffing on his Regal King Size. The substance called snout that his stumpy Earthling friend, whom he towered over, had introduced them to; it was a truly wondrous experience. He remembered that first time, when he had coughed up his virgin lungs. Now he was on forty a day.

Mikey scrutinised the faces, zeroing in on a few recognisable ones. — That wee cunt Ally Masters, used tae run wi the Baby Crew. Looks like ehs a top boy now. Nae fuckin sign ay the wee brar bit, eh.

Tazak smiled at his friend. — Well, we pey these cunts a visit the night. See what thir up tae, eh?

Mikey knew what that familiar glow in his friend's large brown eyes meant. He was up for some serious mischief. But there was a bigger issue. The time was at hand. His time, their time, and Tazak's adventurism could not be allowed to fuck things up. Whether you were in space with internal or external technology at your disposal which could obliterate solar systems, or on the streets looking for a row, it was timing that was important. Mikey Devlin was a top boy. He knew the same rules applied anywhere in warfare. — Ah'm playin it cool first, mind. Ah'll stey up here until ye git the cunts tae see things oor wey, then ah'll come doon. Once they fuckin tubes see who organised the whole deal, they'll accept me as the main man. N wir no jist talkin aboot the cashies here. Wir talkin the whole fuckin Planet Earth, ya cunt.

— As long as this fuckin scam ay yours works oot, ya cunt.

A smile played across Tazak's small mouth, as he held his Regal King Size in his long, thin fingers.

— Course it will. Wir no jist joyridin here, gaun doon thaire n takin some cunts in thair sleep n stickin fuckin tubes up thair erses fir the crack. This is when we formally announce oor presence. This is whaire we brek aw yir Cyrastorian rules. Youse goat the boatil?

— Too right wi fuckin huv, Tazak said, somewhat defensively.

— You ken the auld cunts back it your place. They dinnae study Earth in great detail any mair. They ken it'll soon be fucked, eh. Aw they want is for you cunts no tae interfere, jist leave thum alain. But if youse go in and install ma crew as top boys oan the planet, then yis kin rule fae a distance and these auld cunts'll pick up fuck-all sign ay any ay youse extraterrestrial radges oan the planet. That's goat tae be the game plan, man.

— Sounds awright n theory . . . Tazak puffed on his tab.

Mikey smiled, flashing his large teeth at the young Cyrastorian. This was a gesture his friend, accustomed as he was to the Earthman's startling appearance, never found less than disturbing.
— It's mair thin awright! Listen tae me, ya cunt! Ah wis the cunt thit organised Anderlecht in the UEFA Cup.

— That's fuckin nowt tae this but, Tazak replied.

— It's the same fuckin thing: a city, Brussels, or a planet, Earth. Jist fuckin specks in the solar system.

— Suppose, Tazak conceded. He had to defer to the maturity of the Earth casual. This had been a worrying development recently.

It had been some time since they had struck up their unlikely friendship. Tazak had been a novice Younger on a ship of Elders who had been sent on an errand to randomly pick one Earthling whom they would study and learn Earth language and culture from. The Earthling, Mikey Devlin, was seized in an Edinburgh club when they had stopped Earth time, and he had, after the shock, proved to be only too willing to assist them. Mikey actually requested to extend his stay, wanted as he was by local police on Earth for a wounding offence at Waverley Station after a full-scale pagger. Mikey Devlin had struck up a deal with the aliens. All they had to do was to go back with him to Earth with him on occasion, and find him some lassies to shag. The Elders were happy to oblige. Mikey, though, had befriended some of the alien youth, particularly Tazak, who would take him to Earth on their old cruising ship, enjoying his company. Mikey was a shrewd cunt and his stock had risen with the aliens and soon he became accepted as one of them. He encouraged the Youngers in the consumption of tobacco, a drug they seemed strongly predisposed towards. Their snout addiction kept them tied in a strange way to Planet Earth, and meant that Mikey would always be able to visit home. For his part, the only thing Tazak couldn't get used to was the rank, sweet smell of the Earth alien's skin.

Mikey thought that the aliens' naive interest in physical technology was a load of shite, and he had studied the power of the Will intensely, learning how to resource some of its wonders. He kept his disdain of the youths' interests to himself as he liked them, and he had to concede that the Cyrastorian Elders were boring cunts.

10

The gathering of the posses and the tribes in the non-salubrious area of old Midlothian and south-east suburban

Edinburgh had puzzled the travellers themselves as much as the authorities. Various New Age sages and pseudo prophets had advanced their theories, but the local authorities could do nothing and the government would not intervene as the population in the makeshift camps rose to over twenty thousand.

I I

The local dealers were having a field day and Jimmy and Semo, high from an anticipated success with Clint Phillips in the criminal injuries scam, thought they'd try their hands at more private enterprise. Semo had a good contact in Leith and they went into town in a nicked car to score some acid, in the hope of punting it to the travellers. They drove into the port and picked up their friend Alec Murphy, who took them down to a flat in the Southside, telling them that they were going to meet a guy Murphy simply referred to as the 'Student Cunt'.

— The Student Cunt's awright. Eh isnae really a student at aw, Alec explained. — He's no been tae a college or nowt like that fir years n years. Bit ehs goat a degree: economics, or some shite. But it's like, eh still sounds like a fuckin student, ken?

The boys nodded in a vague comprehension.

Alec warned them about the Student Cunt, who, he felt, tended to formulate the most banal observations as rambling, philosophical propositions worthy of further speculation. On his day, Murphy observed, in optimum conditions, and in the right company, the Student Cunt could be mildly amusing.

Such days, circumstances and companies were, he felt, increasingly few.

Mounting the steps of the dealer's flat with growing anticipation and excitement, Jimmy Mulgrew felt that he had made the big time. He swaggered in like a gangster, checking his look in a mirror in the hallway. He would see Shelley down the chippy later, drop a few hints about 'business'. She couldn't fail to be impressed. Alan Devlin was yesterday's man, Jimmy thought, with a vigorous rush of confidence. A fuckin garage attendant! Top boy my hole! He'd lost it, and the cunt was just treading water. Jimmy's time had yet to come.

Jimmy's fantasies deflated quickly as a guy with a mop of curly hair and black-rimmed glasses ushered them into the front room. There was a woman with lank brown hair and a vesty red top who was feeding a baby from a bottle. She didn't even register their presence.

— Alec . . . hi . . . said the Student Cunt, seeming a little put out at the observation of Alec's friends' relative youth. — Can I have a private word?

Alec turned back to Jimmy and Semo. — Hud oan a minute, boys, he said, disappearing into the kitchen with the Student Cunt. Alec knew he shouldn't have brought them up to the Student Cunt's pad. He hadn't really been thinking.

— How old are these guys? the Student Cunt asked.

— Sixteen and seventeen, Alec said. — Young team, fae oot at Rosewell, but sound cunts, like. Ah mean, ah mind you said that ah could jist bring any cunt ah wanted sorted up here.

— That's all very well *ceteris paribus*, Alec, the Student Cunt said, — but it's a truism that youth are always impressed by new things and therefore tend to run off at the fucking mouth and I can do without labdicks up my fucking arse.

— These boys ken the score, Alec shrugged.

The Student Cunt's eyes rolled doubtfully behind his spectacles.

In the living room, Jimmy was feeling the embarrassed silence with the mother and the baby. He reckoned Semo must have been too, because he was compelled to break it. — How auld's the bairn? he asked.

The woman looked up at him, her eyes cold and detached. — Three months, she said uninterestedly.

Semo nodded thoughtfully. Then he pointed at the woman. — Listen, see whin ye hud the bairn, he asked, — wis it sair?

— What? The woman looked at him in a more focused manner.

— Whin ye hud the bairn, wis it sair?

She looked him up and down. Jimmy gave an involuntary snigger, feeling as if a small motor which he couldn't switch off was oscillating his shoulders from a space in his chest cavity.

— Naw, Semo began seriously, — it's jist, like, ah cannae imagine what it must be like tae huv tae dae something like that . . . it's too freaky, eh? Ah mean, ye cannae really think aboot a livin thing growin inside ay ye, cause it wid like freak ye oot, ken what ah mean?

— Ye just git on wi it, the woman shrugged.

— Ye jist git oan wi it, Semo repeated, nodding reflectively. Then he turned to Jimmy. — Ah suppose ye fuckin well huv tae, eh! He laughed. — Cannae take it back! He looked at the woman. — It's true bit, eh?

Jimmy started sniggering again, as the woman on the couch shook her head and picked a bit of fluff out of the baby's ear. The Student Cunt came through and, with a startled, apologetic expression aimed at the woman, ushered the boys from the Rosewell young team through to the kitchen.

Alec winked at them as the Student Cunt opened a cupboard, pulled out a clay jar marked SUGAR, lifted a bag out of it and rummaged inside, producing some tabs. — Fifty strawberries, he smiled.

— Sound, Jimmy grinned, and settled up.

They went back through to the living room and sat down. The Student Cunt put a tape on. As it started, Jimmy stole a glance at the woman with the baby, before clamping his jaw shut to stop himself from sniggering. He thought of Clint's jaw wired up, and heard soft, appreciative wheezes coming from inside his chest as he vibrated softly on the couch.

The Student Cunt thought that Jimmy was vibing to the music. — East Coast Project, he said, then, turning to Alec, added with great sincerity, — Some pri-tay interesting things going down there.

— Mmm, Alec said non-committally.

The Student Cunt then turned to Semo. — Your neck of the woods, that's where all those posses have gathered, isn't it?

The woman feeding the baby looked up with interest for the first time.

— Aye, Semo nodded. — It's too fuckin radge.

This was the Student Cunt's opportunity to launch into a spiel concerning his view of what was happening in contemporary society. It was the others' cue to make their excuses and go. Jimmy winced when he heard the Student Cunt describe himself to Alec as 'working class' , making it sound like 'wehking closs'. They departed as quickly as they could, going on to a snooker club for a couple of frames and a few beers. Then Alec left, so they thieved another motor to get back out to the sticks.

In the car, Jimmy couldn't resist trying one of the tabs. After a few minutes, the whole place seemed to go crazy and he could barely see Semo sitting next to him in the driver's seat.

— Just as well you never took any ay these, Semo, Jimmy

gasped, as the car turned and sped down the city roads into a wall of blinding light which shot up from the catseyes. They were flying. — Ah'm sayin, jist as well you never hud yin, eh, Semo?

— Shut the fuck up . . . ah'm tryin tae concentrate oan the road . . . ah necked yin ay they tabs n aw n it's kickin in fine style! Semo moaned.

— STOAP! STOAP THE FUCKIN CAR! Jimmy felt the unremitting pulse of raw terror in every cell of his body. ·

— Fuck off! Ah kin see fine. Dinnae fuckin nudge ays! Semo snapped as Jimmy gripped his arm. — Ah kin see by the catseyes in the road . . . pit oan the fuckin cassette . . .

Jimmy clicked on the play button.

Wonderwall by Oasis came on, Liam Gallagher singing about winding roads and blinding lights.

— GIT THAT OAF! Semo roared. — Switch oan the fuckin radio!

— Right . . . Jimmy shivered. He switched oan the radio, bur Liam kept singing about those winding roads and blinding lights, the song Jimmy's old man claimed was a Beatles rip-off, although he said that about all Oasis songs.

— Ah said switch it oaf! Pit oan the fuckin radio! Semo hissed.

— Ah did! That is the radio! It's oan the fuckin radio n aw! Same song!

— Fuck sakes . . . How mad is that, man, eh? Semo groaned. He couldn't stop the car. Try as he might, he couldn't stop it. — This fuckin car willnae fuckin well stoap!

Jimmy had his hands over his eyes. He looked through them. They weren't moving. — It . . . it hus stoaped. Wir no movin. Wir stoaped, ya daft cunt!

Semo realised that he had parked the car by the side of the road. They got out and made their way tentatively down the street. He looked at the objects that littered the urban landscape through a distorted lens. His limbs were leaden; it was like everything was an effort. Just to keep walking. Just to keep moving. Then they stopped dead.

12

Tazak and Mikey walked down the three-dimensional film set that was Princes Street, absorbing the frozen stillness of the humans, their pets and their vehicles.

Mikey observed some girls, shopping smiles caught in suspended animation. — Hmmm . . . no bad . . .

This was one of the best things in this space game for Mikey Devlin: to just stop Earth time and check every cunt out. Tazak was getting impatient though. It was too much of a psychic energy outlay and it could even send a vibe to the Elders who would investigate and their game would be up before it really started. The best way to halt Earth time was to pick a small, rural spot at night and freeze proceedings in the locality. Operating on this sort of scale was crazy. Tazak was growing irritated with Mikey's fannying about. — C'moan, ya cunt! he shouted. — Wuv goat tae fuckin nash!

— Aye . . . aye . . . Mikey was looking a slim, dark-haired girl up and down. — No bad, he commented, no bad at aw.

Tazak stared with disgust at this chunky, hairy Earth female, with its ugly strips of fur above its tiny eyes; its weird head, with its large, protruding nose and that horrible swelling around the lips of the big mouth. They were truly a repulsive-looking race, yet biologically not so different from his own people. He remembered back to his studies at the Foundation as a Younger, where the others had mocked his small eyes and called him the 'Earthling'. It was ironic that he should be down here now, mixing with them.

He shuddered in recall at the occasion, when, with Mikey, he had coupled with one of these creatures, a small, almost hairless female. They were all in a very high transcendental state at the time, but he had felt disgusted with himself afterwards. Even more irritated at this recall, he hissed at his Earth host, – Ah sais nash! Wuv goat things tae dae!

— Aye, right then, ya cunt, Mikey moaned. He had to concede, there *were* things to do.

13

Shelley was dreaming again. She was on the ship and the alien was standing over her. There was a man there this time, a human being. It wasn't Liam. It looked a little bit like Alan Devlin.

14

Ally Masters was having the dream also. He was coming home with Denny McEwan and Bri Garratt through the city centre. Soul Fusion had been a good one but the fanny werenae biting and, if the truth be told, the Es were a bit smacky. He was feeling them. Everything seemed to be slowing down. Then, through a blurred haze, a strange light flooded into Ally's eyes.

At first he thought it was just the inappropriate appreciation of a distant street lamp brought on by the pills, but its intensity and ubiquity was too overwhelming. This was growing into an amorphous mass of protoplasm and he was heading through it, even as it seemed to be forming a structure around him. He sensed that others were walking alongside him, but he couldn't turn his head. He tried to shout to Denny and Bri but nothing came out.

Then, in a strange instant, he found himself fully awake and in what seemed like an immense white amphitheatre.

— Is this the fuckin whitey tae end aw whiteys or what? Ally asked, looking at Bri and Denny. His friends' eyes had shrunk to pinpricks. He felt a strong ammonia-like sting in his nostrils.

— No fuckin real, man! Denny said, tentatively touching the white walls, which had looked smooth but on closer examination and touch seemed to be composed of tightly packed, glowing encrustations.

Then, where there had previously only seemed to be a wall, a door opened and two large aliens, naked save for a loincloth to cover their genitals, and devoid of bodily hair, walked into the huge amphitheatre. — Awright, boys. How yis daein? one of them said.

The Earth thugs were too shocked to reply. Then, without looking at his friends, Bri Garratt asked, – Aw, fuckin hell, man . . . what the fuck've wi goat here . . . ?

— Fuckin aliens, man! Wild! Denny McEwan gasped.

— Well, fuckin aliens or nae fuckin aliens, nae cunt fucks wi the Hibs crew, Ally snarled, then turned to the Cyrastorian youths. — Ah dinnae ken what youse cunts are aboot, but if yis fuckin well want bother yis uv came tae the right fuckin place . . . The East Terracing top boy pulled out his Stanley knife and advanced towards the tall, thin creatures.

The aliens remained unfazed by Ally Masters' approach. The Earth Casual sensed his hosts' dismissive arrogance. He lashed out at the spokesperson, only to feel his blade bounce against an invisible wall which the Hibs boy could just about visualise as a quivering and pulsing translucent membrane, just a few inches from his would-be victim.

— Yir shitey fuckin Stanley knives are fuck-all use against oor force field, eh, Earth cunt?! the alien sneered.

— Fuck . . . Ally moaned.

— No sae fuckin wide now, ya fuckin Earth tube, another alien laughed.

The top alien gestured languidly and the Stanley knife tore out of Ally's grip and stuck in the wall. — See, Earth cunt, youse think thit yir a hard crew but yir jist a bunch ay fuckin shitein cunts in the whole intergalactic scheme ay things. We've no even started here yit. Whaire's yir top boys hing oot?

— What the fuck dae youse cunts want? Ally demanded.

— You tae shut yir mooth fir a second, the alien smiled through his thin lips. — Ah'm Tazak, by the way. Ah ken youse cunts so dinnae bother wi the introductions. Tazak lit up a cigarette. — Ah'd crash the ash, bit ah'm runnin a wee bit low. Anywey, here's how it is: thaire's nae fuckin wey that youse cunts'll run us, so dinnae even think aboot it. But we're here tae help youse. We need cunts doon here tae run the fuckin show fir us. We want youse cunts, cause youse speak oor fuckin language. Could've landed in California in the desert like in aw they crap films ay yours, but we went tae Midlothian but, eh.

— How here but? Ally asked.

— Goat tae land somewhere. Might as well be here as anywhere else, eh? Besides, we ken the score. It's only Scotland. Nae cunt listens tae youse dippit fuckers. Anywey, we'll make every cunt listen tae us. Whae runs things doon here now?

— Like, the main men n that? Ally asked.

— Aye.

— Well, that's like in London, or Washington, eh? Denny turned to Ally, who nodded.

— Fuck off, these cunts dinnae rule us. Bri tapped his chest.

— Aye, but that's the fuckin government, ya cunt. Like Westminster . . . or the White Hoose. That's whaire the real power is.

— The only fuckin White Hoose ah ken is the one in Niddrie . . . Denny laughed.

Tazak was growing impatient. — Shut it the now, Earth cunt! Wir talkin serious business here! We'll fuckin gie they cunts a wee demonstration ay what we kin dae. They kin pit the polis oan as much fuckin OT as they like – this is the mentalist crew in the universe thir dealin wi here! They've no seen real fuckin swedgin yit! We'll fuckin show thum swedgin! Swedgin thit could tear a fuckin solar system apart!

The top boys looked at each other. This alien cunt, this Tazak, talked a good pagger. They would bide their time and see if the cunt could deliver. They could feel the adrenalin pumping through their bodies. Masters and his crew sensed that they had been preparing themselves all their lives for something like this to go off, and they were determined not to let the colours down.

15

The chippy was doing great business. Not from the travellers who were barred by the growing number of police from crossing over the flyover, but from the reporters and camera crews who had come to observe the phenomenon. However, Vincent, the proprietor, was still a far from happy man. There had been a break-in the other night. The fags and cash had been secured in a strongroom and the lock was intact. The thieves, in their frustration at only being able to get some confectionery, had splashed the contents of industrial-sized chip-sauce containers all over his shop. He had an idea who the culprits were. It had to be that Ian Simpson and that Jimmy Mulgrew. He'd see Drysdale about this.

16

The energy was there. It was telling them to come to Scotland. In London, in Amsterdam, in Sydney, in San Francisco, the posses on their comedown heard the message. They would all head to Rosewell in Midlothian for the greatest ever gathering of human spirits. The energy crackled in the air. Posse leaders, seemingly driven, pointed the way to this small settlement on the fringes of Northern Europe. The authorities, sensing something was in the air, watched and waited.

At the chippy, Vincent was dumbfounded. The lock for the strongroom was intact and all the cash was present, but, miraculously, the cigarettes seemed to have vanished.

17

It's almost 4 a.m. and Andrew, Jimmy's dad, feels that his son should be asleep and his mates should be home, instead of upstairs in Jimmy's room playing those cheap tartan techno tapes which they buy in the Asian discount store up the South Bridge. Parental control had become a blurred concept since Jimmy had filled out and met his old man's warning gazes with challenging, hardened eyes.

Jimmy's dad is not too sensitive though, and as long as it's low enough for him to hear the telly, then it's not a problem. The doctor's Valium has taken the edge of Andrew's pain. His wife is long gone. She got fed up with Andrew's depression, impotence and lack of cash since his redundancy from Bilston Glen, and went to live with a day-centre worker in Penicuik.

Jimmy should be sleeping. Fuckin school, Andrew thinks, then remembers that his son left last year. Andrew feels that Jimmy's mother must be giving their son money. Money which goes on drugs, when Andrew finds himself lucky to manage a fuckin pint down the club on a giro day. That selfish wee cunt and his mates were always off their tits on something or other. Like the other night; they had come back in some state. Acid. He knew what it was. These wee cunts thought they had invented drugs.

It's ten years since he was made redundant from the pit. History had vindicated Scargill, sure, but that counted for fuck all. The era had been about selfishness and greed and Scargill was simply out of time and Thatcher was in. Andrew had put in his shift on the picket lines, went on demos, but had sensed from the off that it wasn't going to be a glorious time for the old industrial proletariat. The vibe was important. The vibe then was small and petty and fearful, with too many people eager to embrace the false certainties their masters and assorted lackeys bleated out.

In a way it is healthier now: nobody believes in anything these lying bastards ever spout. Even the politicians themselves seem to rap out the old bullshit with more desperation than the traditional smug conviction everyone's grown accustomed to. The vibe is changing alright, but what is it changing into?

Boom boom boom. The tartan techno beat thuds insistently. Boom boom boom. Andrew hits the volume button on the handset, but the fuckin tartan techno, it's moving up too, keeping pace. Then Mrs Mooney next door is thumping on the wall. Andrew lets his knuckles go white on the rests of the chair.

Upstairs, Jimmy and the boys are celebrating. The duty cop at the substation, PC Drysdale, had given them the coveted crime number they required to advance their criminal injuries claim. Drysdale had taken in the young team's fictitious rantings all too eagerly. He had little time for the local yobs, but far less for those fucking travellers who were making life on his patch a complete misery. It would only take one flashpoint incident for something horrendous to go off, then his promotion board chances would be well and truly jeopardised. This sensitive-policing bollocks had its limitations. Drysdale's instincts told him to wade in and bang up some likely-looking crusties. However, he knew the line that Cowan, the head guy on the promotion board, would be taking.

18

The Hibs boys were being less than cooperative with the aliens.
— How the fuck should we help youse? Ally Masters asked Tazak.

The alien puffed thoughtfully on his cigarette. — Youse kin dae what yis fuckin well like –

He was interrupted by another voice: — Cause we're daein you a favour, ya fuckin radge! The Earthlings stood shocked at the presence of one of their own kind.

The Hibs boys stared in disbelief. It was Mikey Devlin, Alan Devlin's brother. The cunt that vanished. Now he was back. He was still clad in Nikes!

— Mikey Devlin! Ally Masters said, looking Mikey up and down. — Very . . . eh, eighties gear, ma man. The trainers like. Whaire ye been hidin?

— Hyperspace, eh, Mikey smiled, — n ah've goat a tale tae tell youse cunts thit's a loat mair important thin fuckin labels.

He told the boys the story.

— But how could ye just leave like that? Bri Garratt demanded.

— Turn yir back oan yir mates? Ally asked.

— Turnt ehs back oan Scotland, Denny McEwan sneered.

The parochialism of his old crew was getting on Mikey's tits. — Fuck Scotland, ya daft cunt! Ah've been aw ower the fuckin universe! Seen things youse cunts couldnae fuckin well see in yir wildest dreams!

Denny held his ground. — Fuck it, Mikey. Dinnae come back here n slag off Scotland, that's aw ah'm sayin.

Mikey looked tiredly at Tazak. These cunts were just not getting the message. — Scotland . . . he scoffed, — it's jist a fuckin spec ay dust tae me. Shut the fuck up aboot Scotland. Ah'm back here tae make us the top fuckin crew oan Planet Earth!

19

The weather had broken. It pished rain from the heavens. Trevor Drysdale tried to get a good night's sleep for his promotion board interview the next day. Only the thought of those crusty bastards, drenched in a cold field, gave him the warm satisfaction to lull him into soft dreams. As anxious as he was the next morning, Drysdale had prepared well. Interviews were all about cracking codes, finding the current vogue; one minute liberal rhetoric, the next the hard line. The best professional in any bureaucracy was always the one who could control his or her prejudices and learn the dominant spiel with conviction. How one acted, of course, was totally irrelevant, as long as the espousal was effective. With Cowan, it was the liberal bullshit he wanted, so Drysdale would give him it, in shovel-loads. For Cowan, toeing the line was almost as important as personal tidiness.

20

Clint Phillips has been body-swerving Jimmy and Semo since his hospital discharge and the registration of the crime with PC Drysdale. They meet up with Dunky by the quarry, who tells them that Clint has intimated to them that he does not intend to share out the proceeds from the Criminal Injuries Compensation Board. A very aggrieved Jimmy and Semo decide to put the frighteners on Clint. They will steal a car and drive it at speed at him, across the forecourt in the garage. — Show the cunt wir no fuckin aboot here, Semo said.

21

Trevor Drysdale looks at his reflection in the mirror. He has backcombed and blow-dried his hair. He looks a bit poofy with a quiff, Drysdale thinks, but Cowan would approve of the softer image, which is much less severe than his normal Brylcreemed look. Drysdale considers that he cuts quite a dash in his light grey Moss Bros suit. He was moving out of this ugly hellhole, taking on supervisory responsibilities. The South Side Area Station was calling.

Drysdale noted that the heavy rain has stopped. He takes the car into the city, allowing himself plenty of time. He parks about half a mile away from that huge, pristine, structure; a true temple of law enforcement, that is the South Side Area Station. Drysdale wanted to walk, so that he will come upon the building that would surely be his new home, orientating himself slowly and gradually to his new surroundings.

22

Jimmy and Semo's attempted scare on Clint didn't quite go as planned. As they parked in waiting across the road, Clint was nowhere to be seen. Instead, Jimmy's anger rose as he saw Shelley and Sarah go into the garage shop and disappear into the back shop with Alan Devlin.

— That Devlin cunt . . . Jimmy hissed.

— Hud on the now, Semo smiled, — we'll show that fucker.

Alan Devlin was fucking Sarah across the table, and Shelley was watching them, thinking how uncomfortable it looked compared to how it actually felt when she was in the same position.

Devlin was well into his stride when a loud, repetitive car horn blasted from the forecourt. — Fuck! Marshall! He snarled, aggrieved at having to pull out of a tense Sarah, who tugged her dress down and her knickers on in almost one movement. Devlin janked on his trousers and ran into the front shop. Jimmy and Semo were in the car, with the window wound down. They were waving bags of crisps and some other stock they had taken from the shop while Devlin had been on the job.

— YOUSE UR FUCKIN DEID, YA WEE CUNTS! Alan yelled, charging towards the car, but the boys sped off down the road.

At this point Clint came across the forecourt, licking an ice-cream cone.

— Whair the fuck've you been? Devlin hissed.

— Ah jist goat a cone . . . fae the van . . . Clint gasped weakly, as Shelley and Sarah giggled in the shop doorway.

— Ah fuckin well telt ye tae keep shoatie! Devlin snapped, and in a swiping movement knocked Clint's cone from his hand onto the oily forecourt.

The younger man's face flushed red and his eyes watered as he registered the chuckles emanating from the girls.

Jimmy and Semo had decided to keep the car and go into town to score more drugs. They had managed to success-fully punt the acid to a posse of travellers. The stolen car, a white Nissan Micra, was, by coincidence, exactly the same colour and year as that driven by Allister Farmer, a member of the local police promotion board for the South Side of Edinburgh. The coincidence became a cruel one as Farmer, heading up to the South Side Area Station to conduct some promotion interviews, was overtaken by Jimmy and Semo's car as they sped up into town to head down to Alec Murphy's at Leith.

They ripped past Farmer along St Leonard's Street, Jimmy giving the outraged plain-clothed cop a languid V-sign. As

Trevor Drysdale was walking along the pavement, thinking of his responses to the questions that would be asked at the interview, he was unaware that he was passing a huge, murky, oily puddle, which spilled onto the road from a blocked drain. Drysdale had little time to react as a white Nissan Micra sent a sheet of filthy liquid flying over him. In an instant Drysdale's quiff was plastered to his cranium, and one side of light grey suit had turned a wet black.

Drysdale could only look himself up and down. He let out an anguished, primal scream from the depths of his sickened soul: — YA BASTARD! YA FUCKEN BASTARD! as he looked up to see the back of the white Nissan Micra recede up the street.

The police promotional applicant was unaware, however, that there were two white Nissan Micras, and that the offending one had got through the lights at the top of the road. But the second one, containing the innocent Allister Farmer, had stopped at red. For his part, Farmer had been so full of anger at the careless driving from the car ahead, he'd failed to notice what had happened to the unfortunate pedestrian on St Leonard's Street.

On noticing that the lights had changed to red and that the Nissan Micra had halted, Drysdale embarked on a lung-bursting run towards the stationary car. On catching up to it, he tapped the side window. Allister Farmer rolled it down, only to be met with a choking throaty roar of: — YOU FUCKIN BASTARD! and a clenched fist, which crashed into him, bursting his nose.

Drysdale was off. He had extracted his revenge, now he had to save the situation. He still had ten minutes left. He ran into a pub and attempted to clean himself up as best he could. He looked at himself in the mirror. He was a mess, an absolute fucking mess. All he could do was to try and explain to Cowan, and hope that the chairman of the promotion board would accept his story and turn a blind eye to his appearance.

Allister Farmer stemmed the blood with a hanky. The police inspector was shaken. He had investigated many such arbitrary assaults, but had never, ever conceived of himself as the victim of one, particularly in broad daylight, on a busy road, near a main police station. Farmer had been too stunned to see where the culprit had escaped to. He shakily started up his car, passed through the lights and parked outside the area station.

— Allister! What happened? Are you okay? a concerned Tom Cowan asked, as a first-aider treated Farmer's nosebleed. A couple of investigating officers were straight onto the street, looking for the culprit.

— God, Tom, I was assaulted, in my own car, just outside the bloody station, by some fucking community-care jakey who tapped on my window . . . Anyway . . . we've got our interviews. The show must go on.

— What did the guy look like?

— Later, Tom, later. Let's not keep the interviewees waiting.

Cowan gestured affirmatively, ushering Farmer and Des Thorpe from personnel into the interview room. They had another quick look at the forms they had already studied in detail. In terms of experience, background and lodge membership, they agreed that Trevor Drysdale was an excellent candidate for one of the posts. — I know Drysdale, Cowan said, brushing a distasteful white thread off his jacket sleeve. — A Craft stalwart and a damn fine polisman.

They sent for Drysdale who trooped timidly in. Cowan's jaw fell, but not as far as Farmer's.

Drysdale just covered his eyes and burst into tears. Another decade at the substation loomed.

23

Gezra, the Appropriate Behaviour Compliance Elder, found it hard to fathom today's youngsters. He had, perhaps, been around too long, he considered again, but what satisfaction they got from going to backward places like Earth in their beat-up spacecrafts and kidnapping hapless aliens and sticking anal probes into them was beyond his understanding. It was just one of these things that youths did, he supposed. Once it got into the culture and the telepathic media got a hold of it, it spread like a bush fire. These kids were harmless really, but the animals on Earth had rights too, something it was difficult for youngsters nowadays to grasp.

His people had learned all about Earth culture from a native of the planet called Mikey Devlin, whom they had kidnapped for cultural study five years ago. He opted to stay with them rather than undergo memory wipe, provided they could supply him with young Earthwomen, the dangerous and highly addictive substance called snout and the odd takeaway. Several top Hollywood actresses and international models, *Sun* Page Three girls and females who frequented Buster Brown's nightclub in Edinburgh had claimed that aliens had come for them in the night, but nobody made the connection or took the complaints seriously. They all said that one of the creatures looked human. Well, that was Devlin, thought the Appropriate Behaviour Compliance Elder: a fanny merchant of the first order.

Mikey had been okay when he stuck to the official tours. He was sound, a plausible cunt, and they liked having him around. But, Gezra reflected, the Earthman had fallen in with a crowd of rebellious youngsters and they took him on illicit trips back home. They weren't bad really, but they were silly.

Once they entered the procreative years, this behaviour would cease. But, for now, the Earthman was with them. Gezra was concerned that Mikey might try to tempt them to make contact with his old friends on Earth; this was strictly forbidden without a memory wipe. But then there would be the imperative that Tazak and Mikey would need to replenish their supplies of the drug snout! Gezra would go now, and to avoid being detected, he would travel by technology rather than by the Will. With thin, trembling fingers, he set his controls.

24

Jimmy and Semo were unable to score anything from Alec other than some temazapam capsules and a little bit of hash. They were pretty disappointed as they drove back out from the city.

25

And all the people who had converged on the fields near the old mine works, spreading out from as far as the eye could see, were listening to the music, the sweet music, which filled the air. As the sky darkened, the exhilarated rushes were intensified by the awesome sight of the spacecraft coming down to Earth. It was like a giant white seashell, as if it was composed of other, smaller shells, and it hovered silently some seventy feet above the site.

Some who weren't religious crossed themselves; others who were quickly renounced everything they'd been taught.

The ship, in its magnificent splendour, did not move. It just stayed put. This was it, this was the moment all the travellers had been waiting for.

26

Jimmy and Semo first noticed delays at the Newcraighall round-about. Then the police were turning everyone back. — But we live ower thaire, Semo pleaded, suddenly realising that they were in a stolen car. But the cop had other things on his mind. He pointed to the huge disc that hung in the sky over the other side of the bypass.

Semo turned to Jimmy. — Thaire's a fuckin flying saucer oan toap ay ma hoose!

27

At the hastily convened conference in Washington, the world's leaders were finding it difficult to understand the alien spokespersons. They had enlisted some of the CCS top boys, who had the confidence of the aliens, to help with the translation.

— We could fuckin run youse like that. Tazak snapped his fingers. — Aw yir fuckin weapons, thir fuckin nowt against us, eh.

The world leaders looked far more concerned than the impassive, square-jawed security men from the federal forces, who surrounded them.

— Fuckin shitein cunts, another alien sneered, picking up on the psychic vibe of fear.

— I don't see that this – the British Prime Minister started.

— You shut yir fuckin mooth, ya specky cunt! Tazak snapped. — Nae cunt's fuckin talkin tae you! Right! Fuckin wide-o!

The PM looked nervously at his feet. The Special Air Services officer who flanked him tensed up.

— What ah wis fuckin sayin before this cunt started wis – Tazak looked at the PM who was silent, — we could fuckin annihilate youse in a swedge. Nae fuckin problem. We've goat the fuckin technology, eh. And the fuckin willpower. So the wey we see it is, youse cunts dae as yis ur fuckin well telt and that's it. Endy fuckin story.

Ally from the CCS stood up. For all that they spoke the same language, the aliens' arrogance still jarred. If only he could get that cunt with his force field down. — No in a square go yis couldnae.

— Eh? What's this cunt sayin? one alien asked Tazak.

The American President put his hand on Ally's shoulders to force him to sit down. — Sit on your goddamn ass, will you, they got us over a barrel!

Ally's head crashed into the leader of the Western World's nose. The President fell back into his chair, dazed, pulling a handkerchief from his inside pocket to stem blood and tears. Two security men from the FBI moved swiftly forward as Masters sneered, bracing himself for a straightener, but the alien raised his hand and the President ushered his guards to stop.

— Nae cunt fuckin pills me up, Ally said.

— Boy's right enough, Tazak considered. — Ah'm hearin a loat ay talk fae youse cunts aboot this n that, but these boys are the only ones that huv stuck up fir thumselves. He looked at Ally. — Yir no tryin tae tell me thit youse cunts ur feart ay they cunts, his large almond eyes sweeping over the world's leaders.

— That'll be fuckin right, Ally said, looking challengingly at the late-middle-aged posse of suits who led the world.

— Bit these cunts are the top boys, they tell every cunt what tae dae but, Tazak said.

The Chancellor of Germany cut in. — But ziss in a democracy. Ze process of choosing leaders is not based on physical fighting abilities but on ze vill of all ze people.

— Is it fuck, Ally said, quickly putting the cunt right. — If that's right, he said, pointing at the British Prime Minister, — how is it that nae cunt in Scotland voted for these bastards and we git thaim rulin us? Answer ays that! If ye fuckin well kin!

— Right enough, said Bri. Then he turned to the German Chancellor. — You keep yir fuckin nose oot ay things ye ken nowt aboot, right?

There followed a series of loud arguments. At one stage, it looked as if it was going to go off between the top boys of the Capital City Service and the security forces of the FBI.

— Fuckin shut it! Tazak, the alien leader, shouted, pointing at the world's leaders. — Listen, ah cannae handle they radge cunts nippin ma heid. — Fae now oan, he nodded over to the casuals, — youse cunts are in charge here. The alien leader threw a transmitter over to Ally. The startled football thug jumped back, letting the device drop on the floor. — It's only a fuckin mobby, ya radge! Pick it up!

Ally tentatively picked up the transmitter.

— Wi that yis kin bell us at any time, day or night. See, if these cunts – he swept his hand contemptuously around at the world's leaders, — if they fuckin well gie yis any grief, just bell us and we'll sort the cunts right oot. Fuckin surein wi will. Sort the cunts oot fir good, eh?

— Sound, Ally smiled. — Listen though . . . youse cunts say thit yis kin destroy anything on Earth fae space wi yir weapons?

— Aye . . . yis ur welcome tae come aboard n huv a shot, eh.

28

From the alien ship, Mikey Devlin looked down on the thousands of ravers making their excited pilgrimage below. He willed the monitor to pan out, across the green and brown hills of the Pentlands, and over the cityscape.

Something had twinged in a corner of Mikey's psyche. He retraced, focusing on the bypass, almost directly underneath them. He could see the garage. Closing in, Mikey was elated to spy his brother, Alan, operating the car wash.

Alan wanted to get rid of the driver, a PC Drysdale, as soon as possible. He had a young woman called Abigail Ford in a state of semi-undress in the back shop. Drysdale seemed away with it though. Probably this space thing had freaked him. Loads of them were like that. He had to concede that it was pretty mind-blowing. Then, at the corner of his eye, Alan saw something move in the front shop. He was concerned that Abby was getting ready to go. It wasn't her though, it was those wee wide cunts Jimmy Mulgrew and Semo!

— These cunts are fuckin well robbin us blind, ya useless tube! he shouted at Drysdale, who wouldn't react. Alan ran towards the shop, and Semo got out just in time, but he cornered Jimmy Mulgrew. The younger man tried to swing at him, but he was overpowered by the senior thug, who dragged him outside and proceded to boot him all over the forecourt. Semo jumped on Alan's back, but he was thrown off, and had to frantically scramble to his feet and swiftly retreat in order to escape a similar fate to his now semi-conscious friend.

Alan raked the battered young man's pockets and found only some change and a handful of jellies, which he confiscated. Drysdale drove out without making an arrest.

From his vessel, Mikey watched approvingly as his brother fucked the young girl in the back shop, as Jimmy Mulgrew stood up and staggered along the street. He waited until his brother had finished and the girl had departed, before freezing local time and carrying him onto the craft.

Alan was delighted to see his brother again. — Mikey! Ah dinnae believe it! You're behind aw this shite! Ah knew it! Ah'm no jokin, man, somethin telt ays tae come tae this fuckin place! That was how ah couldnae leave here! It wis you, man! He studied his older brother. — Fuck sake, man, ye look younger thin me!

— Clean livin, Mikey smiled, — no like you, ya cunt! It was useless to try to explain the concept of controlling cellular elasticity and form through the use of the Will.

— No goat any blaw, huv ye? Mikey asked.

— Naw, ah took some jellies oaf this wee cunt.

— What are they? Mikey asked. As Alan explained, Mikey's eyes grew wider. He took some of the capsules from Alan. — Jist ma fuckin ticket these, eh.

29

The day after the conference in Washington had effectively installed the Casual Administration as the new unitary Earth Government, there followed a series of disasters unprecedented in British sporting history. The board of directors of Heart of Midlothian FC were devastated to find that the stadium, which boasted three brand-new stands, had been completely vaporised by a beam from outer space. In Glasgow, Ibrox, so long Scotland's showcase arena, suffered a similar fate. The next horror was the destruction of Wembley Stadium and its famous twin towers. Then, sequentially, all the football grounds in the country, with the exception of Easter Road in Edinburgh, were obliterated. Ally and his mates made their centre for Earth Government at the stadium, using the funds of various Earth nation states to completely refurbish the stadium and embark on a massively expensive team-building programme.

In several Leith pubs a few terracing diehards whinged on about 'these fuckin casual cunts' in charge of the club, but the new regime was generally welcomed. The outgoing board had been even less happy than the international heads of state in standing down in favour of the top boys, but had little option in the face of the power the hoolies now wielded.

— Cool gig this, eh? Tazak said, as Mikey watched on the monitor. They still had made no contact with the dancing crowds below the craft. However, the time was nearly right.

— Aye, and it hus tae be said that they've done a better joab wi the club than the cunts they hud in charge. It's aw doon tae resources though, the eighties top boy sagely conceded.

Tazak looked at his friend. — Wi ready tae hit it?

30

Cheers went up as a thrashing telepathic bass line rocked the planet and the crowd jumped and swayed as a series of blinding lasers shot out from the craft. An Earth voice, a Scottish voice, asked: 'Are we havin a fuckin good one?' and the crowd screamed in unison: 'Yes!' They certainly were, the only dissenting voices coming from the Fubar crew who were signalling for more. — Lenny D! some cunt shouted.

An opening appeared in the craft and a small balcony extended from it. An Earthman walked out onto it. A huge cheer filled the air as his image was beamed for miles around. — We've goat the best fuckin sound system in the universe here! Mikey roared.

Shelley looked up from the crowd. This man was even more fantastic than Liam from Oasis . . . he was the man of her dreams.

At that point the man said: — And now gies a top Planet Earth welcome tae this big, skinny, spammy cunt whae's made it aw possible! Fae acroas the cosmos, Planet Cyrastor, massive respect for our fuckin main man, Tazaaaak!

Tazak joined Mikey on the balcony. He felt humbled by the reception the Earth crowd gave him. No way was the big alien cunt about to lose the floor with the stakes so high, and punters jumping about for as far as his large brown eyes could see. Vibing like fuck, he unleashed a psychic virus of beautiful and powerful sound unequalled anywhere in the universe.

The Earth crowd had known nothing like it. Even those who had been privileged to attend some of the biggest and most happening events since 1988's summer of love had to concede that this one was a bit special. Even club snobs agreed that the almost non-existent toilet and catering facilities failed to put a downer on the awesome nature of this event.

When he was exhausted, Tazak brought it down, and staggered from the balcony, back into the craft, to a tumultuous reception. — Cheers . . . that's me fucked . . . he telepathically flashed to the hordes below.

Inside the craft, Mikey was devastated. This was to be his big moment, but there was no way he could match that. The Earthman went out and did his best, using the full range of the psychic powers he'd developed, even extending himself past his breaking point, but very quickly into his set some groups were already chanting for the return of the big alien. He cut his performance short and returned to the interior of the craft, totally humiliated.

— Good one, Mikey conceded to his show-stealing friend, as he entered the amphitheatre which was the craft's central Will propulsion temple.

— It wis the fuckin best! Ah fuckin blew these Earth cunts away! Tell ays that wisnae something else! Tazak roared triumphantly.

— Aye, right, Mikey moped.

Tazak turned to his friend. — Listen, mate, you goat any snout oan ye? Ah'm gantin oan a fag, eh.

— Naw, Mikey said, reaching in his pocket and producing one of the jellies his brother had taken from Jimmy. — Take one ay these.

— What are they? Tazak asked, examining the egg-shaped capsules.

— Thir jist pills. They take away the snout cravin until wi kin go doon and git sorted, eh, Mikey shrugged. His face twisted into a smile, when, from the corner of his eye, he saw the alien neck the capsule.

31

Tazak was still recovering from the gig when Ally, Denny and Bri came through a door into the craft's central Will propulsion temple. There was another human with the casual mob. Tazak, who had grown used to differentiating members of the species, thought he looked like Mikey. The Cyrastorian glanced over at his colleague. — What the fuck are these cunts daein here? They've no goat authorisation.

Mikey smiled. — Ah gied thum authorisation but, eh. That's ma brar. He nodded at Alan, who smiled at Tazak, showing a full set of Earth teeth like Mikey's.

— You dinnae fuckin gie nae cunt authorisation oan this fuckin ship, Mikey! Tazak pointed at himself. — Ah'm the only cunt that gies any cunt authorisation! Right?!

Mikey stood up. — Naw, it's no right, mate. Ye see, thaire's gaunny be some fuckin changes roond here. This is ma fuckin ship now.

— Fuck off, Piltonian, dinnae you start gittin wide oan ays, Tazak scoffed, as Mikey squared up to him.

— You're no the only cunt wi psychic powers, Tazak. Mind that, Mikey warned.

Tazak laughed like a drain. This would be fuckin sad if it wasn't so funny. It was time this so-called top boy was put in his place. — Huh, huh, huh! Ye saw what happened tae your psychic powers oot thaire! Tazak turned to the Hibs crew and pointed to the hull of the craft. — Eh loast the fuckin flair! He shook his head forlornly at Mikey. — Listen, Earth cunt, ah might have taught ye aw that you ken, bit ah nivir taught ye aw thit *ah* ken!

This was true. Despite his immersion into Cyrastorian culture, Tazak, with that show outside, had painfully demonstrated to

Mikey that he had a repertoire and volume of psychic skills which the Hibs boy could never hope to emulate.

However, the ex-CCS man had one trick up his sleeve. — See that fuckin pill ah gied ye the now? Fir the snout cravin?

Tazak looked hestitant. Mikey flashed his teeth. Ally and the other boys looked lairy.

— Well, it wis nowt tae dae wi fags. It wis a jelly. Any minute now, aw your psychic powers'll be fuckin useless, eh. The only Will you'll be able tae access'll be the one ah hope yuv made oot fir yir next ay kin, ya cunt!

At these words Tazak felt his senses spinning out of control. He tried to orientate himself through the exercise of the Will, but he was unsteady on his long legs. — . . . Ughn . . . feel . . . suddenly . . . cunted . . . he gasped, staggering backwards against the glistening, encrusted hull of the ship.

The Hibs boy seized his chance and decked the gangling, foal-like alien with a chunky fist to the side of the creature's face, toppling the frail Cyrastorian like a stacked tower of playing cards. — No sae fuckin wide now, ya fuckin streak ay alien pish! Lesson in life: nae cunt fucks wi the Hibees boys! The cosmic thug grinned arrogantly as he sank the boot into his old intergalactic comrade's skinny ribcage.

Ally Masters and the boys moved in for the kill. — Nice one, Mikey! Lit's fuckin well stomp this cunt!

Mikey, though, halted the advancing Hibs boys. He looked down at his friend, who was shaking, making a high, agonised noise that he had never heard before, and his skin was losing its indigo-blue hue, becoming a sickly pink. — Leave um! The cunt's fucked!

Mikey backed away in horror from Tazak's high-pitched, resonant squeals which produced no intelligent words, although it was obvious the Cyrastorian was trying to speak them.

— What is it? Ally said.

— These cunts arenae used tae bein touched physically. That's how thir that weak-lookin. They cannae survive withoot their psychic shields! Ah've probably fuckin killed um! Mikey fell to his knees. — Tazak mate . . . ah'm fuckin sorry . . . ah didnae mean tae −

— Keep away from him!

Mikey turned to see an advancing Elder. He wore the white robes of the Appropriate Behaviour Compliance. Although this Cyrastorian looked the same as the rest of the race to the other top boys, Mikey had learned to distinguish them and he knew this one. — Gezra . . . he whispered.

— You've caused a fair bit ay bother, eh, Earth cunt . . .

— Ah didnae mean tae . . . Mikey stuttered.

The Appropriate Behaviour Compliance Elder had heard it all before. — Now it's time fir ye tae pey bit, eh.

The other Hibs boys tried to run the Cyrastorian Elder, but there was nothing the football thugs could do as light and sound burst and ripped all around them. They shut their eyes and held their ears to try to block out the shattering pain, but it seemed to be inside of them; twisting, ripping and splintering their bones. Unconsciousness mercifully took them, one by one, Ally Masters defiantly the last man to pass out.

32

Gezra had a lot of work to do. Firstly, Tazak had to be repaired, otherwise the youth would be reduced to the carrion phase, which was unacceptable. It had been centuries since any Cyrastorian had expired before their allocated time span. Death was not appropriate behaviour for one so young. Fortunately, the reparations proved non-problematic for such an experienced master of the Will.

The next phase he needed help with. He had to send for a Cyrastorian task force. This was unprecedented, but the behaviour of Mikey and Tazak meant that the entire inhabitants of Planet Earth needed memory-wiping. It was a big job, and the Principal Elders at the Foundation would not be amused at this state of affairs.

33

Shelley woke up feeling as if her head was going to explode. Her guts were in a turmoil, and she had shooting, stabbing pains in her abdomen. She made her way unsteadily to the toilet, unsure of which orifice to put towards the bowl. In the end she sat on it and felt a sickening shudder followed by a violent excretion of the life she had within her. She fell to the floor, her blood trailing across the bathroom lino. Before she slid into unconsciousness, the young woman had the strength to pull the flush, so that she would never have to look at the matter she had miscarried.

Lillian heard the screams and was quickly at her daughter's side. Ascertaining that Shelley was still breathing, she ran downstairs and called an ambulance. When she got back to the bathroom, the young girl was semi-conscious. She looked at her mother and said, — Sorry, Mum . . . I didnae even like the boy . . .

— It's okay, darlin, it's okay . . . Lillian wheezed in a soft mantra, mopping her sick child's brow, awaiting the ambulance's arrival.

They took Shelley into the hospital, where they kept her for a few days. The doctors told Lillian that she had had a miscarriage with some bad internal bleeding, but there would be no lasting damage. They advised her to put the girl on the pill. Lillian was too relieved to have strong words with her daughter; they would come later.

Sarah visited Shelley and told her that Jimmy was asking after her. Shelley was pleased to hear this. Jimmy was okay. Not as cool as Liam, but better than that Alan Devlin, who had just used her, getting her pregnant like that. She felt relieved. Whatever she told herself, she hadn't really wanted a baby.

34

Alan Devlin was upset. He had rediscovered his long-lost brother, only to find that Mikey had been sent to jail. The polis had finally caught up with him for that wounding offence at Waverley Station, all those years ago. Alan jacked in the garage job – there seemed little point in hanging around such a dump as Rosewell. These wee lassies from the school were fuckin jailbait and he wanted none of that; he saw what prison was doing to his brother.

Alan went back into the city. Working as a barman in a Rose Street hostelry, he met a trendy woman from London who was up for the Edinburgh Festival. Romance blossomed and he moved down to her place in Camden Town, and currently works behind a bar in Tufnell Park. He regularly returns to Edinburgh, to visit his brother Mikey in Saughton Prison, but he finds the visits very distressing. Mikey has lost his marbles a little, going on about aliens who come to his cell in the night and insert all sorts of probes into his orifices.

It hurts Alan to admit it, but he reckons that his brother has become a bit of a shirtlifter on the inside, and all this aliens stuff is just a form of denial.

But in the chilling silence of frozen Earth time, Mikey's anguished soul screams its mute pleas for assistance and clemency as Tazak's crew remove his immobilised body from his cell, and take it to their craft for further investigation.

The State of the Party

Crooky and Calum sat in a spartan but popular pub on Leith Walk arguing about whether or not it was a good idea to put something on the jukebox.

— Pump up the jukey, Cal, your turn tae feed the beast, Crooky ventured. He'd just bunged in a quid and he knew that Calum had money.

— Waste ay fuckin dosh, Calum said.

Crooky grimaced. He hoped that this cunt wasn't going to be in one of his tight-arsed moods. — Ah bit c'moan, ya cunt, pump up the fuckin jukey! he implored. — Ah cannae handle this nae-sounds-in-a-pub shite, man.

— Hud yir hoarses. Some daft cunt'll pit something oan in a minute. Ah'm no wastin fuckin poppy oan a jukey.

— You're fuckin flush, ya cunt.

Calum was about to continue the argument but his attention was arrested by the presence of a figure who shambled over from the bar to the corner of the pub, tentatively clutching a soda water and lime. Reaching his destination, this apparition just let his legs collapse, slumping down onto the padded seat. He sat in a still trance, broken only by an intermittent twitch.

— Deek the cunt thaire, man. That's wee Boaby Preston. Boaby! Calum shouted over, but the small, grey-fleshed figure in the old leather jacket ignored him.

— Shut up, fir fuck sakes. That cunt's a fuckin junkie.

Dinnae want somebody like that in tow. Paupin cunt, Crooky said. — Nae fuckin passengers the night, Cally, eh?

Calum scrutinised Boaby Preston. In the dirty, diminished figure staring at the glass, he caught sight of someone else, someone Boaby Preston had once been. Childhood and adolescent memories bounced around in his head. — Naw, man, you dinnae really ken the cunt. Sound fuckin guy. Boaby, Boaby Preston, he repeated. It was as if by saying his name often enough, Calum felt that he could somehow summon back the old incarnation. — The stories ah could tell ye aboot that cunt . . . BOABY!

Boaby Preston stared over at them. After straining for recall for a moment or two, he nodded a bemused half-acknowledgement. Calum experienced a depressing sadness at this lack of recognition and an embarrassment that, in front of Crooky, his familiarity had not been reciprocated by his old friend. Recovering from this setback, he rose and went over to Boaby. Crooky reluctantly joined them.

— Boaby . . . ya daft cunt . . . yir still no banging up, ur ye? Calum asked in weary compassion.

Boaby smiled slowly and made a non-committal gesture with one hand.

Uneasy at this reaction, Calum stormed into an anecdote. Surely, he thought, if he could whip up enough gusto, enough enthusiasm for bygone days, he might entice the old Boaby Preston to come out from his lair deep within the recesses of this parcel of jagged bone and gaunt, grey flesh which approximated him. — Ken whae ah saw the other day thaire, Boab? The boy thit stabbed ehs auld man cause eh widnae gie um the money fir a Mars bar. Mind ay him? Cunt fae doon the scheme: funny glesses, bit ay a spazzy cunt?

Boaby said nothing, but forced an inane grin.

Calum turned back to Crooky. — This wis whin we wir

wee laddies like, back doon the scheme, eh. Thaire wis this cunt . . . cannae mind ay the boy's name, but eh stabbed ehs auld man cause eh widnae gie um the money for a Mars bar, fae the ice-cream van, ken? Well, one time we wis in the Marshall – this wis years later like – me, Boaby here n Tam McGovern. Tam clocks this wee cunt n goes: that's the cunt that stabbed ehs auld man cause eh widnae gie um the money for a Mars bar. Ah goes, naw, that's no the boy. Mind, Boaby? Calum appealed to his wasted old friend.

Boaby nodded, the smile stuck to his face like it had been painted on.

Calum continued. — Bit Tam's gaun: naw, that's the cunt. This boy's jist sittin oan ehs puff readin the *News*, ken? Bit me n Boaby, we wirnae sure, eh no, Boab? So Tam goes: ah'm jist gaun ower tae ask the cunt. Well, ah sais tae Tam: if it wis the boy, ye'd better watch oot cause the cunt's fuckin tapped. Well, Tam goes: fuck off, that wee specky cunt? n goes ower. Well, the next thing we ken is thit the wee cunt's glessed Tam, cut the side ay ays face open. It wisnae that bad, bit it looked it at the the time. So the boy runs oot ay the pub n we wir right ower n chasin efter the cunt, bit eh bombed up the road. Tae tell ye the truth, we wirnae gaun that fast, eh no, Boab? This wis donks ago now though. Bit ah saw that cunt the other day; oan the 16 comin doon the Walk, eh.

Crooky was starting to get bored. Junkies bored him. Pests, if in need, dull if their needs had been met. Certainly, they were to be avoided at all costs. What the fuck was Calum playing at here? Auld mates or no, you couldnae play the social worker tae a skag merchant, he thought in irritation. So Crooky was pleased when he noted a sallow-skinned guy with dirty black locks and a large hooked nose come into the pub and take a stance up at the bar. — Thaire's the Raven.

Mibbe see if the cunt's goat any eckies, eh? Whoa, whoa, whoa, whoa, whoa! He raised his thick eyebrows.

— Thaire's supposed tae be somethin happenin at the Citrus the night, eh, Calum told him, turning from the impassive Boaby.

— Ye wantin any Es if ehs goat thum? Crooky asked.

— Aye . . . no if it's they doves but. Ah hud yin in the Sub Club in Glesgay last week. Yir up fir an ooir then yir jist fucked. Buzz jist goes like that. He snapped his fingers. — Aw they Weedgie cunts wir oan the Malcolm Xs n aw, pure fuckin buzzin, n thaire's me aw frustrated n comin doon.

A concerned frown moulded Crooky's face. — Aye, right. No wantin nane ay that.

He made his way to the Raven. They briefly exchanged pleasantries, then hit the gents' toilet.

Calum turned back to Boaby. — Hi, Boab, listen, man, really great tae see ye again. Mind whin it wis you, me, Tam, Ian n Scooby? That wis some fuckin squad, eh? Dae anything, any time. Ah'm no bein a borin cunt or nowt like that, Boaby, bit it's, likes, ah've been wi Helen fir four years now, ken? Ah'm still intae gittin oot ay ma face n that, bit no the smack n that, ken? Look at perr Ian now: deid likes. The virus, Aids n that, ken?

— Yeah . . . Ian . . . Gilroy . . . said Boaby. — Nivir really liked the boy, ken? he mumbled, an old grievance briefly animating him through his smack apathy.

— Dinnae talk like that, Boab . . . fuck sake . . . the boy's deid! Dinnae talk like that.

— Ripped me oaf . . . Boaby slurred.

— Aye, bit ye cannae hud that against the boy, Boaby, ken? No whin the boy's deid, that's aw ah'm sayin. Like ah sais, ye cannae hud nowt against a boy that's deid.

Crooky came back from the toilets. — Goat some acid, eh. Microdot. Ye intae trippin?

— Naw, no really. Wantin an ecky, eh, Calum said uneasily. He was thinking of Ian Gilroy, of Boaby, as they once were. Boaby had put a lot of badness in his head. Then there was Helen, his girlfriend: things hadn't been going well between them. It would be stupid to trip in this frame of mind. Trips were best left to long, hot summer days, with the right vibe and the right company, preferably in a park or, better still, out in the country. Not in these circumstances.

— Moan, Cally, thaire's a perty oan the night, at this cunt Chizzie's. You ken Chizzie, eh?

— Aye . . . Chizzie, Calum replied blankly. He didn't really know Chizzie. He didn't feel so good. However, he wanted to get out of his face. This acid probably would just give a mild buzz; eighties acid rather than sixties acid, as some of the old sages might disdainfully say. There wasn't a lot that could happen to you on that kind of trip. — Like ah sais, ah'd rather huv an E, eh . . . but, well . . .

They swallowed the trips as surreptitiously as their haste allowed. Boaby, dictated to by distress signals from his pain centres, hauled himself up and went to the toilet. He was gone quite a long time anyway, but it could have been months for Crooky and Calum, for by the time he came back, they were seized by a massive trip.

The pub mirrors distorted, seeming to arc and form a strange bubble around them, cutting them off from the rest of the clientele who looked twisted, as their images reflected through these strange, warped lenses. The sense of isolation this gave them was briefly comforting, but it quickly grew suffocating and oppressive. They became aware of their body rhythms, the pounding of their hearts, the circulating of their blood. They had a sense of themselves as machines. Calum, a plumber, thought of himself as a plumbing system; this made him want to shit. Crooky had seen the video *Terminator* recently, and his vision became as through the Schwarzenegger robot's red-tinted viewfinder, the lettering spelling out alternatives which flashed up before his eyes.

ACID TRIP NO. 372
PSYCHOLOGICAL SURVIVAL PROGRAMME
ACTIVATED

1. Go to bar and get pished.   [ ]
2. Leave immediately and go home.   [ ]
3. Go to bogs and lock self in trap.   [ ]
4. Phone someone to come and talk you down.   [ ]
5. Chizzie's party.   [ ]

— Fuckin hell . . . he gasped, — ah'm a fuckin robot, man . . .

— It's either the end ay the world or the start ay a new one, Calum said, turning away from a distorting grin that transformed Boaby into a cartoon wolf, to watch some creature crawl slowly across the floor of the pub.

It's only really a dug . . . or a cat . . . but ye dinnae get cats in pubs, mibbe sometimes in country pubs in Ireland where they sit in front ay the coal fire, but this yin must be a fuckin dug . . .

— These trips, man, how fuckin wild are they, eh? Crooky shook his head.

— Aye, said Calum, — n Boaby's jist fuckin banged up, the dirty wee cunt. In the bogs like. Look at um! Calum was grateful to Boaby for providing an external focus, before he felt a surge of blood course through fragile veins and he visualised these veins popping under the bubbling power of that blood, like a turbulent river bursting its banks. This was how you died, he thought, this was how life ended. — Goat tae git oot ay here, man!

— Aye, lit's git ootside, Crooky nervously agreed.

It took them a while to actually manage to stand up. The pub was spinning around them, people's faces were distorting wildly. At one moment all was light; at the next they seemed ready to black out, due to the awesome overload of the trip on their senses. Calum felt reality slipping away from him like a rope which was pulled through greased hands by an irresistible force. Crooky felt his psyche peeling away rapidly, like the skins on a multilayered banana, believing that this process was stripping him down, fundamentally altering him into some different form of life.

When they got outside they were immediately all but overwhelmed by a wall of sound and light. Crooky felt himself leaving his mortal flesh and shooting off into space, then snapping with great force back into his body. He glanced back down the street, a buzzing cacophony of strange but familiar sounds and a whizzing kaleidoscope of flashing neon; both producing a bizarre and overpowering interface which drenched their senses. Roughly tangible through this flood was the solitary figure of Boaby who they saw shuffling along behind them.

— C'moan, ya junkie cunt! Calum shouted, then turned to Crooky. — Fuckin waste ay space yon cunt! Despite his aggression Calum was glad that Boaby had tagged on as he did, providing a much-needed source of reality orientation.

They made their tentative way through an obviously familiar terrain, yet the drug had given it an alien hue. When Leith Walk did look like its old self, it was only for short bursts of time, which popped like bubbles to reveal a newer, different reality. Then they found themselves walking through Dresden after the bombings; the flame and smoke and smells of charred flesh around them. They stopped, looked back, and Boaby emerged from the fire, like, Crooky thought, the

Terminator robot from the gasoline explosion. — Too fuckin risky . . .

Once again, Crooky and Calum felt themselves drift out of, then snap back into their bodies from a long way out in space. Reality briefly asserted itself as Calum gasped, — Ah cannae handle this, man . . . it's like thaire's some kind ay fuckin nuclear war gaun oan . . .

— Aye, right. They always droap the fuckin bomb whinivir you droap a tab. They dae it just tae fuckin spite ye. Nivir mind that Saddam-whit's-the-cunt's-face, Cally's jist droaped a fuckin tab, Crooky mocked.

Calum laughed loudly and therapeutically. It settled him down. Crooky was a sound cunt to trip with. No freakouts with Crooky. A cool cunt. This was fuckin brilliant.

They moved into a tunnel of golden light which pulsed and resonated as they looked on in bewilderment. — Fuckin no real, ya cunt. How good is this? Crooky commented, his mouth open.

Calum could not speak. Thoughts came into his head, but they were related to undefinable objects. It was if he was a baby again and had rediscovered pre-speech thought. The objects were distorted household artefacts; a lamp, a table, a chair, but they were the lamp, table and chair that had furnished the house he lived in as a baby, when he was trying to get to grips with his environment. He'd forgotten about them, never really consciously remembered them. Rhymes and rhythms flashed incessantly through his mind, but he couldn't say them, as these thoughts had no proximity to traditional spoken language. It would all be lost when he came down; this secret mental language, this pre-speech thought. He began to feel terrible, deflated at the prospect of losing this great insight. He was on the threshold of some superior knowledge, some great insight. If he could get even further back, beyond consciousness, birth, into past lives . . . but no, there was no way to break through. You could look, that was all, but you couldn't learn as there was no point of reference. He felt it slipping through his psyche like sand through his fingers. There was no way to break through, if you wanted to come back. And he did. — We ken nowt, we ken fuck all . . . nane ay us ken fuck all . . .

— Take it easy, Cal, c'moan, man, Crooky implored. — All hands on deck. Look, wir nearly at Chizzie's. Here's Boaby, fir fuck sakes. Boab! Stick in, ya cunt! Ye awright?

— Ah cannae speak . . . ah'm on heroin, man. Heroin, Boaby slurred.

— Daft cunt. Should've taken one ay they microdots, eh? The Raven said that they were the business and jist tae take a half, but ah thought that wis jist the usual fancy sales talk. But naw. How good is this, Cal?

— It's good . . . Calum said doubtfully. This was not acid. This was something else. He'd been tripping for years, thought he'd seen it all; become blasé about the drug. Old fucked-up sages who now never touched the stuff because of that one-too-crazy trip had warned him: just when you think you've got the measure of it, you get hit with a trip which changes your life. They were right. Everything else he'd taken was just a preparation for this moment, and it was no preparation at all. Whatever happened, things would be different after this.

They walked on, with the minutes feeling more like hours. They seemed to be constantly double-backing, as if in the type of dream where you appeared to be going one step forward and two steps in reverse. They would pass narrow roads with pubs on the corner. Sometimes it was same pub and road they'd just passed, sometimes a different one. Eventually, however, they seemed to arrive at Chizzie's stair door without recognising any of the landmarks between the pub and their destination.

— Eh . . . ah dinnae ken which yin . . . Crooky tried to read the faded tags on the stair intercom system. — Thaire's nae Chizzie.

— What's ehs real name? Calum asked, as Boaby boaked up some bile. The pubs were beginning to leak drunks. It was important to get into the flat. Calum felt the presence of demons in the streets around them. At first it had just been a suggestion. Now it was unbearable. — Jist git the fuck in, the demons ur oot here, man!

— Dinnae talk fuckin shite! Crooky snapped. It was a thing they had when they were talking about tripping, about how tripping always brought out the demons. That was fine *after* a trip, but they'd always tacitly agreed never to mention it *on* the trip itself, and now this fucked-up cunt was . . . Crooky composed himself. — It's, eh, Chisholm, ah think . . .

— Fuck, shouted Calum, — jist press the fuckin loat! Press the toap yins! Whin some cunt opens git in the stair n follay the sound fir the perty!

— Aye! Right! Crooky did this and they gained entry to the stair. Their rubber legs carried them up towards the sound.

They were relieved to see a distorted but discernible Chizzie standing on the top landing. — Awright, chavvy! Chizzie roared. — Good tae see yis! Good night, aye?

— No bad . . . wir really trippin likes, Crooky admitted, slightly guilty about showing up without a carry-out or drugs.

— Whit yis fuckin like, ya daft cunts thit yis are? Chizzie laughed, then noted that they were empty-handed. — C'moan in, he said, with less enthusiasm.

The flat appeared claustrophobic to Crooky and Calum.

They sat by the fireplace, drinking cans of lager, looking into the imitation coal fire, trying to blot out the party that was going on around them. Boaby, who had shuffled up behind them, went to the toilet and lurched back half an hour later, depositing himself in a pine rocking chair.

A square-jawed guy with a moustache approached Crooky and Calum. — Awright, boys. Raffle tickets fir sale. Club 86. First prize, Rover Metro. Second Prize, five-hundred-pound hoaliday voucher fae Sphere Travel, eh. Third prize, Chrismiss hamper worth a hundred bar. Pound a ticket likes.

— Eh, ah'm no wantin a ticket . . . Crooky said.

The guy looked at them with an expression of beligerent outrage. — Chrismiss draw-aw, he snapped, swishing the book of tickets in front of them.

— Eh, aye . . . Crooky fumbled in his pockets. Calum thought that he'd better do likewise.

— Chrismiss fuckin draw then, cunt . . . A pound a fuckin ticket fir a hamper or a hoaliday or a motor – dinnae dae ays any fuckin favours!

— Eh, ah'll take yin . . . Calum started to hand over a pound coin.

— Eh! One fuckin ticket! Moan tae fuck, ya tight cunt! Chrismiss fuckin draaaww! Club 86. Hibernian Youth Development . . . Yir no fuckin Jambos, ur yis?

— Eh . . . naw . . . ah'll take five! Calum shouted, with a sudden surge of enthusiasm.

— That's ma man! said the guy with the moustache.

Crooky, who was a Jambo, reluctantly handed over two pounds.

— Ye gaun oan Setirday? Calum asked the salesman.

— Eh? The man looked at him with hostility.

— Easter Road.

The man stared at Calum for a moment and shook his head

in an aggressive, surly manner. — Ah'm here fir a fuckin perty n tae sell fuckin tickets, no tae talk aboot fuckin fitba.

He departed, leaving Crooky and Calum feeling extremely paranoid.

— Bevvy's the only thing for a trip like this. It's a depressant, brings ye back doon, Crooky said, raising the can of lager to his lips.

— Ah jist wish we'd fuckin brought some along, Calum nodded nervously as he drank.

— Thaire's a wee pile behind ays, but whin thir finished, it's your turn tae go through the kitchen n nab some mair, Crooky told him.

Calum swallowed heavily.

After about an hour, however, they began to feel better, and decided that they would be less conspicuously out of things if they got up and started dancing with some of the others. Somebody had put on a trancy tape, which went well with the acid. Calum moved to the music, looking at some girls, then at Boaby, who was fast asleep in the rocking chair.

A wiry guy with a crew cut was shouting: — CHIZZIE! PIT MA FUCKIN TAPE OAN! MA FUCKIN TAPE, YA CUNT! PRIMAL SCREAM, CHIZZIE! He held up a red cassette box with a blue splash in the middle, stabbing at it with the index finger of his other hand.

— Naw . . . Finitribe, eh, a skinny guy with hair in his eyes mumbled. Crooky thought he recognised the guy from somewhere.

Calum was starting to feel a bit paranoid again. He didn't really know anyone at the party and he began to feel more and more out of place, as if he wasn't welcome. They should have brought along a carry-out. It was out of order, coming empty-handed like that. He sat down alongside Boaby.

— Boab man, this is really fuckin weird. Ah ken it's just

the gear n that bit thaire's a couple ay cunts fae Lochend
here n ah think one ay thum's the brar ay that radge Keith
Allison, the cunt that chibbed Mooby. That whole family,
man, total blade merchants. Ah heard a story that one time
some cunt tried tae gless one ay they Allisons doon at the
Poast Oaffice Club n eh jist took the gless oaf ay the boy,
cool as fuck, and ripped the cunt's face apart wi it . . . ah
mean, total psycho like, eh . . . thaire's that many bad things
in ma life right now, Boab . . . a bad time tae take the acid . . .
ken Helen, like? She's ma bird, ah mean, ah dinnae think
you've met her like, Boaby, but she's goat this sister called
Julia . . .

Boaby said nothing.

— MA FUCKIN TAPE THEN, CHIZZIE, YA CUNT!
PRIMAL FUCKIN SCREAM! The wiry guy with the crew
cut screamed, but not particularly at Chizzie, and then started
frantically dancing to the tape that was on.

Calum turned back to the silent Boaby. — . . . it's no that
ah fancy her, Boab, Helen's sister Julia like, ah mean, no really.
It's jist thit me n Helen, wirnae really speakin, n thaire ah wis
up the toon n jist sortay ended up at Buster's, n her sister Julia
likes, well, she wis thaire wi some ay her mates. Well, the thing
wis, nowt happened, no really. Ah mean, ah wee bit a neckin
n that . . . thing wis, ah wanted somethin tae happen. Ah did
n ah didnae, if ye ken what ah mean, eh? Ah mean, you ken
how it is, eh, Boab?

Boaby said nothing.

— See me, Boab, ma trouble is thit ah dinnae really ken
whit ah want oot ay ma life. That's whit it aw comes doon
tae . . . fuck this gear . . . every cunt looks fuckin ancient . . .
aw decrepit likes . . . even that Sandra lassie, she's here, mind
her that used tae go oot wi Kev MacKay . . . you legged her
one time, Boab, ya dirty cunt . . . ah mind ay that . . .

—Yi'll git fuck all oot ay that cunt, a skinny guy with black hair said to Calum, — he wis bangin up smack in the bogs. Bangin up in thaire whin thaire's lassies tryin tae git in fir a fuckin pish.

This guy looked hideous. He was like something from a concentration camp: he was skeletal. As soon as Calum got a sense of this, the guy actually *was* a skeleton.

— Eh . . . whaire's Crooky? Calum asked him.

— Yir mate? The skeleton's jaw rattled.

— Aye . . .

— He's through in the kitchen, ootay his fuckin nut. Bit ay a lippy cunt is eh no?

— Naw . . . eh . . . aye . . . ah mean, whit's eh been sayin?

— Too much ay a fuckin lippy cunt, eh.

— Aye . . .

The skeleton departed, leaving Calum wondering how to get out of this nightmare.

— Hi, Boaby, mibbe wi should go . . . eh, Boab? No that struck oan the vibes here, eh.

Boaby said nothing.

Then a girl in a red dress came over and sat down beside Calum. She had short blonde hair with light brown roots. He thought that her face was pretty, but her bare arms seemed sinewy and scraggy. — You here wi that Crooky? she asked.

— Eh, aye. Eh, ah'm Calum, likes.

— You're no Ricky Prentice's brother, are ye?

Calum felt as if he had been electrocuted. Everyone knew his brother Ricky was an arsehole. If they knew that he was Ricky's brother, then they would think he was an arsehole.

— Aye . . . bit ah'm no the same as Ricky . . .

— Nivir says ye wir, the girl shrugged.

— Aye, bit what ah mean tae say is thit Ricky's Ricky n

ah'm me. Ricky's nowt tae dae wi me. Ah mean, he goes his wey n ah go mine, eh. Ken whit ah mean likes?

— You're ootay yir face.

— They microdots . . . eh, what's yir name?

— Gillian.

— They microdots, Gillian, no real.

— Ah nivir touch acid. Maist people that dae acid end up in the funny farm. They jist cannae handle it. Ah ken one guy thit did acid n went intae a coma . . .

— Eh . . . aye . . . no bad perty but, eh, Calum bleated nervously.

— Hud oan the now, Gillian said, suddenly distracted. — Be back in a minute.

As she rose, the guy with the crew cut started shouting again. — CHIZ-AY-AY! GIT MA FUCKIN TAPE OAN! PRI-MIL FUGH-KIN SCREEEM!

— Aye, Chizzie, pit Omelette's tape oan, Gillian agreed.

The loud guy called Omelette turned to Gillian, nodding in stern vindication. — See that. He looked over at Chizzie, who was rolling a joint on an album cover, and pointed back at Gillian. — Listen tae that! GIT MA FUCKIN TAPE OAN!

— In a bit, chavvy. Chizzie looked up and winked at Omelette.

Crooky came over to Calum. — This is too fuckin mad, Cally . . . n there's you chattin up that Gillian lassie n aw, ya dirty cunt . . .

— Ye ken ur, like? Calum asked.

— Yir well in thaire, a fuckin easy lay, Crooky smiled.

— She's awright, Calum said, slightly agog. — Seems a nice lassie, like . . .

— Filled mair jars wi abortions thin yir granny hus wi jam, ya cunt, Crooky sneered.

Gillian was coming back. Crooky felt a twinge of guilt as

his eye caught hers and he smiled sheepishly at her before departing to the kitchen.

— Listen, Gillian said to Calum, — ye wantin tae buy tickets fir the Christmas draw? Club 86, she smiled, — Hibernian Youth Development.

— Aye, Calum replied, before remembering that he had already bought some. She seemed so pleased, though, he just couldn't refuse. He bought another five tickets.

— What wis ah oan aboot? Aye, the guy who went intae the coma eftir the trip . . .

Calum began perspiring. He could feel his heart beating wildly. He nudged Boaby gently, but Boaby fell out of the rocking chair and leadenly hit the floor with a heavy crash.

— Fuckin hell, Calum gasped, as Boaby lay prostrate.

People gathered round him. The guy with the moustache who had sold Calum the first batch of Club 86 tickets felt for his pulse.

Chizzie grabbed the guy by the shoulder. — Hi, Geggs! Lit me in thaire, he shouted. — You've no goat ma medical trainin. C'moan, Geggsie, ya cunt.

— Hud oan the now. Geggsie waved him away. To Calum, Geggsie's hair across Boaby's sickly chest looked like ugly, rat-tailed tentacles that were draining the life from Boaby's body. Then Geggsie sat upright. — This cunt's deid. Your mate. He turned to Calum accusingly, as if it was Calum who had murdered him. — Fuckin deid, eh.

— Aw fuck . . . dinnae muck aboot . . . Calum pleaded.

Chizzie bent over Boaby's body. — Aye, ehs fuckin deid awright. Ah should ken; medical trainin, registered first-aider at Ferranti's. They sent ays oan tae this course at Haymarket wi that St Andrew's ambulance crowd. Certificate, the fuckin loat, he said smugly. Then he sprang up. — Crooky! Sorry, chavvy, youse broat the cunt here. Ah'm no wantin the

fuckin bizzies roond here, man. Yill huv tae take the cunt
wi yis.

— Aw . . . Crooky said.

— Nowt else ah kin dae, chav. Try seein it ma wey. No intae
the fuckin bizzies comin roond here, eh.

— GIT THE CUNT OOTAY HERE! the guy called
Geggsie roared.

— Wi cannae . . . ah mean . . . whaire we gaunny take the
cunt? Crooky gasped.

— That's up tae youse. Fuckin radges. Bringing a fuckin
junkie roond tae some cunt's hoose. Geggsie shook his head
bitterly.

— Nivir even brought a fuckin cairry-oot, another voice
sneered. It was the guy with the blond crew cut, the one called
Omelette. — Mibbe git ma fuckin tape oan now then, eh.
Fuckin saw whit that yin did tae the boy, he laughed.

Crooky looked at Calum and nodded. They got on either
side of Boaby, picked him up under his arms and carried him
out the flat and into the stair.

— Sorry aboot the wey this's panned oot, chavvy. Yir mate
thaire, sound boy, wis eh? Chizzie asked. Calum and Crooky
just stared at him. — Listen, mate, ah ken now might no be
the right time, but ah meant tae ask ye, ah'm floggin they
tickets fir the Chrismiss draw –

— Goat thum, Calum snorted.

— Aye, well, right then, Chizzie said bitterly.

They began to carry Boaby's body downstairs. Thankfully,
he was light and small. Gillian and another girl followed
them.

— Half the fuckin fanny's away wi these cunts, Omelette
moaned, before the door slammed shut.

— This is too mad, the other girl said. — Is it cool for us
tae come, aye?

Neither Crooky or Calum responded. The worst of the hallucinations had gone, but everything was still a bit distorted and their legs felt rubbery and unsteady under Boaby's weight.

— Ah want tae see what they'll dae tae him, Gillian said.

— Whit are we gaunny dae? Calum asked, as they carried Boaby down the stair. While he was not heavy, it was as if he was a sackful of water, his weight constantly shifting. They adjusted their grip, and as they walked down the stairs Boaby's legs trailed down the steps behind them.

— Fuck knows! Lit's jist git the fuck away fae this fuckin place, Crooky nipped.

— Euugghh! Euugghh! Dinnae ken how yis kin even touch um, the other girl said.

— Tsk, shut up, Michelle, Gillian nudged her.

They got Boaby out the stair and carried him down the dark, deserted street. His legs and feet dragged along, scrapping his shoes at the toes and sides. Gillian and Michelle at first walked a few feet behind, then alternatively ran in front, or, if they saw someone approach on the same side of the street, would cross the road and make parallel progress. — Ah've never seen anybody deid before, Gillian stated.

— Ah huv. Ma grandad. Ah saw him laid oot, Michelle told her.

— Whae wis it that laid him oot? Gillian asked. She visualised somebody killing Michelle's grandad with one punch.

— The priest . . . at the church, Michelle said, in a strange, sad voice.

— Aw aye . . . Gillian nodded in realisation. Then she looked at Boaby. — He goat any money oan um?

Crooky and Calum, and therefore Boaby, stopped suddenly.

— What dae ye mean? Calum asked.

— Well, it's no much good tae him now. Better get him intae a taxi or something.

Calum and Crooky considered this for a while. Then Calum said, — The perr cunt's deid! We could be done fir murder! Wi cannae git him intae a fuckin taxi!

— Jist sayin, Gillian said.

— Aye, Crooky snapped at Calum, — the lassie's jist sayin. It's cool, Cal. Dinnae take it oot oan the lassie . . .

Calum was ready to explode. This was Boaby . . . Boaby's body. He thought of Bonfire Night. He remembered raiding other bonies in the scheme with Boaby. Boaby. Boaby Preston. He recalled playing IRA and UDA with Boaby. He remembered shooting him and Boaby playing dead, lying on the grassy bank by the main road. When he got up, the back of his T-shirt was covered in dogshite.

Now Boaby wasn't playing dead and they were all in the shit.

— Ah'm no takin this . . . THIS IS BOABY . . . aw fuck . . . Calum moaned, then once again they stopped suddenly, as a car pulled up alongside them. They froze in a communal terror as they realised that it was a police car. Calum's thoughts quickly turned from Boaby to himself. He could feel his life disintegrating before him, as sure as Boaby's had, silently in that chair, taken by the overdose, too junked to know that he was slowly dying. Calum wondered about his girlfriend Helen; whether he'd ever see her again.

A cop got out of the car, leaving his mate at the wheel. — Awright, folks? He looked at Boaby, then turned to Crooky. — Yir mate looks like he's had a skinful.

Crooky and Calum just stared at him. The policeman had a squashed nose with two large holes in it. His skin was the sickly pink of uncooked pork sausage and his eyes were dulled, slanted and set far back into a large, bulbous head. It must be the acid, Crooky kept thinking, it hus tae be the fuckin trip.

Calum and Crooky shot a fearful glance at each other, over Boaby's lolling neck. — Aye, Crooky said weakly.

— Youse huvnae seen any bother roond here the night, huv ye? Bunch ay nutters huv been fillin in shoap windaes.

— Naw, we've no seen nowt, Michelle said.

— Well, yir mate's no seen nowt by the looks ay him. The policeman looked contemptuously at Boaby's corpse. — Ah'd git him hame if ah wis youse.

Shaking a chunky head a couple of times, the cop snorted with disgust before departing.

They were relieved to see the car speed up the street. — Fuckin hell . . . we're fucked here, man . . . totally fucked, Calum whined.

— That's an idea bit, what that polisman sais likes, Crooky considered.

— Eh? Michelle said as Calum looked incredulously at Crooky.

— Jist listen tae this, Crooky elaborated, — if we git pilled up wi the boady, we're fucked. See, if we could git the cunt tae his hoose but —

— Shite. Calum shook his head. — better jist dumpin him.

— Naw, naw, Crooky said, — bound tae be a polis investigation, ken?

— Ah cannae fuckin think straight, it's this acid . . . Calum gasped.

— Mad takin acid, Gillian said, chewing on a piece of gum.

Crooky watched the side of her face swell and ripple as she chewed.

— Ah ken whit we should dae. Take um tae the infirmary. The casualty. Tell thum eh passed oot, Calum said, suddenly animated.

— Naw, they kin tell. Time ay death, Crooky told him.

— Time ah death, Calum repeated in a ghostly echo, —
. . . ah mean, ah dinnae even ken the cunt really, well, no
that well. Ah mean, wi wir mates donks ago bit wi drifted
apart, ken? First time ah seen the cunt in years, eh. Junkie
now, ken?

Gillian pulled Boaby's head back. His skin looked sickly
and his eyes were shut. She spread the lids open with her
fingers.

— Euugghh . . . euugghh . . . euugghh . . . Michelle half
moaned, half-sneered.

— Fuck off! Calum snapped.

— Eh's deid fir fuck sakes, Gillian dismissed him, closing
Boaby's eyes. She took a compact from her bag and began
dabbing Boaby's face. — Make um look a bit less creepy. In
case wi git stoaped again, likes.

— Barry idea, Crooky nodded in stern approval.

Calum looked across the dark blue sky, over to the dead,
dulled tenements. The burning street lamps only seemed to
emphasise the lifelessness of the ghostly city that surrounded
them. There was one shop light, though, that beamed on
ahead of them. It was the all-night kebab.

— Ah'm starvin, Michelle ventured.

— Aye, me n aw, Gillian said.

They lowered Boaby onto a municipal bench which lay
under some trees at the entrance to a small park. — Wi'll
leave Boab here wi you, Cally, n wi'll go ower n get some
doners, Crooky suggested.

— Hud oan a bit, Calum started, but they were moving
across the road to the kebab shop, — . . . how's it always me
that hus tae –

— Stey cool, Cally, dinnae strop oot oan ays. Be back in
a minute, Crooky explained.

Cunts, thought Calum. This was a bad move, him left on his jack. He turned to Boaby, whom he was supporting upright with his arm round him. — Listen, Boab, really sorry aboot this, man . . . like ah ken ye cannae hear ays . . . it's like Ian n aw that auld crowd . . . nae cunt kent aboot the virus n that, Boab, every cunt thought thit ye could only git it through shaggin, mind? It wis like only poofs in London, accordin tae they adverts, no junkies up here. Some boys like Ian, they wir jist oan it fir a few months, Boab . . . jist bad fuckin luck, Boab . . . Ah took the test, eftir Ian, ken? Clear, Calum observed, blankly pondering the implications. For the first time, he realised, it didn't seem to matter.

A drunkard in an old overcoat that smelt of stale spirits and pish approached the bench. He stood staring at them for a bit, seemingly rooted to the spot. Then he sat down on the other side of Boaby. — VAT's the thing nowadays, he mused, — VAT, my friend. He winked at Calum.

— Eh? Calum said irritably.

— A rerr baked tattie ye git in that shoap in Cockburn Street son, a rerr baked tattie. That's whair ah eywis go. That shoap in Cockburn Street. Nice people workin in thaire, like, ken? Young yins like yirsel. Aye, students. Students, ken?

— Aye, Calum rolled his eyes in exasperation. It was cold. Boaby's neck felt cold.

— Philadelphia . . . the city ay brotherly love. The Kennedys. J. F. Kennedy, the drunk said smugly. — Philadelphia. Brotherly love, he wheezed.

— Boston bit, Calum said.

— Aye . . . Philadelphia, the drunkard croaked.

— Naw . . . the Kennedys came fae Boston. That wis thair home toon.

— I FUCKEN KNOW THAT, SON! DON'T FUCKEN PREACH HISTORY AT ME! the old drunkard roared into the night. Calum watched his spittle splash against Boaby's face. Then he nudged Boaby. — You'll ken! Tell yir fucken friend here! Boaby slumped against Calum, who pushed him back upright, then pulled on his body to stop him from sliding against the drunkard.

— Leave the boy, ehs fucked, Calum said.

— Ah kin tell ye whair ah wis whin John Lennon wis shot . . . the man wheezed, — . . . the exact fucken spot. He pointed briskly at the ground under his feet.

Calum shook his head in derision. — Wir talkin aboot the fuckin Kennedys, ya tube!

— AH KEN THAT, SON, BIT AH'M FUCKEN TALKIN ABOOT JOHN FUCKEN LENNON! The drunk stood up and started singing: — *End so this is Cris-mehhsss and what have we done . . . a veh-ray meh-ray Cris-mehhsss end a hah-pee new yeh-ur . . .*

He moved unsteadily down the road. Calum watched him vanish into the night, his voice still audible long after he was out of sight.

The others returned with the kebabs. Crooky handed Calum one. He still had a spare one in his hand. — Fuck! He spat between his teeth. — Ah forgot thit that cunt wis deid, wasted a fuckin kebab! He looked gravely at the spare doner in his hand.

— Oh aye, fuckin selfish ay the cunt tae go n die like that, Calum glared at Crooky, — waste ay a fuckin kebab! Listen tae yirsel, Crooky, ya cunt! Boaby's fuckin died!

Crooky stood with his mouth open for a bit. — Sorry, man, ah ken eh wis ah mate ay yours.

Gillian looked down at Boaby. — If eh wis a junkie, eh widnae huv wanted it anywey. They nivir eat.

Crooky considered this. — Aye, that's true, bit no aw the time though. Remember Fat Phil Cameron? Eh, Cal?

— Aye, Calum nodded, — Fat Phil.

— The only cunt ah've ivir kent whae goat intae smack n pit weight oan, Crooky smiled.

— Bullshit, Gillian scoffed.

— Naw, it's true though, eh, Cal? Crooky appealed to Calum.

Calum shrugged and then nodded in acknowledgement.

— Fat Phil used tae take ehs shot, then go radge for a sugar fix. Eh'd head up tae the Bronx Cafe n buy a huge bag ay donuts. Ye couldnae git near they fuckin donuts n aw. Better chance ay gittin the cunt's skag oaf ay um thin one ay they donuts. He goat better though, goat cleaned up . . . no like poor Boaby. Calum looked sadly at the greying corpse of his friend.

They silently finished their kebabs. Crooky took a bite out of the extra one, then slung it over a hedge. Looking at Boaby's body, Gillian seemed sad for a bit, then she put a little lipstick on his blue-tinted lips.

— Nivir hud a chance, Calum said, — boy like him. The cunt goat in too deep, ken? Thaire wis that many ay they boys, good fuckin guys n aw, well, some ay them, bit jist like any other cunts, good n bad in every crowd, ken . . . ?

— Mibbe ehs goat that Aids anywey, Gillian speculated.

— Euuggghh . . . Michelle screwed her face up, then, looking thoughtful, said, — What a shame. Imagine how ehs ma must feel.

Their deliberations were disturbed by noises coming from down the street. Calum and Crooky tensed up. There was no time to run or manoeuvre. They sensed instantly that the owners of the voices, manically screaming a medley of drunken football songs at each other, were just indulging in a spot of practice for the time when they could vent their aggression on some external force.

— Better nash, eh, Calum said. He saw the dark demons come into full view, illuminated by a shining moon and the sparkling street lamps. How many there were he could not be sure, but he knew that they had him fixed in their sights.

— HI, YOUSE! one of them shouted.

— Who the fuck ur you shoutin at? Gillian sneered too loudly.

— Shhh! Calum hissed. — Lit us handle this, he pleaded. He was panicking. Fuckin daft slags, he thought, it's no thaim thit gits the fuckin doin. It's us. Me.

— HI! ANY AY YOUSE CUNTS SEEN THE FUCKIN POLIS? one guy shouted. He was tall and powerfully built with shoulder-length greasy hair and blazing eyes devoid of reason.

— Eh, naw . . . Crooky said.

— WHAIRE YIS FUCKIN BEEN? the greasy-haired guy shouted.

— Eh, a perty, Crooky nervously told him. — The mate's flat n that, eh.

— That yir felly, doll? another guy with a pork-pie hat said to Gillian, while looking Calum up and down.

Gillian stood silently for a moment. Her stare never left the face of her questioner. With a harsh contempt in her voice she said, — Might be. What's it tae you?

Calum felt a simultaneous eruption of pride and fear. Magnified by the acid, it was almost overwhelming. He felt a muscle in his face twitch wildly.

The guy in the pork-pie hat put his hands on his hips. He bent his head forward and shook it slowly. Then he looked at Calum. — Listen, pal, he said, attempting to sound reasonable through his obvious anger, — if that's yir burd ah'd tell her tae watch her fuckin mooth, right?

Calum nodded sheepishly. The youth's face had distorted

into that of a cruel gargoyle. He had seen that image before; on a postcard of Notre-Dame Cathedral in Paris. The demon had been looking down on the city, crouched high up on a ledge; now it had come to Earth.

— What's this cunt goat tae say fir ehsel? The greasy-haired guy looked at Crooky and pointed to the body of Boaby. — Eh's goat fuckin lipstick oan! YOU A FUCKIN POOF, MATE?

— Eh, the boy's – Crooky began.

— LIT THE CUNT SPEAK FIR EHSEL! HI, PAL, WHAIRE'S IT YIR FAE? the greasy-haired guy asked Boaby.

No response was forthcoming.

— WIDE CUNT! He lashed out and slammed a chunky fist into Boaby's face. Crooky and Calum relaxed their grip completely and the body fell heavily to the ground.

— EH'S DEID! EH'S FUCKIN DEID! Michelle screamed.

— Eh fuckin well will be in a minute, the greasy-haired guy said, pointing down at the body. — C'MOAN THEN, YA CUNT! YOU N ME! SQUARE FUCKIN GO! GIT UP THEN, YA RADGE! He started booting up the corpse. — THE CUNT'S FUCKED! SEE THAT, YA CUNTS! He turned in triumph to his mates.

The pork-pie hat guy upturned his palms, then extended his hand to his greasy-haired pal. — One fuckin punch, Doogie, cannae say fairer than that. He curled his lower lip and half shut his eyes. — Took the daft cunt oot wi one fuckin punch.

The guy called Doogie, swollen with a belligerent pride, looked at Crooky and Calum. — Whae's next?

Calum's eyes furtively scanned around for potential weapons. He could see nothing.

— Eh . . . we're no wantin any bother like . . . Crooky said in a weak gasp.

The guy called Doogie stood immobilised for a second. His face contorted as if he was trying to assimilate a barely digestible concept.

— Fuck off, ya radge! You're a fuckin arsehole, son! Gillian snapped at him.

— WHAE YOU FUCKIN TALKIN TAE? he roared at her.

— Dinnae ken, the label's fell oaf, Gillian said unfazed, chewing steadily and looking him up and down with scorn on her face.

— IT'S FUCKIN . . . IT'S FUCKIN BURDS LIKE YOU THIT DESERVED TAE GIT FUCKIN RAPED . . . SLAGS WI A FUCKIN MOOTH! Doogie had never been dismissed in this manner by a woman.

— HOW THE FUCK WID YOU KEN ABOOT ANYTHIN! YUV NIVIR HUD A FUCKIN FANNY THIT WISNAE YIR MA'S IN YIR LIFE, YA FUCKIN PRICK! AWAY N SHAG YIR POOFY MATES UP THAIR FUCKIN ERSES! Gillian screamed like a banshee: no fucker talked to her like that.

Doogie stood hyperventilating, seemingly rooted to the spot. His face distorted in uncomprehending disbelief. It was like he had seized up. — You dinnae ken . . . you dinnae ken nowt aboot meee . . . he moaned like a wounded animal, pleading and raging at the same time.

For Crooky, the distortion of the guy's face was magnified twentyfold by the acid. He felt a surge of raw fear which transformed into anger and he ran at Doogie, throwing punches. In no time at all he was overpowered and beaten to the ground, where Doogie and two others began trying to kick lumps out of him. At the same time, the guy with the pork-pie hat exchanged blows with Calum, who was then chased around a car. He pulled at an aerial which came away in his hand and he whipped his pursuer across the face with it, opening up his cheek. The pork-pie-hat guy screamed with pain but mainly frustration and anger as Calum rolled under the car. He felt some boots in his side as he crawled into its centre and safety, but, to his horror, he felt somebody getting under with him. He started kicking and punching, flaying out in a frenzy, before he realised that it was Crooky.

— CAL! IT'S ME, YA CUNT! FUCKIN COOL IT!

They lay breathing heavily, bonded in a state of abject terror, listening to the voices:

— BREK INTAE THAT FUCKIN CAR! START THE MOTOR! KILL THE CUNTS!

Fuck sakes, Crooky thought.

— Gang-bang the fuckin slags! A fuckin line-up!

Aw fuck . . . but they daft cows started it, they caused everything, Calum thought.

— Aye, jist fuckin try, ya cunts! That was Gillian's voice.

Naw, Calum thought, they didnae start nowt. Gillian. She was just sticking up for herself. Cannae let them touch her but.

— Lit's jist git the fuck oot ay here! one voice shouted.

Yea-ehs! Crooky and Calum thought together. Go. Just fuckin go. Please. Go.

— Git the cunt Doogie decked!

Daft cunts.

A consensus quickly formed around this. From under the car Crooky and Calum watched the gang kicking Boaby's body around.

One guy stuck a lighted cigarette against the prostrate figure's red lips. Boaby didn't respond in any way.

— EH'S FUCKED! THAT'S ENOUGH! one voice shouted, and they stopped.

They panicked and departed hastily, one guy in a blue jacket shouting back at Michelle and Gillian: — Youse fuckin boots say anything aboot this n yis ur deid! Right!

— Sure, Michelle voiced sarcastically.

The guy ran back and struck her across the face. Gillian stole across and punched him in the mouth. She made to do the same again, but he blocked her blow and restrained her arm. Michelle had pulled off her high heel and, in a tearing, upward sweep, tore the jagged seg of its point across his cheek, up into his eye.

The boy staggered back in pain, stemming the blood with his hand. — Fuckin slag! Could've hud ma fuckin eye oot! he whined, before moving away with increasing haste as they came slowly towards him, like two small predators circling a larger, wounded animal.

— YOU FUCKIN DIE, YA CUNT! MA BRARS'LL FUCKIN KILL YOU! ANDY N STEVIE FARMER! THAT'S MA FUCKIN BRARS, YA CUNT! Gillian screamed.

The boy gave a frightened, bemused look and turned to trot after his pals.

— GIT OOT FAE UNDER THAIRE, YA FUCKIN ARSEHOLES! Gillian screamed at Crooky and Calum.

— Nup, Calum said weakly. It felt good under the car. Safe. Crooky, though, was starting to feel as if he was being buried alive, as if he was sharing a coffin with Calum.

— Thir away, Michelle said.

— We're sound here. It's the acid . . . aw this shit . . . cannae hack it. Youse jist go hame . . . Calum rambled.

— AH SAIS, GIT FUCKIN OOT! Gillian shrieked, her voice scrapping on their raw nerve endings.

Compliant with shame and fear, they wriggled out from under the car. — Shh, Calum moaned, — yi'll huv the polis here, eh.

— Eh, nice one. Eh, thanks, girls, Crooky said. — . . . Ah mean, eh, yis did awright stickin up fir yirsels against these cunts.

— Aye, well done, Calum agreed.

— That prick hit Michelle. Gillian pointed at her friend, who was putting her shoe back on and sobbing wretchedly.

Crooky's bushy eyebrows knotted in pity. — We'll git the cunts eftir, eh, Cally? Git a squad thegither. Couldnae huv hacked swedgin oan the acid bit, ken? Cunts obviously dinnae ken whae thir dealin wi. They wirnae hard cunts. Fuckin wankers. Mind you, ah thoat ah wis fucked whin they goat ays doon, bit they wir kickin each other mair thin me, the daft cunts. Ah'll git they cunts though. See, if it hudnae been fir that acid, eh, Cal!

— Mad tae take acid, Gillian said.

They looked over at Boaby. His face was bashed in at one side, like his cheekbone and jawbone had collapsed. Calum thought again about the time he had pretend-shot Boaby in Niddrie, as a child, when Boaby had played dead. — Lit's jist go, he said.

— Cannae jist leave um, Crooky ventured, shuddering. That could've been ma fuckin face, he thought.

— Aye, we'd better go. The polis'll git they bastards fir it. They killed um really, Michelle said tearfully. — Everything dies, thaire's nowt naebody kin dae aboot it . . .

They walked away from the body in a silence punctuated only by Michelle's sobs, through the night, towards Crooky's place in Fountainbridge. Crooky and Calum staggered wearily on ahead, Gillian had a comforting arm around Michelle, a few yards behind them.

— Thinking aboot Alan? Gillian asked her. — Time ye goat him oot ay yir system, it really is, Michelle. Ye think he's greetin aboot you now? Huh! she sneered. — Ye should jist git the first guy ye see tae screw yir fuckin brains oot. That's your problem, ye need tae git laid.

— Ah loast that joab in the bank thanks tae him . . . Michelle whimpered, — . . . a good joab. The Royal Bank.

— Forget him. Start enjoyin yir life, Gillian said.

Michelle gave Gillian a hostile pout then forced a smile. Gillian nodded at Crooky and Calum who were still lurching on ahead. The two women started laughing loudly. — Which one dae you fancy? Michelle asked.

— Nane ay them really, bit ah cannae stand him wi the eyebrows. Gillian pointed at Crooky.

— Naw, he's awright, Michelle said, — it's ehs mate, that Calum . . . eh's no really goat any erse oan um.

Gillian considered this. Michelle was right. Calum didn't really have much of an arse. — As long as he's goat a fuckin cock, she laughed, flushing with a hormonal itch.

Michelle joined in with the laughter.

Gillian kept her stare on Calum. He was quite skinny, and had both big hands, big feet and a big nose. These factors combined, surely, she thought, made it odds-on that he would have a big cock.

— Right, well, you fire intae that Crooky n ah'll fire intae his mate, Gillian whispered to Michelle.

— Suppose, Michelle shrugged.

They went up to Crooky's flat and sat around the gas fire. The flat was frozen and they kept their coats on. Gillian got up on the couch and began massaging Calum's neck. He was coming down from the acid and her touch felt good. — Yir awfay tense, she said.

— Ah feel tense, was all Calum could say. Ah wonder why, he thought, recounting the events of the night. — Ah feel tense, he repeated in a nervous snigger.

Michelle and Crooky were crouched on the floor, whispering to each other.

— Yi'll probably think ah'm a slag n that, just say if ye do, Michelle said softly to Crooky.

— Naw . . . Crooky said, doubtfully.

— Ah used tae work in the bank, the head oafice, Michelle said, as if underlining her inherent respectability, — the Royal Bank. She emphasised the 'Royal'. — Ken the Royal Bank ay Scotland?

— Aye, in the Mound, likes, Crooky nodded.

— Naw, this is the *Royal* Bank, that's jist the *Bank* ay Scotland you're thinkin ay. This is the *Royal* Bank ay Scotland thit ah used tae work fir. The head oafice. St Andrew's Square.

— The *Royal* Bank . . . Crooky acknowledged. — . . . Aye . . . the Royal Bank, he repeated, looking into her dark eyes. She looked beautiful to him; those eyes, her red lips. The lipstick. The visuals from her lipstick, even coming down. Crooky realised that he loved women who knew how to wear lipstick and he thought that Michelle certainly came into that category.

Michelle sensed his desire. — You n me through thaire then, she said, nodding urgently at the door.

— Yeah . . . sound . . . the bedroom. Aye, the bedroom, Crooky smiled, raising his bushy brows.

They got to their feet, Michelle eagerly, Crooky tentatively, and crept across to the door. Crooky caught Calum's eye and puckered his lips and fluttered his brows at him as they departed.

— That leaves you n me, Gillian smiled.

— Eh, aye, Calum said.

They lay out on the couch. Gillian took her coat off, and draped it over them. It was a large, brown imitation fur. Calum liked the way she looked in her short red dress.

Her arms seemed okay now; he realised that it must have been the acid.

Gillian was aroused by the hardness of his body. She couldn't make out whether it was muscle or just large bones under his skin. She began touching him; rubbing his crotch through his jeans. He felt himself go hard. — Feel ays, feel ays well, she said in a soft, low hiss.

He began kissing her and twisted his hand down her cleavage. Her dress and bra were so tight he couldn't expose any tit without his activities causing her to wince in discomfort. So he disentangled his hand and ran it up her thigh, getting his fingers inside her pants. She pulled away from him, springing from the couch, but only to undress. Gillian ushered him to do the same. Calum got his clothes off quickly, but his erection had gone. Gillian got back on the couch and pulled him to her and he achieved stiffness again for a bit, but he couldn't sustain the hard-on.

— What is it? What's wrong? she snapped.

— It's just the acid . . . it's like . . . it's like ah've goat a girlfriend, ken? Helen. Ah mean, it's like ah dunno if wir still gaun thegither like, cause, eh, well, wuv no been really gittin oan n ah've moved oot, the flat n that, likes, bit wir still sortay seein each other like . . .

— Ah'm no wantin tae fuckin mairray ye, ah just want a shag, right?

— Eh, aye. He ran his gaze over her nakedness and got hard without feeling himself stiffening.

They pulled the coat over their naked bodies and went for it. The union was based on a grinding genital interaction rather than any deep psychic communion, but it was hard and intense and Gillian came quite quickly, Calum shortly after. He felt pleased with himself. At one stage he had wondered whether he'd be able to hold on for her.

He could do a lot better than that, he thought ruefully. It was the acid, Boaby, all the shit in his head. He could do a lot better, but this wisnae bad under the circumstances, he thought happily.

Gillian was content. She thought she wouldn't have minded getting there again, but at least he'd managed to keep it up until she'd come. It was okay, it had cleared things out a wee bit. — That wisnae too bad, she conceded, as they fell into a post-coital slumber.

Later, Calum felt Gillian moving, but pretended to be dead to the world. She had got up from the couch and had started to get dressed. Calum then heard whispering conversations and realised that Michelle had come into the room. This made him feel embarrassed at his nakedness under the coat. He tugged it tighter to ensure that his genitals were completely covered.

— How was your night? Calum heard Gillian whisper softly to Michelle.

— Shite. He didnae ken what tae dae. Like a fuckin virgin. Couldnae git it up. Kept gaun oan aboot the fuckin acid . . . Calum could hear Michelle dissolve into tears. Then she asked, with a sudden eagerness, — What was he like?

Gillian struggled into her dress, then considered, for what to Calum's ears was a painfully long time. — No bad. A bit ay a grunter likes . . . Aw, perr Michelle . . . it didnae happen for ye . . . ah should've gied ye him, she gestured a thumb at Calum, who felt a twinge behind his genitals.

Michelle rubbed her tearful eyes, smearing thick eyeliner around the sockets. Gillian went to speak but couldn't get a word in before Michelle started talking. — It wis jist thit wi Alan, well, it wis brilliant. At the start it wis brilliant. It goat crap later oan, whin eh wis wi that fuckin hoor, bit see, at the start . . . nuthin could beat it.

— Aw, Gillian said softly, considering Alan and contemplating his sexuality for the first time. She would mention Michelle's eyes later. She turned to Calum, shaking him gently. — Hi, Calum, wakey-wakey! Yir gaunny huv tae wake up. Ah need ma coat. We're oaf now.

— Eh, right . . . Calum mumbled, opening his eyes. He felt as if his brain had been pickled and his body seemed to have been battered all over. At least he was back down, though, free from the acid and its malevolent games. — Lit's ays git me keks oan then, he pleaded.

They went behind the couch. — Wi'll no look, honest, Gillian said.

This sparked off a laugh from Michelle which to Calum's ears had a disturbing predatory harshness to it, particularly with her dark eye sockets, but he pulled on his pants, then his jeans and handed Gillian the coat.

— Well, eh, cheers then . . . Michelle, eh, Gillian. Eh, Gillian, ye goat a number? he asked tentatively. Calum didn't know whether or not he wanted to see her again, but it seemed a good idea to at least offer. He thought that Gillian was a bit of a nutter.

— Yir no gittin ma number. You gie ays yours, she said, passing him a pen and a piece of scrap paper from her bag. It was a voucher for the Club 86 Hibernian Youth Development Christmas Draw. — Did ah flog ye one ay they raffle tickets? she asked.

— Aye, ah bought five, he replied, writing down his number on the back.

Gillian looked at Calum, then at Michelle, then back at Calum. — That wey if ah want tae see you, ah kin. Ah dinnae like laddies hasslin ays oan the phone: Come oan oot, Gilli-ihhnnn, she said scornfully in a creepy, insipid voice. Then she went over and kissed Calum and wrapped her arms around his naked torso. She whispered in his ear, — You're gaunny fuck me again, really soon. Right?

— Eh, mmh, he muttered incoherently, — eh, aye . . . yeah . . . likes. Calum remembered that point in a nature programme he'd seen where the female praying mantis ate the male praying mantis's head during sex. He watched Gillian departing with Michelle and could certainly imagine her French-kissing praying-mantis-style.

Alone in the front room, Calum sat watching morning television and smoking cigarettes. He rummaged in his jeans and pants, rubbing at his penis and balls and smelt Gillian on his hand. He thought of Helen and Boaby and started to feel depressed and lonely. Then he forced himself to make some tea before Crooky came in.

— Good night? he asked Crooky whose face was split by a hatchet-wound grin.

— The best, mate, the best. That Michelle, man; the Royal Bank, whoa, ya cunt ye! Takes it aw weys! She wis fuckin gantin oan it, bit Crooky wis up tae the joab.

— Gie her the message, aye? Calum asked, his face ashen.

— Ah fuckin split her right up the middle, man. The Royal Bank'll no be able tae sit oan a bicycle seat eftir that! Crooky here, he drummed his chest with his index finger, — ah'm well in credit wi the Royal Bank. Ah only made one with-drawal, but no before ah hud pit in quite a few fuckin big deposits, if ye catch ma drift. Wir talkin high interest n aw, ya cunt! Ah should've telt her, if ye want any ay yir mates sorted oot, take the address doon n send thum up tae Crooky . . . he's simply the best . . . do . . . do . . . Crooky burst into song, thrusting his hips: — *He's beh-rah thehn aw-wil the rest . . . he's beh-rah thehn eh-eh-he-one, thehn eh-ne-one ah've eh-eh-vah met . . . he's simply the best . . . do . . . do . . .*

Calum left Crooky to his dancing. He couldn't be bothered

slagging him off. A sadness had gripped him, Boaby relentlessly intruding into his thoughts. When had Boaby really died? Sometime long before last night.

— What aboot you, Cal? How wis it wi Gillian? Crooky suddenly asked, with a smirk on his face.

— No up tae much really, ma fault likes. The acid, ken?

Crooky shot him an expression of theatrical disdain. — That's a poor excuse, Cally ma man. Take Crooky here, he pointed at himself, — or tae gie him his official title: SIMPLY THE BEST, nae amount ay drugs kin knock this boy oot ay his stride. That's whit sorts oot the highly skilled time-served men fae the also-rans.

— Suppose yuv either goat it or yuv no, Calum acknowledged wearily.

— That's it, Cal, natural talent. Aw the coachin manuals in the world cannae instil that.

Calum was thinkin about Boaby, and about Gillian. — Ah once saw this documentary aboot insects, n thaire wis this prayin mantis, ken they big, radge insects?

— Aye . . . fuckin evil-lookin cunts, eh.

— Well, the lassie prayin mantis eats the laddie prayin mantis's heid whin thir shaggin . . . ah dinnae mean the lassie prayin mantis n the laddie prayin mantis . . . ah mean, like, male n female, ken?

Crooky looked at Calum. — What the fuck's that tae dae wi anything?

Calum bowed his head and put his hand in front of it. Crooky saw that he was trying to cover his face from him. When he finally spoke, Calum's voice was urgent and breathless. — We . . . saw Boaby . . . Boaby . . . we saw Boaby die . . . it shouldnae be like this, it shouldnae be like nowt's jist happened . . . ah mean . . .

Crooky slid onto the couch beside Calum. He felt stiff

and awkward. He tried to speak a couple of times but he was gripped by a paralysis. Maybe that was to stop you from rabbiting, from talking shite, he thought. Maybe it was right that he couldn't say anything to his friend, who kept his face turned away from him. After a long silence he looked at the telly and asked, — What's this shite?

Calum lifted his head up, and turned it towards his friend. — Breakfast telly. Now aw wi need is breakfast, eh?

— Aye, aye, aw right, ya cunt! Ah'll go doon for some rolls n milk in a bit. Then Crooky looked at Calum, glad that the tension between them had ebbed. — Wonder what'll happen aboot last night?

Calum thought about Boaby, about how you could never ever tell that arrogant little cunt anything, how he always strode along with that petulant twist to his lip, as though the world owed the stupid wee fucker a living. — Fuck knows. Nowt tae dae wi us though. We jist say thit we thoat thit Boaby wis fucked; we tried tae help um doon the road, eh? Gillian n Michelle'll vouch fir that. We jist huv tae say thit we goat chased by they boys. They'll be the ones tae git done.

— Bit Boaby OD'd, Crooky said.

— Bit it serves they cunts right. They nutters, they might've killed um. Whaes tae say? It's thaim or us, n it's better thaim.

Crooky watched the sunlight rise from behind the tenements opposite. The city was coming back to life. The demons he and Calum always talked about were in retreat: the guys at the party, the gang of nutters, Boaby, Gillian and Michelle the Royal Bank, even. Especially that slag the Royal Bank. It was just the acid. He should've fucked the slut though, she wisnae bad-lookin, he thought bitterly. But now the nightmare was over. The sun was here, they were still here.

— Aye, Crooky agreed, — better thaim thin us.

Calum thought that he heard a car pull up outside. He was convinced that there were at least a couple of sets of heavy footsteps coming up the stair. Paranoia, he thought, it's just the residue of the acid, he told himself, just the comedown.

Victor Spoils

S he should have been enjoying herself.
      The light blue wall, the back of the old, brown corduroy
settee in front of her, her elbows on its cushions and him
behind her, his large hands not that far from circling her entire
waist. His prick inside her, moving in a strange insistent rhythm
and his encouraging sounds.

Sarah was thinking that she should have been enjoying
herself.

She should have been enjoying herself but she most certainly
wasn't. When she thought why, Sarah reckoned that it could
have been because it was too cold to be naked. But that
shouldn't have been an issue, and it wouldn't have been an issue,
not if her tooth hadn't been hurting. Now she was feeling self-
conscious, aware of herself on this couch, sprawled out in front
of Gavin, like an extension of his prick, and the whole point
of sex was *not* to feel self-conscious. It was difficult, though,
when your tooth was hurting and you were the recipient of
Gavin's Hollywood-style seduction techniques; so obviously
gleaned from the sections in formula videos when the music
changes and the leading couple get it on. First, the foreplay;
second, the penetration; third, the positions; fourth, the orgasms
(simultaneous of course). When Gavin mumbled 'you're gorgeous'
or 'you've got a great body', Sarah imagined that she should
have been flattered, but this was done with the concentrated
detachment of a wooden actor trying to remember his lines.

Gavin hoped that the sheer force of ceremony and ritual, the expression of the appropriate word and gesture, was going to weave together the new suit that would take pride of place in that wardrobe crammed with his life's social fabric. While he was imaginative enough, Gavin knew that he possessed the exclusive imagination of the only child quietly amusing himself by setting up armies of soldiers for battles on the carpet and that this training had not given him the essential speed of thought to enable him to make contingency plans if anything went amiss in his psychologically storyboarded seduction routine.

In the club last night he had been full of Ecstasy, which always helped. Gavin had made the point of kissing every girl in the company (which on this particular night meant every girl in the club), but with Sarah he'd slipped a bit of tongue into her mouth, soul into her eyes and let his hand linger on the small of her back where it seemed determined to set up residence.

To Sarah, such attentions were a welcome source of affirmation since her split from Victor. She'd recently grown half aware that guys were mistaking her pissed-off look for the less ambiguous 'keep-the-fuck-away-from-me' variety. So as the clubbers danced under the flashing lights and the loudspeakers pumped the latest throbbing bass lines through their bodies, Gavin and Sarah found themselves in an embrace as welcoming as it was surprising.

Gavin was entranced by the fluid suggestiveness of Sarah's eyes and the mesmerising movement of her red-glossed lips as she spoke. She, in turn, was surprised by how much she fancied Gavin, his big, soulful eyes, his easy, if slightly cheesy grin, simply because she had always disliked him when he was with that Linsey.

But last night she had enjoyed his touch. Although often

intimate, it had no sense of the sewer in it. She reciprocated by giving him a massage, starting off by gently stroking the tendons of his neck, then increasing with an imperceptible force to knead the MDMA through his body until it pulsed like an open wound.

They went out into the early-morning chill and took a taxi to his place where they sat up hugging, kissing and talking, removing articles of clothing as they went, losing themselves in long, shared journeys as they snogged. Gavin explained that penetrative sex would be out of the question for a while, which Sarah felt less than chuffed about, but accepted. Later, with the MDMA running down and the tiredness setting into their bodies, they fell into a comatose sleep on the couch in front of the gas fire.

Sarah awoke to Gavin's caresses. Her body immediately responded but something was not right in her head. This was now post-MDMA, another set of circumstances, and Gavin, she felt, hadn't acknowledged this. She didn't want to start all over again, but she did want Gavin to make some sort of affirmation that things were now different, terms had to be restated as much as renegotiated. And her toothache. She thought it had left her alone, this wisdom tooth problem. But those things never went away, you just got a bit of remission.

And now it was back.

It was back alright, with a persistent, spiteful vengeance.

Gavin had woken up with his cock stiff and throbbing. He pulled the throw cover from them, at first mildly surprised at his and Sarah's nakedness. Then he drew in a deep breath and felt a surge of wonder rise in him. It was like winning the lottery. Then mild paranoia that his inarticulacy and arousal would take off on different tangents settled into his psyche. It had to happen now, otherwise she would think there was something weird about him. He has to show her a good time as well, especially after all the things they had said last night. The way he hadn't been able to go for it, in a penetrative sense, and was there really any other? he considered, the thought disturbing him slightly. He knew that women liked guys who had a bit of imagination and who knew how to use their tongues and their fingers, but at the end of the day they still wanted fucking and he hadn't been able to deliver the goods last night. Yes, he had to show her a good time. That was crucial. Gavin's tongue ripped his dry lips apart as he felt consciousness submerge and movement take over, his hands gliding like heat-seeking missiles towards her.

So it was that Sarah found herself being bent and moved like a mechanical doll while Gavin thrust himself into her from different angles, all the time with his accompanying banal bleatings, which jarred at any sense of abandon. Worse, every time she threatened to get into it and just as it seemed to be transcending the pain of her toothache, he would stop, withdraw and change positions like an assembly worker on job rotation. At one point she wanted to scream with frustration. Almost to her surprise, they did achieve close to simultaneous orgasm, her coming first and Gavin just after, her thrashings against him, against the toothache, against the frustrations of the situation, telling him, — Don't fuckin move and don't fuckin come!

Gavin dug in, thinking that it would be a brave man who did either in the face of such ferocity, as she brought herself off against him.

So while the eventual destination was satisfactory, the nagging toothache prevented Sarah from basking in the afterglow and forced her to reflect that she wasn't sure whether or not she wanted to make this particular kind of trip in Gavin's company again.

She twisted and writhed in his proprietary arms, then pulled away and sat on the couch.

— What is it? he moaned in a drowsy petulance, like a child confronted by a bigger kid with designs on his sweets.

Sarah put her hand to her jaw, and let her tongue probe the back of her mouth. A spasm of sharp pain shot through the dull, omnipresent ache. — Ughhhh . . . she groaned.

— Eh? Gavin prompted, his eyes widening.

— I've got toothache, she said. It hurt to talk, but as soon as she stated this, she realised that it was unbearable.

— Want a paracetamol?

— Ah want a fuckin dentist! she snapped through the agony, holding her jaw to support that effort. That was the worst thing about pain of this sort: it seemed to draw strength from the first acknowledgement of how bad it was. Now it was becoming as bad as she could imagine pain getting.

— Aye . . . eh, right . . . Gavin stood up. The toothache, he remembered, she had mentioned it last night. It was okay then, but it must be kicking in now. — I'll see if ah kin git a number. It'll need tae be one ay they emergency punters, this bein a Sunday n that.

— I just need a dentist, she howled.

Gavin sat down on a chair and started thumbing through a Thomson Local. There was a tatty notepad with numbers and some doodlings on it. He had put a thick box round the bold lettering FEED SPARKY. His mother's cat. He had said he would. The poor bastard was probably starving.

He found a number in the Thomson's and dialled it. The book flipped shut. The cat on the cover picture of the directory seemed to judge him on Sparky's behalf.

Then there was a voice on the end of the line.

He looked strange, just sitting there naked, Sarah thought, talking on the phone to the dentist or a receptionist. His circumcised cock. The first time she had ever been with a guy with a circumcised cock, the first time she had *seen* a circumcised cock. She wanted to ask him why he'd got it done. Religious reasons? Medical ones? Hygiene? Sexual? She'd read in magazines that women enjoyed it better with circumcised cocks, but it hadn't felt different to her. She would ask —

A spasm of pain —

The fuckin pain . . .

Gavin still talking on the phone. — Yes, it *is* an emergency. No way can it wait.

Sarah looked up and felt good about Gavin, his positiveness, his lack of wavering, his resolute putting of her needs first in this situation. She tried to flash some message of gratitude, but her gaze didn't catch his eye and her hair fell over her face.

— Right, that's 25 Drumsheugh Gardens. Twelve o'clock. Is that as soon as ye can manage? Okay . . . right, thank you.

He put the phone down and looked up at her. — They kin take ye in an hour, doon the New Town. It wis the quickest the guy oan call could git oot tae the surgery. If we head off now we can stop at Mulligan's for a drink. Dae ye think ye could swallay a paracetamol?

— I don't know . . . aye, ah could.

— Ye swallayed enough pills last night, Gavin laughed.

Sarah tried to smile, but it hurt too much. She did, however, manage to swallow a pill and they made their way down the road, Sarah moving in a grim deliberation, Gavin in a tense symbiosis.

The bright autumn sun nipped their eyes as they walked down Cockburn Street. Gavin looked at the street sign, Cockburn Street. Though it was pronounced Co-burn Gavin felt the rawness in his genitals. Cock-burn right enough. He looked at Sarah; she had taken her hand from her face. She was fuckin lovely, sure she was. He didn't even want to look at her tits or her arse or anything, although they were fuckin beautiful, as he'd seen last night, but now they were just swamped by the essence of her. When you can feel the essence, not visualise the constituent parts, Gavin considered, that's when you know you are falling in love. Fuck, when did it happen? Maybe when he was on the phone. You could never tell with these things! Fuckin hell. Sarah!

Sarah.

He wanted to take care of her, help her through this.

Just to be there with her. For her.

Gavin 4 Sarah.

Maybe he should hold her hand. But he was jumping ahead of himself. God, he'd just fucked her every way! Why couldn't he hold her hand? What was wrong with this fucking world? How had we come to get so perverse that holding the hand of a lassie you were in love with was a heavier deal than shagging her doggy-style across your settee?

And what was he doing saying that they'd go to Mulligan's? The whole posse would be there, carrying on, keeping it going, some of them buying more pills. A few had probably been in the Boundary Bar since five this morning. Gavin tried to distance himself from a growing unease by loftily considering that he had all the chemicals he needed, the natural chemicals of love. The self-loathing was growing though. It wouldn't go away. It was like toothache. Was he really such a bastard that he wanted to parade her like a trophy in Mulligan's? I FUCKED SARAH McWILLIAMS LAST NIGHT. No, it wasn't like that; he just wanted the world to know that they were, as they say, an item. But were they? What did she think?

Maybe he should take her hand, just do it.

Sarah thought *dentist dentist dentist*. The steps that had to be taken, the streets that needed to be crossed in order to narrow that terrifying distance between pain and treatment. There was one bad, traffic-infested roundabout in the way. She didn't know if she could do, if she could cross over that roundabout.

The cars seemed to slow down and speed up, play a cat-and-mouse game with you, dare you to try and cross. It was just the way they came down to it off the steep hill. But they were over in no time. Sunday. It was quieter. Then there was Princes Street, then Mulligan's. She couldn't go to Mulligan's! What the fuck was she thinking about? But Louise and Joanne would be there. They'd chum her. Yes, Mulligan's.

Then she felt him grab her hand. What was he doing?

— Ye okay? he asked, concern scribbled on his face in the broad strokes of a crayon in an infant's fist. Expressions of sincerity were something she always found painful in men she didn't know that well. There was something so obvious about Gavin, so overplayed, not so much that of a person who was false as of one who had never learned to be comfortable being real and —

AGHHHH!

A bigger spasm of pain, *real* pain; and her squeezing on his hand.

— It's okay, we'll be there soon. Yir really suffering, eh? Gavin asked. Of course she was. He should shut up. Inappropriate, that was him, everything about him. His friends were inappropriate. His friends.

He never saw Renton now, nobody did, nor that much of Begbie, thank fuck, or Sick Boy or Nelly or Spud or Second Prize. His core mates he grew up with had evaporated from being a tight wee crew into stars of their own psychodramas. It happened to everybody. But they were inappropriate. Higher Executive Officers in the Department of Employment do not have friends like that. Executive Officers perhaps, at one time, before they find their limits, but HEOs have never had friends like that. No HEO has ever had a pal like Spud Murphy. He would never be an HEO, he was tainted by associations he didn't even have any more! They'd made their mark on him though. This manifested itself by him drinking too much, coming in obviously cunted on a Monday. But it was the Tuesday that did you. You can go through Monday still on a bit of a high, especially if other drugs were in the weekend picture, but the comedown always kicked in on the Tuesday. And they noticed. They always noticed. They had to have noticed, over the years. It was their *raison d'être*. Thus no HEO. Perhaps he shouldn't have stayed a weekend waster. Perhaps he should have gone full-time like the others, he thought bitterly.

Sarah hadn't even bothered to respond because this was hell and it couldn't get any worse but it *was* getting worse, much worse because she sensed a presence. Sensed it before she saw it. It was him.

Sarah looked up as they crossed Market Street, because Victor was coming towards them. His face, pinched and hard, his classical self-absorbed look, which broke into one of disbelief, then outraged pain, as he registered them coming towards him hand in hand.

Gavin saw him too. With a guilty instinct both regretted their hands flew apart. But it was over, her and Victor, and he'd have to know about it sooner or later. He liked Victor; they were mates. They'd drunk together, partied together, gone to the fitba together. Always in company, mind you, never just the two of them on their own, but they'd done it for long enough over the years for them to be more than just acquaintances. And Gavin liked him, he really did. He knew that Vic was what his dad would have called a man's man, which Gavin supposed was a sort of euphemism by omission for maybe not the type of guy a lassie would get much joy from in a relationship. But Gavin liked him. Vic had to know about him and Sarah, he had to know sometime. Gavin wished that it could have been sometime later, but it wasn't to be.

— Awright, Victor said, his hands resting on his hips.

— Vic, Gavin nodded. He looked at Sarah, then back at Victor, who was still in the gunfighter stance.

Sarah folded her arms and turned away.

— Oot last night? Gavin asked tepidly.

— See you wir, aye? Victor looked Gavin scornfully up and down, then turned to Sarah. His hateful gaze burned her so much that for a moment she forgot her toothache.

— Ah've goat nowt tae say tae you, she mumbled.

— Mibbe ah've goat something tae say tae you!

— Vic, look, Gavin said, — we've goat tae git tae the dentist –

— You shut yir fuckin mooth, lover boy! Victor pointed at Gavin, who felt the blood draining from his face. — Ah'll knock yir fuckin teeth oot then yi'll huv tae go tae the fuckin dentist awright!

The fear rose within. Yet part of Gavin's mind was working coldly, detached from what was going on around him. He thought that he should assault Victor first, in order to prevent Vic from hitting him. Yet he felt guilt towards Victor. And there was the self-preservation instinct. Would he be able to take Victor? Doubtful, but the outcome hardly mattered. What would Sarah want? – that was the question: the dentist. They had to get to the dentist.

— That's your answer tae everything, eh! Sarah said, screwing up her eyes and nose.

— How long's this been gaun oan? Eh? How long ye been seein that cunt?! Victor demanded.

— It's none ay your business what ah dae!

— How fuckin long? Victor roared, lunging forward, grabbing her by the arm and shaking her.

Gavin sprang at him and smacked Victor on the jaw. Victor's head jerked back as Gavin tensed, ready to follow up. Victor put one hand to his face and raised his other, signalling for Gavin to hold off. Blood spilled in droplets onto the pavement from his mouth.

— Sorry, Vic . . . sorry, man . . . Gavin felt confused. He'd hit Victor. A mate. He'd fucked his mate's bird, and then he'd panelled the boy for being upset. That was out of order. But he loved Sarah. Victor grabbing her like that, him ever having his hands on Sarah, over her, his *cock* in her, for fuck's sake. His large, ugly, sweaty cock that he held languidly as he pished next to Gavin in the East Stand toilets; expelling the cloudy, stagnant pill-filled lager urine into the latrine. His face twisted with a drunken belligerence that announced to the world that he was off on one for the weekend. It was too much, the idea of their cocks being in the same place, in Sarah's beautiful, beautiful cunt, no, not cunt, he thought, what a horrible word to use for her wonderful fanny. God, he wanted to kill this Victor fucker; just obliterate every fucking trace of him from this planet . . .

Sarah wanted the dentist's. She wanted it now. She was off down the road. Gavin and Victor started off after her at the same time. The three of them stumbled down the street in a confused and tense silence and ended up walking into the surgery together.

— Hello . . . the dentist, Mr Ormiston said. — Are you all together? He was a tall, thin man, with a red face and a shock of white, wavy hair. He had large blue eyes, which were magnified by his specs, giving him a crazed look.

— I'm wi her, Gavin said.

— *Ah'm* wi her! Victor snapped.

— Well, if you could both wait in here. Come through, my dear, Mr Ormiston smiled benignly, his toothy smile expanding as he ushered Sarah into his consulting room.

Gavin and Victor were left in the waiting room.

They sat in silence for a while, which Gavin broke. — Listen, man, sorry aboot aw that. We werenae seein each other behind yir back. We jist went hame thegither last night.

— Did ye fuck her? Victor said in a low, ugly voice. The side of his jaw was swelling up. He'd bitten into his tongue and the sour trickle of blood was running down his throat. Victor was bobbing around in the pool of his own misery, testing its depths, seeing how far out he was from the edge.

— That's fuck all tae dae wi you, Gavin replied, feeling his anger rising again.

— She's ma fuckin bird!

— Look, mate, ah ken yir upset, bit she's no your fuckin bird. She's goat a mind ay her ain n she's finished wi ye. Youse ur finished, ye understand that? That's how she wis wi me last night, cause youse ur finished!

Victor's face twisted into a leery smile. He looked at Gavin in a different way, like Gavin was the sad case, the imbecile.
— Ye dinnae git it, dae ye, mate?

— Naw, you dinnae git it, Gavin retorted, but he could feel his confidence waning. He tried to work out why he was feeling fearful of Victor, who had backed down after he had struck him with just one blow. It was because, Gavin realised, because he could never sustain violence. It came to him in a reactive way, an instinctive blow, but he lacked the mental stamina for a real battle. Gavin couldn't bear the thought of winners and losers, but with everyone in the gutter, everyone debased: violence, the warped sibling of economics. It was a good thing Victor had backed down.

Victor shook his head. Felt the satisfying range of his physical and psychological pain. In it, he measured the extent of his coming retribution. He'd get Mr Gavin fuckin lover-boy Temperley later, but the aggression of his old pal had shocked him. It seemed so out of character. What he had done with Sarah, that was out of character as well. Gav was okay. Gav was sound. There was talk about him grassing up cunts to his work at the dole, but he could never, ever believe that of Gav, even if those DoE fuckers put him in that position. A resignation issue, surely, it would be. Surely. But swinging for him like that, that wisnae Gav. Anyway, Victor rationalised, it had been better to let Sarah see him get hurt, the sympathy vote, he could tell it had put a bit of doubt in her. Gavin could be taken out in other ways. — This has happened before, Gav. She's been wi other guys. But she eywis comes back tae me. Ah'm no sayin that it doesnae — Victor's voice rose and his fist smashed against the table, — GIT OAN MA FUCKIN TITS . . . cause it does. It hurts cause it's ma fuckin woman.

Gavin felt deflated. He went to speak, but stopped, knowing that his voice would come out biscuit-ersed, that the uncertainty would be threaded right through it.

Victor continued. — She went wi Billy Stevenson the last time. You ken him. The time before that it wis that Paul. Paul Younger . . . He spat out the names like poison and Gavin shook under them as though they were thunderbolts. He didn't like Billy Stevenson, a smart, arrogant cunt. Him with Sarah: it was a horrific thought. Victor's cheesy spunk-and-lager urinating cock inside her now seemed quite a pleasant consideration. Paul Younger was *okay*, but so fuckin anodyne. How could a woman like Sarah go with a fucking nobody like that? Paul fuckin Younger! Victor couldn't have mentioned two more hurtful names if he'd tried.

— Billy Stevenson? Gavin repeated, hoping that he'd somehow heard wrongly.

— She did it tae git at me, for when ah went wi Lizzie McIntosh.

So Victor had shagged Lizzie as well. Gavin liked Lizzie. He knew that she punted around a bit. It was hardly a surprise that Victor and her had got together. It was strange. Prior to a few moments ago Gavin had never thought of Victor and him having had their cocks in the same place, bar some club, pub and football-ground urinals. Now they had shagged not one, but at least two of the same women. He started to think about other girls he had been with that Victor might know. Edinburgh, what a fuckin place: everybody had shagged everybody else. No wonder Aids spread so fast. They blamed it on the skag, but the shagging was as much to blame. It had to be. The myth that junkies didn't have a sex life. Plenty of birds wasting away in the hospice whose only injection had been of the meat variety could testify otherwise. He thought of his old deceased mate Tommy, Lizzie's ex, his paranoia after shagging her last year. He couldn't ask her though. Not about her and Tommy. He knew that Tommy and her split up prior to Tommy getting into the junk, but he had to go and take the test. The demons came in the night. They always came.

— It meant fuck all tae me, man, it wis jist a ride, eh? Ye ken what it's like whin yir aw eckied up, Victor continued. Gavin found himself nodding, stopping when it seemed too self-incriminating. Victor didn't miss the opportunity. — That wid be whit it wis like wi you n her but, eh?

— Naw it wisnae! It fuckin well wisnae, right!

— Well, that's the wey ye'd best remember it then, mate, cause that's it finished.

— Naw, you n her's fuckin well finished, that's whit's fuckin well finished, Vic. This isnae the same is her shaggin some twat like Billy Stevenson or some arsehole like Younger, she'd jist be a ride tae they cunts, this is somebody who cares aboot her, right!

— Naw it's no fuckin well right! Find yir ain fuckin bird tae care aboot! Sarah's mine! Ah love her!

— *Ah* fuckin love her!

— Yuv only kent her five fuckin minutes! Three fuckin *years!* Victor thrashed his chest with his fist. — Three fuckin years!

Ormiston the dentist came running through. — Please! Keep the noise down or go away! I'm having to extract two wisdom teeth here.

Gavin swiftly raised his hand to silence the dentist, then stood up over Victor. — It's her n me now, ya cunt! Right?! Git used tae it, cause that's the fuckin wey it is!

Victor stood up. Gavin moved back and Victor punched the air in front of him. — IS IT FUCK!

— Right! Out of here! I'm going to call the police, Mr Ormiston shouted. — Out! Now! You can wait outside! Just get the hell out of my surgery! I'm trying to extract two wisdom teeth . . . The dentist's voice disintegrated into a woeful, bewildered plea.

Victor and Gavin reluctantly shuffled outside. They stood apart from each other, then Gavin sat on the steps while Victor continued leaning on the wrought-iron railings of the Georgian building.

They stared at each other for a minute, then looked away. Gavin felt himself chuckling lightly, his trickle of laughter soon becoming an uncontrollable cascade. Victor started to join in. — What are we fuckin well laughin at here? he asked, shaking his head.

— This is mad, man, totally fuckin mad.

— Aye . . . lit's git a drink ower thaire. Victor pointed to a basement pub on the corner.

They went in and Gavin bought two pints of lager. He thought that he'd better pay, feeling guilty as he did about Victor's chin. Besides, Victor wasn't working, as far as he knew, though he hadn't been signing on at the Leith office.

They sat in the corner, slightly apart.

Victor stared hard at his bubbling pint of lager. — Tae me,

he said, without looking up. — Ah dinnae see how ye kin say ye love her. He raised his head in a plea and met Gavin's eyes. — Ye wir E'd up, man.

— This wis the next day but.

— It's still in yir system.

— No that long. We didnae . . . we didnae dae anything that night . . . ah mean, ah cannae make love when ah'm E'd up, ah mean, ah kin make love but no git it up, if ye ken what ah mean . . . Gavin stopped, seeing Victor's face contort in rage.

— Still dinnae believe ye love her, he exhaled, gripping the table, his knuckles whitening.

Gavin shrugged, then suddenly looked inspired. — Look, man, they say that Ecstasy's like a truth drug. They gie it tae couples in therapy n that . . .

— So?

— So ah *do* fuckin well love her. Ah'll prove it. Gavin pulled a small plastic bag out of the watch pocket of his jeans, tentatively extracted then swallowed a pill, washing it down with a mouthful of lager. He grimaced, then said, — It's you that doesnae love her, it's jist a habit wi you n ye cannae lit go. Feart ay rejection. That's aw it is, Vic, fuckin male ego. You take one ay they pills n then tell ays ye love her when it kicks in.

Victor looked doubtfully at him. — Ah've no goat the hireys, man . . .

— Fuck the hireys, this is important, this is oan me!

Feeling inflated and virtuous, Gavin dug into his bag for another pill.

— C'moan then. Victor held out his hand and took the pill from Gavin, which he quickly necked.

The pub was strangely deserted for Sunday lunchtime, except for an old guy who was drinking a pint and reading a newspaper, looking a model of contentment. — Quiet in here the day, eh, mate? Gavin smiled at him.

The man regarded him with mild suspicion. — New management. They've no started the bar meals yet.

— Right . . .

Gavin went up to feed the jukebox. It was switched off. A tape of easy-listening music was playing. It was Simply Red's *Greatest Hits*. — It's a tape, eh, he said to Victor, who gave an uncomfortable scowl, before spinning in his seat and springing up to the bar. — What's the story wi the jukey? he asked the youngish woman behind the bar, who was washing some glasses.

— Broken, she said.

Victor felt in his pocket of his bomber jacket for a tape. It was the Metalheadz' *Platinum Breaks*. — Goan, stick this oan fir ays.

— What is it? the barmaid asked.

— Bass n drum but, eh.

The woman looked over in some trepidation at the old guy reading his paper, but succumbed and put the tape on the deck.

Twenty minutes later Victor and Gavin were cunted and shaking their stuff around the floor of the deserted pub. The old guy with the pint looked up at them. Victor gave him the thumbs up and he turned away. The music was leaking into them from all sides. It was an excellent pill.

— J Majik. Wait till ye hear this cunt, Victor shouted at Gavin.

After a bop they sat down to vibe out and chat.

— Whoa, man, these are fuckin strong pills, better than that shite ah hud last night, Victor acknowledged.

— Aw aye, thir something else.

— Listen, mate, this isnae aboot you n me, ye ken that, eh?

Victor was at some pains to express. After all, this was him and Gav.

— Tell ye what, Victor, n ah'm bein honest here, ah respect ye, man. Always huv, n aye, ah love ye. Yir a mate. Ah ken we're eywis in company, likesay Tommy when he wis here likes, Keezbo, Nelly, Spud n aw that, but that's jist the wey it goes. Ah love ye, man. Gavin hugged Victor hard and his friend reciprocated.

— Ah like you n aw, Gav man, ye ken that . . . if the truth be telt yir one ay the soundest cunts ah ken. Naebody's ever goat a bad word tae say against ye, man.

— Tell ye what though, man, Billy Stevenson . . . that fuckin shocked me, man . . .

— It cut ays up . . . it really cut ays up. Ah'd rather she went n screwed some fuckin jakey thin that cunt.

— Me n aw. Ah nivir could stick that wanker.

— That's his wey though but, wait fir a bird tae be feelin a bit vulnerable, a bit low, then steam in wi the smarm . . .

— Bit ah'm no like that, Gavin said, — it wisnae how it wis wi her n me. Ah widnae huv moved in if ah didnae think that youse wir history, Vic. Ah'd nivir move in oan a mate's bird. Ah mean, ah didnae even think ay her at aw until last night up Tribal, man. Believe it, man, ah'm fuckin tellin ye. Oan muh ma's life.

— Ah believe ye, man, it's jist hard tae take, eftir three years . . .

— Bit listen, mate, are ye sure thaire's love left? Hus it no jist gone sour? Mibbe yir jist haudin oan, fir whatever reason, mibbe ye ken yirself deep doon inside . . . ah mean . . . it wis like wi me n Lynda, man . . . ah huv tae be honest, it wis like . . . it wis gone, man, it wis gone n ah wis jist hudin oan. Ah dinnae ken what fir, bit ah wis.

Victor thought for a bit. He kept hold of Gavin; it seemed

important to do so. The pain in his jaw was now a delicious throb. He had his arm around Gavin's shoulder and the throb in his jaw seemed to pulse with the afterglow of some deep communion. Maybe it was possible, maybe it really was over with him and Sarah. They'd been having some terrible rows. There was a tension and distrust between them, which, since both their infidelities had been exposed, now seemed more than just a malaise they could get out of. Maybe he had to let go, and move on.

Photek rattled around them. — Some fuckin tape, eh, Gavin acknowledged.

— Metalheidz, man, the fuckin best. Thuv no seen drum n bass here in Scotland, man, no real drum n bass.

Gavin knew that Victor headed down to London at least once a month for the Sunday Metalheadz sessions in the Blue Note. He hadn't been able to get the vibe before, being more of a garage and soul man, but now it was obvious. This was film music. Their film. Two friends, two comrades, two Hibernian urban warriors in a battle for the heart of the beautiful woman both loved. This was the soundtrack of that horrible, wonderful movie. Life. It was sick, gorgeous nonsense. — Listen, mate, whatever happens between us and Sarah, ah want us tae stay mates. Ah want tae go doon tae London wi ye tae one ay they Metalheidz dos.

— Cool. Victor squeezed Gavin tightly.

Gavin kissed Victor on the jaw. — Sorry, man, sorry ah hit ye, Vic.

— Goat tae admit, Gav, it wis a cracker. The first time ah've ever seen ye gub some cunt. Eywis thought ay ye as a gentle giant. Spud said ye wir a tidy cunt, at the school n that, bit that's Spud but, eh. Great cunt, bit ye take whit eh sais wi a pinch ay salt. Ah wis a bit shocked, man, tae be honest likes. Fuckin Gav, man, bang! Victor rubbed his jaw.

— Tell ye what though, Gav, it feels fuckin nice now, the throb n aw that.

— That's good. Gled it's like . . . positive, ken what ah'm sayin? Gled ah've done something positive fir ye, man. Ah mean, that's aw ah want tae dae in life, man, spread a positive vibe. That's ma sole ambition. N what dae ah dae? Ah go n hurt a mate. That's no me, Vic, ye ken it's no me. Gavin shook his head and tears welled up in his eyes.

— Ah ken that, Gav. Listen, Gav . . . love, man, that's the fuckin thing. Victor extended his hand and Gavin shook it, then held it and opened it, letting his index finger trace the long, deep lifeline on Victor's palm. — Lit's see what she wants tae dae, let's lit love decide, Victor urged.

Gavin looked into Victor's clear, wide pupils. His soul was pure, there was no duplicity about Vic. — Lit's dae it, he whispered, then embraced Victor again.

— Right, Victor said, his smile beaming broadly.

— Tae the victor the spoils, Gavin said grandly, then laughed. — Tae the Gavin the spoils it should be! Naw . . . may the best cunt win!

They clinked their glasses together.

Dr Ormiston had Sarah on the chair. He was looking down at her as she fretfully stared up at the ceiling. She was a fetching girl alright, her long legs in that short skirt, her hands clasped across what looked like a very nice chest, and that chesnut hair swept back from her face cascading out across the headrest of his chair. Yes, he conceded, he could see what all the hoo-ha was about with those two young bucks. He felt a flutter in his chest, as her scent filled his nostrils. There was nothing like the succulent flesh of a young female, he thought, licking his lips. — Open wider, he gasped, as his pulse skipped a beat and his cock stiffened.

There was no drill, she was thinking, thank fuck there was no drill. But there was the knife, and the sound it made; picking, prodding, rending and sawing at her flesh. She couldn't feel the damage, but she could hear it.

A beautiful mouth. It was the thing Ormiston noticed in a woman. Full lips, strong, white teeth. There was a bit of neglect inside here, however. A shameful waste. A woman like this should floss.

Sarah looked at the dentist's intense electric-blue eyes, the white hairs in his eyebrows which joined in the middle. It seemed that he was looking right into her, sharing a strange kind of intimacy with her that no man ever had. She saw her mouth in his mirror. But not the wound. She couldn't look at the wound. Nor the pliers – especially not the pliers. Something hard was digging into her thigh. It might have been a rest on the chair. The man's breathing was becoming irregular under the exertion. Ormiston was her saviour. This was the man who would liberate her from the sickening, all-pervading pain. This man, with his education, his skill and, yes, compassion, for a man capable of success in the field of dentistry could surely have chosen a more lucrative sphere. How much did they get paid? This man would sweep aside the misery and everything would be as it was. Victor would do nothing, Gavin could do nothing, but this man, he would take away the pain.

— It's got to come out now. He yanked and twisted, ripping into numbed flesh around the back of her gums. It was a shame to lose those wisdom teeth and Ormiston always mourned what he gloomily referred to as the death of a tooth, but in this case there was just no alternative. The girl simply had too many teeth for her head. The extraction of both bottom wisdom teeth was essential. He leaned into her and let his free hand rest on her hip. She squirmed a little and he apologised. — Sorry, I just need to get leverage . . .

The suction tube removed the saliva from her mouth. He moved his free hand up and pulled it languidly around inside her, poking it into every cavity, sucking all her sweet, sweet juices, oh God, her gorgeous mouth . . . he couldn't help but imagine his tongue in that mouth, the clean, sharp probing tongue of a man who used all the proven to be effective rather than gimmicky dental products on the market, and he let his hand move down, and why was she wearing that skirt, he could feel her naked thigh against his hand, the hairs on the back of it bristling and him now imagining it going between her legs and his fingers inside her wee cotton briefs and her hungry dripping pussy eating them and one more wrench and her tooth came free in his pliers as he ejaculated into his pants.

— That was a hard one, he gasped, as his cock spurted spasmodically into his trousers. He turned away as the spunk pumped into his flannels and his raw prick throbbed. — Ah . . . ah . . . a satisfactory extraction . . . he wheezed, trying to compose himself.

Sarah felt uncomfortable and went to mumble something, but he told her to keep quiet. He worked away at the second tooth and extracted it more easily than the first one.

He took great care cleaning and packing her wounds. Her mouth was numb as she spat out the wash but Sarah felt a tremendous relief.

— I thought I'd better get them both out at the same time to save you going through the same rigmarole again shortly, Ormiston explained.

— Thanks, Sarah said.

— No, the pleasure was all mine . . . I mean, you have beautiful teeth and you really should floss them. Now that those wisdom teeth are out, they shouldn't be so tightly packed together. There's no excuse now! Get that floss working!

— Aye, I will, she told him.

— Lovely teeth, Ormiston shuddered. — No wonder you have those young men fighting over you!

Sarah blushed and felt bad for blushing. It was just the man's way, however. He wasn't being creepy, he was a professional, it was just another mouth to him.

Ormiston *was* a professional man, and as such not wont to letting aesthetic or sexual considerations take precedence over finance, and he composed himself sufficiently to charge Sarah one hundred and twenty pounds, for which she had to write out a cheque.

— I'd like to see you again in a fortnight's time, Ormiston smiled. — Unfortunately, because it's an emergency call-out, we don't have a duty receptionist. But if you give me a note of your address and phone number, I'll arrange for an appointment to be made for you.

— Thanks, Sarah said. Even the loss of the money couldn't take away the sense of relief. — Sorry to get you out on a Sunday, I hope I didn't spoil your day.

— Not at all, my dear, not at all, Ormiston smiled. He watched her depart, and his face sank into a frown as he contemplated the mind-numbing tedium of a family Sunday afternoon at Ravelston Dykes. — Bugger it, he hissed softly, then went to the toilet to clean himself up.

Sarah heard her name being called. She looked across the road, where Victor and Gavin were standing, outside the pub. She moved towards them. They were both regarding her brightly, but they seemed oddly at peace with each other.

— How did it go? Gavin asked. — Are ye okay?

— Much better, jist a bit numb. He took ma wisdom teeth oot.

— Come in and sit doon, Victor implored.

As Sarah entered the bar and sat down Gavin gave her a full embrace. It felt a bit strange to her. For Gavin it was great to hold her and smell her hair and perfume and feel her warmth. Then he saw Victor out the corner of his eye and he felt bad that he was excluded. He pulled Victor towards them and they had a group hug with Sarah feeling awkward and self-conscious in the middle. — Sarah . . . Victor . . . Sarah . . . Victor . . . Gavin moaned, kissing their faces alternately.

She looked out across the pub at the old guy with the pint and smiled in benign embarrassment. He tetchily looked away. Two younger guys came in and looked, then shrugged and smiled.

— Sarah . . . Sarah . . . Sarah . . . Victor started in a sad mantra, — aw, doll, ah'm really sorry. Ah'm a prick, a total fuckin prick.

Sarah considered that it was a contention hard to dispute.

— Ah love ye, Sarah. Ah'm in love wi ye, Gavin was mumbling in her other ear.

For a few brief moments it seemed to her that it was like sticking a load of After Eight mints into your mouth: you were lulled by the sudden sweetness of it, until the sickness and self-loathing overwhelmed you. — Fuckin let go ay me! she snapped, pulling away and looking at Victor's raised hands and Gavin's forlorn, sad eyes. — What are yis fuckin like! Yis are E'd up!

— Ah love ye, Sarah, ah mean it, Gavin said.

— Ah love ye, but ah think it isnae workin oot. Ah want ye tae be happy and if this cunt's makin ye mair happy thin ah kin, well, that's the wey it is. Ah want tae ken though, what's the story, doll?

The story was that these things were invading her space, like huge, creepy, twisting plants wrapping around her as the come-down kicked in and her nerve ends, twisted and raw, rebelled against their insinuation. They didn't get it; it was as if she didn't exist in her own right, like she was a thing to be fought over. Territory. Land. Possession. That was Victor. That was him.

When they made up, after she had went with that guy from Yip Yap, the way he had fucked her, hard, rampantly, in every orifice, as if to reclaim territory lost, devoid of any tenderness or sensuality. She'd lain there on the floor, trying to hide the tears she knew he'd seen but hadn't acknowledged. She felt like she had been beaten, punished, used; like he'd tried to fuck out of her anything the other guy may have left in. And that was just the sex. No way was Sarah going to be on the receiving end of Victor's sexual and psychological scorched-earth policy again. Him and Gavin together. Colluding now. At first, conflict over territory, but now the fraternal brothers realise that it cannot be resolved by military means. Let's get round the table and thrash this out. The only thing missing was her perspective.

It was not (a) leaves Victor and falls in love with Gavin and lives happily ever after, or (b) fucks Gavin but realises error of ways and goes back to Victor and lives happily ever after. It was (c) left Victor, fucked Gavin. Past tense in both cases. It's over, you silly wee laddies, well fuckin over, you sad, self-mythologising egotistical ratbags.

She slipped free from them, stood up and shook her head. It was too much. She looked at Victor. — You're a prick, you're right enough there. Git oot ma fuckin face. How many times dae ah huv tae tell ye? It's over! N you, she fumed to Gavin whose eyes had gone even more baleful, — we had a fuckin shag, that's aw. If it wis any mair tae you, tell *me* aboot it, no him, n tell ays whin yir no aw fill ay chemicals. Now fuck off and leave ays alaine, the pair ay yis! She stood up and moved towards the exit of the pub.

— Ah'll gie ye a bell the night . . . Gavin said, hearing his voice crack like a light bulb and the 'night' part become incomprehensible.

— Jist fuck off! she fumed and sneered, and left.

— Well, Gavin said, turning to Victor with a hint of self-satisfaction, — there it is. You're bombed oot fir good, bit ah'm still in thaire. Ah jist see her whin ah'm straight n pit her in the picture.

Victor shook his head. — Ye dinnae ken Sarah but, eh. That's no what ah goat fae it at aw.

They argued for a while, punctuating their points with friendly squeezes on each other's wrists to maintain their communion.

A man entered the pub at this point, a man whom they both recognised. It was the dentist, Mr Ormiston. He bought a half-pint of heavy and sat at a table close to them reading *Scotland on Sunday*. He noticed them out of the corner of his eye. Gavin grinned and Victor raised his pint glass. Ormiston gave a weary smile back. It was the two young bucks. Where was the girl?

— Sorry aboot the Edinburgh, mate, Victor said. — Bet ye wir fuckin well zorba'd at that, eh?

— Pardon? Orminston looked puzzled.

— Didnae mean tae involve ye in aw that nonsense in yir surgery. Sorted her oot but, mate, eh?

— Oh yes. Pretty nasty but routine extractions. Wisdom teeth can be tricky, but it's all in a day's work.

— Victor moved closer to Ormiston. — Some joab yuv goat thaire but, mate, eh? Ah couldnae dae that. Lookin in cunts' mooths aw day. He turned to Gavin. — Widnae be me!

Gavin looked thoughtfully at the dentist. — They tell ays thit ye need as much trainin tae be a dentist as ye dae tae be a doaktir. Is that right, mate?

— Well, as a matter of fact it is, Ormiston began, in the somewhat self-justifying air of a man who regards his profession as crassly misunderstood by the lay person.

— Shite! Victor interrupted. — Youse kin fuck oot ay here,

the pair ay yis! A dentist yuv jist goat the mooth tae deal wi, where the likes ay doaktirs, they cunts've goat the whole boady! Yir no tryin tae tell ays that a dentist needs the same amount ay trainin as a doaktir!

— Naw, bit it's no the same thing, Vic. By that fuckin logic, that means that a vet wid need mair trainin thin a doaktir, because they've goat tae learn no jist aboot humans, bit aboot cats n dugs, n rabbits, n cows . . . the physiology ay aw they different animals.

— Ah nivir sais that, Victor insisted, wagging his finger at Gavin.

— Ah'm jist sayin thit it's the same fuckin principles involved here, that's aw ah'm sayin. Tae tend tae a whole creature needs mair trainin than tae tend tae one part ay a creature. That's what yir sayin, right?

— Aye, right, Victor conceded, as Ormiston tried to get back to his paper.

— So by the same logic, tendin tae different creatures'll mean mair trainin than tendin tae jist the one creature, right?

— Uh-uh-uh-uh, Victor halted him. — Doesnae follow. This is human society wir talkin aboot here, right?

— So?

— So it isnae fuckin dug society or cat society –

— Wait the now. What you're sayin is thit in oor society humans are the maist valued species, so the level ay investment in the trainin ay people tae tend tae humans –

— Has goat tae exceed the level ay investment n trainin gied tae people thit tend tae animals. Hus tae be that wey, Gav. Victor turned to Ormiston. — Is that no right but, mate?

— Yes, I suppose it's a point, the dental surgeon said distractedly.

Gavin was thinking about this. There was something that was jarring him. The way people treated animals was out of order. And him too, he hadn't even fed the fuckin cat. Out for two days on one, and he'd forgotten about a promise he'd made to his ma, that he'd go round to hers and feed the cat. She was away up to her sister's at Inverness. She was mad about that cat. She often called it Gavin by mistake, which hurt him more than he let on. He felt a surge of guilt. — Listen, Vic, ah've goat tae nash. You've jist reminded ays, ah said thit ah'd go roond tae muh ma's n feed the cat. The last thing ah promised. He stood up and Victor did too. They had another hug. — Nae hard feelings, eh, mate?

— Naw, man . . . ah jist hope she comes back tae ays, Victor said wearily.

— Well, mate, ye ken ma feelins oan that yin . . . Gavin nodded.

— Aye . . . take care, Gav. We're at hame next Setirday. Aberdeen, eh, the cup.

— Aye. Which effectively means the season's over next week if ye discount the relegation battle.

— It's a tough joab, mate, bit some cunt's goat tae dae it. See ye doon the Four-in-Hand.

— Right.

Gavin turned and left the pub. He walked up the hill at Hanover Street, or Hangover Street, as they called it. The effects of the MDMA were running down in him and a shiver coursed through his body, although it wasn't cold. He pulled a flyer for a club night out of his pocket. Written on it was the name SARAH and a seven-digit phone number. He should just be able to phone that number. It was love. It was. It shouldn't have needed an ideal place and time to be expressed. It should just happen.

There was a phone box. There was an Asian woman in it. He wanted her to finish that call. More than anything. Then he became aware of his heart, thrashing in his chest. He couldn't speak to her like this; he'd fuck it up again. He wanted the woman to stay on the phone forever. Then she put the receiver down on the cradle. Gavin turned away and walked down the road. Now wasn't the time. Now was the time to get to his mother's house and feed Sparky the cat.

I Am Miami

For Dave Beer

I

S itting in the lush garden, Albert Black's eyes glinted as he
sipped his glass of iced tea. The fauna and flora of this
tropical zone were alien to him; a coal-and-rouge bird chirped
a belligerent warning from its vantage point in a eucalyptus
tree, before springing into the air. Black wondered fleetingly
about signs, though the notion of the augur was too Romanist,
too pagan for his tastes, before returning to the palms that
sambaed in the cool breeze. This led his line of vision out
onto the electric blue of Biscayne Bay, and beyond to the
skyscrapers of downtown Miami, glowing brashly in the
morning sun. He found these lofty edifices distasteful. America
seemed, in spite of the fervour of its daytime television evangelists, and the obligatory piety of its politicians, to be the
most godless place he had visited. When he looked over at
the emerging new financial district, he dimly recalled the
magnesium gleam of the first Apollo spaceship as it launched
from close to here, en route to the moon; all the time moving
further from heaven.

Lifting the glass of tea, Black caught sight of his reflection.
Despite his advanced years, his face had retained its bony,
angular structure and pasty complexion. Close-cut grey stubble
grew on each side of his head, the dome of which glistened

leathery pink. He regarded his trademark thick, black spectacles, sitting on a hawklike beak of a nose. They covered small, dark eyes that still sparkled combatively, despite the pathos in them that seemed to invite sympathy. But he was the only person around to offer this, and that was certainly not in his nature. He crushed the weakness from his face with a tightening of his mouth, setting the glass down on the white wrought-iron garden table.

There was the problem of getting William and Christine ready for the church. Every Sunday: always the same problem; the foot-dragging, the procrastination. Nobody, even Marion, seemed to really grasp the issue of punctuality, and how we needed to set a good example. Rudeness to God, through late arrival at His house, could not be accepted. Lateness in general was a curse, the way in which time could be stolen, frittered away . . .

He felt the surge of a familiar malign force rising from within, and fought it down, champing on nothing but his teeth: that terrible burn inside. It was always strongest when he reluctantly woke into a new day and was sabotaged by that cruel jolt of anticipation, that hope that she'd somehow be back.

But Marion was gone.

Forty-one years of marriage over and the best part of him destroyed. He'd watched powerlessly as the cancer thinned her down and hollowed her out, eating her from the inside. Albert Black looked out over the bay. He could have been cast adrift, floundering aimlessly in its waters, as he now was in the thick, warm air around him. Nothing was left; even his basic principles and his faith wavered uncertainly.

Why Marion? Why? Why, Holy Father?

But was it right to expect a just God? Was to do so not merely displaying the vanity of those who would seek to elevate themselves in the grand scheme of things? What a conceit to expect individual justice, when we were blessed by being part of something larger and immortal!

Or were we?

Yes! Forgive me my doubts, oh Father!

The bird had returned, and it cast a sharp, keen eye over Black, before trilling with increased venom.

— Yes, my friend, I hear you.

Yes. We are so slow to consider justice to members of other species on this Earth, yet we are so piteous when our mortality is tampered with by powers greater than us.

The bird seemed satisfied by this response and flew away.

But Marion . . . a world full of sinners, and He took you from me!

No matter how much Old Testament outrage Albert Black tried to summon up in his contempt of what he saw as the forlorn weakness of his species, Marion's face would always appear in his mind's eye. Even in her absence, her grace had the power to subdue his rage. But he'd been forced to recognise a painful, if bitter-sweet, lesson since her death: it was always *her*, not God. He saw that now. It was her love, not his own faith, which had cleansed and saved him. Redeemed him. Made sense of his life.

He always envisioned her as youthful; just as he had known her when they first met at the church back in Lewis, on that cold and squally October Sunday afternoon. And now, following her departure, he'd felt the desertion of another lifelong companion. No matter what chapters and verses of the good book he recited, or which psalms played in his head, however he tried to deflect his rage onto his fellow men, especially the non-believers, doubters, Judases and false prophets, Albert Black had to concede to himself that he was angry at the Creator for Marion's absence.

Estranged from his daughter, Christine, who lived in

Australia, Black had found that coming to Florida and the remnants of his family had offered him far less solace than he could have imagined. His son, William, was an accountant – a traditional and noble profession for a Scots Protestant. But he worked in the film business. Black had always associated that tawdry enterprise with California, but William had explained that some major studios now had operations out in Florida in order to take advantage of the tax incentives and the weather. However, it was clear to him that his son had taken on some of the decadent trappings of that vile industry.

You only had to consider this house and its sickening extravagance. The Caribbean-style, theatrically uplit dwelling on its waterfront setting, the impact-glass windows running from the hardwood and tiled floors to the nine-foot ceilings, those five bedchambers with en suite facilities and walk-in closets, which were rooms themselves in their spacious generosity. The kitchen, with its stone countertops and designer accessories: refrigerator/freezer, stainless-steel appliances, washer-dryer. (Italian, William had called it. Albert had stated that he was unaware a scullery possessed a nationality.) Five luxurious bathrooms, all with marble countertops, baths and showers, toilets and bidets. The largest one, in the master bedroom that William shared with his wife, Darcy, containing a large Whirlpool bath, raised on a stage, and obviously meant for the indulgence of more than one person; Romanist in its decadence. A fitness room with state-of-the-art exercise equipment, an office and library, and a wine vault with dedicated storage spaces. Outside, a rear multi-level landscaped garden with luxurious water features and direct bay access with moorings that berthed a substantial boat, and a four-car garage the size of the old family home back in Edinburgh. When William conversed on the phone to his business associates and friends, it seemed to his father as if he was speaking another language.

William's wife, Darcy (Black had to constantly fight to cast aside images of her and his son cavorting nakedly in that bath), had been such a sweet wee lassie, all he could have wanted in a daughter-in-law. He recalled when the shy and demure and, above all, God-fearing young American student was presented to them by their son, at the old house in Merchiston, some twenty years ago. An exchange student, Darcy was supposedly a committed Christian. But how many times, he considered, had he seen her since they'd first met? Perhaps on half a dozen occasions. Then, when she and William had graduated, it was understood that they would marry and go to live in America.

Now Darcy seemed different: brisk, sly, assertive and worldly. He heard her cackling with her friends who came over and drank alcohol during the day. Their shrill laughter stinging his ears, as they recounted, in a manner that nauseated him, their purchases of rubbish, which seemed to be procured purely for the sake of ownership rather than utility.

Albert Black did not regard it as his place to pass comment on his discomfort. After all, on picking him up at the airport, William had immediately informed him that they didn't attend church any more. His son had obviously been thinking about this declaration; it had the stilted air of rehearsal. Of course, it was sugar-coated: he'd claimed that the Church of Scotland in Miami wasn't suitable, and the American Protestant evangelical churches were littered with egotists and false prophets. But Albert Black had looked into his son's watery-grey eyes and saw treachery.

Black had no relationship with his teenage grandson, Billy. He'd made the effort in the lad's boyhood, even trying to understand baseball, but how could you take seriously a nation that had rounders as its national sport? He'd taken him to the football over in Scotland, which he'd liked. But Billy was grown up now. That girl who came around – from Mexico or somewhere like that. They had told him but he couldn't recall. What he did register were her judging eyes, and that wily little smile stuck on her lips. Pretty, yes; but in a very tarty sort of way. A girl like that was always trouble to a young man. And that music they played! It was surely a travesty referring to that artless, monotonous racket as music. Continually banging out from his room in the basement. Billy seemed to have sole use of that huge area, which ran the length of the house. Living like a mole when there were perfectly good empty bedrooms to choose from. William and Darcy seeming not to bother, not even appearing to hear the continual cacophonous din. But then they were out most of the time. He recalled them mumbling some nonsense about Billy's need for privacy when they took him on the inaugural tour of their home.

So after two weeks in the Sunshine State, human contact was decidedly lacking. Now Albert Black's routine consisted of sitting all day in the shade at the bottom of the garden overlooking the bay, reading his Bible, waiting for his family to come home. Darcy would cook a meal, and they would say grace at the table, which he sensed was contrived and purely for his benefit. Then he'd go for a short evening walk prior to sitting in front of the monstrous plasma television screen before retiring to bed in withering exhaustion, his head blasted by one thousand channels of advertisements with slivers of television broadcast sandwiched in between.

Turning in.

His catchphrase: I think I'll turn in.

I've been turning in all my life.

He looked up to see a large white cruise ship pulling into

the bay. It resembled a block in the housing scheme where he'd taught. From the inside, he supposed that the cabins would be luxurious enough. Perhaps the key difference to the scheme block, though, was in its mobility. It had probably come from the Caribbean. Albert Black found it hard to think of such places; they never seemed vivid in his imagination. It was Canada that had always held exotic sway. He'd thought of emigrating there, long ago, when he and Marion were young. But he felt duty-bound to work in his own country, and he joined the Scots Guards, serving abroad for three years, before returning to Scotland's capital city and taking a degree in divinity and philosophy at Edinburgh University, opting then to go into education via Moray House Teacher Training College.

He'd entered the education system with a Knoxian zeal, believing that it was important for a Scottish Protestant to continue the great democratic tradition of providing the best education for the poorest children. And he'd come to the then new sixties-built comprehensive school in the housing scheme, with high hopes of turning out mission-aries, ministers, engineers, scientists, doctors and educators like himself; making it a bastion of a new Scottish Enlightenment. But, he reflected under the relentless sun that filtered through the shivering palm trees, his aspirations were lunatic. Typists and labourers; they produced them by the barrel-load. Builders, shop assistants and, latterly, once even that work had dried up, small-time gangsters and drug dealers. These days the school couldn't even unearth a decent footballer. It had never boasted a Smith, Stanton, Souness or Strachan, though one or two had made a living from the game. But no longer.

Of course, Albert Black knew the material he was working with – poverty, social disadvantage, broken homes and low expectation – but he strove to provide a disciplinary and ethical framework within the school gates, which might compensate for the lawless immorality in the scheme and beyond. And he'd been mocked for this. Not only turned into a figure of fun by his pupils, but also by other members of staff and by the Marxists on the city's education committee. Even his colleagues in the Association of Christian Teachers, embarrassed by his zeal, had betrayed him, failing to support his protests against the compulsory early retirement visited upon him.

We must have social education and religious knowledge!

2

She wished that she had taken his advice and succumbed to letting him shell out on the first-class ticket he had offered to get her. Sydney to LA to Miami was a nightmare. The economy class would have been okay, but for the toddler who peered over at her from the seat in front, never breaking his stare, despite her attempts to stay buried in her book. And there was his baby sibling next to him, in the arms of its mother; how it screamed and shat with a vengeance, filling the cabin with ear-splitting cries and noxious fumes.

Despite a relief that she wasn't in the woman's shoes – a woman, she noted, not that much older than herself – Helena wasn't volunteering to help out the stressed mother. She wanted nothing to do with anybody else's children.

Sitting back, ignoring the toddler and turning to the plane window, she copied the dozing man next to her and shut her eyes, letting Miami fill her thoughts. All Helena Hulme could think of was what was going to happen with her lover. He was a generous man, too reckless with his cash, she fancied, but it wouldn't have been right to let him pay for a first-class fare. Not with what she had to tell him.

3

The sun burned relentlessly over the bay, with not a single cloud defiling the azure sky. Although his preference was to stroll in the evenings when it was cooler, Albert Black decided to go for a walk and rose from under the parasol. He looked at the panama hat on the table in front of him. He felt somewhat foolish wearing it, but he had to protect his bald pate from the sun, and the alternative of the baseball cap offered by Billy was simply out of the question. Assuming this hat was William's, he picked it up again, and put it on.

Setting off at a steady pace, pleased that he had extricated himself from the house, Black meandered through Miami Beach, down to the art deco district towards Ocean Drive. His problematic right knee was stiff; the walk would be kill or cure. He recalled that fright some five years ago, when it just gave out one afternoon, sending him into recumbent shock onto a pavement in crowded George Street. His puzzlement and fear at how something that he had relied upon for so long could just withdraw its hitherto under-appreciated services in a split second, transforming his life in the process.

The knee was holding up though. Despite the intense heat on his back, causing his shirt to stick uncomfortably to his skin, Black was hitting a decent stride and making good progress. When he came onto Ocean Drive, he immediately cut through the crowds of posing youths and holidaymakers, crossed its Bermuda-grass verges, and approached the sea. He watched the Atlantic lap up against the vanilla sands. The sea was steady, with small breakers rolling in and washing up on the sun-kissed coast. Already, quite a few bathers were out, working on their tans. Yet as soon as Black became aware of a vague sense of idyllic contentment, it was abruptly broken, seized as he was by a vice-like grip inside him. It seemed to crush some of his organs, and he realised what it was: an insinuating thought, pulsing and poignant, that somehow Marion was out there, waiting for him! He struggled for breath, his palpitations big and heavy as his eyes gaped out over the aquamarine prairie.

What am I doing here? I have to go home . . . she might come back . . . everything will be a mess . . . the house . . . the garden . . .

Two bikinied girls, supine on beach towels, caught a glimpse of his stricken figure, and turned to each other and giggled. His schoolteacher's instinct to hone in on sources of mischief got the better of him as Black observed their derision, and saw that he was its object. His face flushed red and he turned away, traipsing dejectedly across the sand, leaving the beach for the bustle of Ocean Drive. At the News Cafe he went to the adjoining shop and picked up a two-day-old *Daily Mail*.

Paying for the paper, he made his way back down the street. He soon became aware of some impending commotion ahead: people were hastily peeling aside as a growling, wild-eyed figure lurched forward, pushing a cart. Unlike the others on the street, Black did not move, maintaining steady eye contact with a skinny, crazed-looking Negro man, as the strutting tourists grimaced and al fresco diners turned away. The man stopped his trolley in front of Black and glared at him in hostility, screaming 'muthafucker' three times in his face.

Albert Black was still, but felt that terrible rage working his insides again, and envisioned picking up the metal fork on the table close to him and ramming it into the man's eye. Driving it into his brain.

This thing alive, spared, while my Marion's gone . . .

Instead, Albert Black stared back at his aggressor with a look of loathing so focused and total that it reached the man's brain through its narcotic icing. With deliberate enunciation, Black spoke the Latin motto of his old regiment, the Scots Guards: — *Nemo me impune lacessit!* The bum lowered his head, picking up the meaning from the body language and tone of the old soldier. *No one assails me with impunity.* He quickly steered his cart round the rigid-spined Black, mumbling inaudible curses as he departed.

That foul creature, beyond sin, walking God's Earth in mortal pain; surely deliverance from its torment would be the act of a righteous man . . .

Terrorised by his thoughts, Albert Black looked around, and turned on his heels, heading back to the News Cafe, where he sat down in a heap at the pavement-side table and looked onto Ocean Drive. A young man minced towards him. — What can I get you? he performed.

— Water . . . Black could only gasp like a man marooned in a desert.

— *Avec gas, sans gas?*

This thing lisping at me! This land of monsters!

— No gas, Black coughed, still shaking at the violence of his thoughts. Wiping the back of his dripping neck with a hanky, he turned to his paper. The news from the UK told him that a child had been kidnapped in Sussex, police suspected a paedophile. This disgusted Black, but then all the news did.

There seemed to be evil, sloth and degenerate behaviour every-where. He recalled the watershed election of 1979 when he'd voted for Thatcher, seeing the free market as a way to enforce discipline on a feckless and destructive working class. Later he realised that she and her ilk had, in consumer capitalism, unleashed a godless, amoral wrecking ball; a satanic genie you couldn't get back into the bottle. Far from delivering the British proletariat from squalor and ignorance, it had reduced them to new depths of despair and immorality. Drugs replaced jobs: Black watched the scheme and the school where he worked, slowly give up and die.

Now with Marion's restraining and calming influence gone, his head was filled by the dark thoughts of violence he'd strug-gled all his life to repress. He thought of his family; how it had all been a sham.

It would be fitting if our souls were taken: my own, William's, Darcy's and the boy's, so that we may join Marion, spared of any further mortal pain and treachery.

No, that was a weak and sinful thought! The thought of a monster! Forgive me.

Restore unto me the joy of Thy salvation; and uphold me with Thy free spirit.

Then will I teach transgressors Thy ways; and sinners shall be converted unto Thee.

At his table, oblivious to the crowds, Black's thoughts raced back to those years of teaching, to that desperate war of attri-tion with other teachers, education committees and, most of all, the pupils.

Such a vain and thankless battle. The waste of a life. Nobody from that school had been a success. Ever.

Not one of them.

No, that wasn't quite right. There was one. Black had seen him. On the television, at some pop-music award ceremony he'd mistakenly tuned into. Sitting up, lost, in the old family house, with Marion in the hospital, vapidly gazing at the television. He'd been about to change channels, but then had instantly recognised an ex-pupil, teetering up onto the stage, obviously drunk, to receive his award. He had that distinctive, almost albino, whiteness that he'd retained. He had mumbled some nonsense to a nervous host before leaving the platform. It was a few days later when Black had seen his image again, this time on the front page of a magazine: silly pop-music tripe for imbeciles, which he'd nonetheless been moved to purchase. The boy – now a man – was staring back at him with the same sneering insolence he recalled from bygone days. Yet, such was his pride in his old school, Black had been rather delighted. It was good to see an old boy doing well. The article told of a number-one hit single with a well-known American singer, Kathryn Joyner. He knew the name, had recalled that Marion had liked her. It said that the ex-pupil was now working with some established artists, one of whom he had heard of from the Sunday papers: a shallow, manipulative woman who had led a selfish, decadent and sinful life before supposedly 'finding God'.

American lies and blasphemy! No man or woman who has sinned can be born again in this life! The sin has to be carried, suffered, prayed against, and then, on the Day of Judgement, we fall upon the blessed mercy of the Lord. No pope or priest or prophet, no mortal man can absolve us!

But Albert Black had nonetheless gone back to the hospital that evening, enthused enough to anticipate telling Marion the story of the ex-pupil. When he got there, the curtains were pulled around her bed. A nurse saw him. He knew everything he needed to know by her face. Marion had gone, and he hadn't even been there. The nurse explained how they'd tried to call him. There was no answerphone. Didn't he have a mobile? Black ignored her, and pulling aside the curtains, kissed his departed wife's still-warm head and said a quick prayer. Then he walked off the ward and into a hospital toilet where he sat down and cried like a madman, in furious, demented rage and abject misery. When a male nurse came to attend to him, knocking on the door, he'd insisted that he was fine, then simply stood up and pulled the flush, washed his hands and unlocked the stall, appearing before the young man. Then he signed the appropriate documentation and went home to organise the funeral.

But when he reached his house something compelled him to read more of the music magazine article and Albert Black dissolved into apoplexy.

I can honestly say that I learned nothing from my school, from my teachers. Fucking zero. In fact, they often went out of their way to discourage me. All I wanted to do was music . . . they make you do all that utterly pointless shit . . . stuff that you've no interest in, nor any aptitude for. We were all treated like factory fodder at our school. Then when the factories shut down, dole and YTS fodder. The only decent teachers I had were in English and Art. It was the only time I was treated like a human being. Other than that school was a concentration camp run by weak, stupid wankers with no morality. No fucking spine.

Black had hoped for affirmation in that article. Instead, he'd found only scorn and contempt. He'd cut out the offending passage, keeping it in his wallet, and no matter how many times he reread it, it never failed to induce rage. Here in a busy cafe in South Florida, shaded from the oppressive heat, he was moved to look at it again. Surely Ewart – that was his name – surely he was joking; it was just the so-called ironic anti-establishment posturing so beloved of such publications, usually owned by the satanic profiteers of the multinational media corporations. Black cast his febrile mind back; dates and faces slowly started to mesh together. The exhalted art teacher would no doubt be the harlot Slaven, with her short skirt and husky voice, unaware that the basis of her supposed 'popularity' lay solely in the boys' hormones. No, it was probable she was aware of this fact only too well.

How could the girls do anything but fall like dominoes to teenage pregnancy, with a wanton slut like that on the staff to set the example?

The English teacher would most likely be Crosby. Sitting back in the staffroom, pontificating and agitating; spreading cynical discord wherever he went.

I crossed swords with that Trotskyite a few times before . . . a trouble-maker.

Like this Carl Ewart character. Not a thuggish type, more of a subversive. Possessing that snide ability to wind up the dimmer pupils with his wilful rebelliousness. He was in cahoots with the wee laddie, Albert Black recalled, the one who'd died. Black had attended the funeral (a tawdry civil service in the crematorium) in order to represent the school. A former pupil had passed over to the mercy of the Lord. The death would have gone unmarked and unrepresented had Miss Norton not said in the staffroom that she'd heard how the lad who had fallen from George VI Bridge after a bout of stupid, drunken horseplay had gone to the school.

He'd looked up the details. Another nobody: a poor, un-remarkable wastrel of a youth. Yet how could pupils feel connected to the school, believe in it, if nobody even acknow-ledged that this boy had been part of it? The school failed the likes of that young man, Galloway, he recalled, and in return, they failed the school. That was it: complacency, laziness, the lack of belief, the absence of standards, it all came down to one thing: secularism.

And now, sitting at the News Cafe in Miami's South Beach, oblivious to the passing crowds, Albert Black's racing brain recalled where he had seen Carl Ewart's name even more recently. It had been on a large poster in his own grandson Billy's basement bedroom! The big emblazoned logo, it had jumped out at him on his brief tour of the subterranean labyrinth of the house: N-SIGN.

That was what Carl Ewart called himself: *N-Sign*. Of course, Ewart wouldn't be aware that this referred to Ensign Charles Ewart, a giant Scot who was a hero of the Battle of Waterloo, single-handedly capturing the French standard of the Eagle. No, doubtless he picked it up from passing by or sitting inside the grubby hostelry on the Royal Mile which exploited that brave soldier's name.

Carl Ewart. A millionaire, and he was a *disc jockey*. This would mean that he played records, presumably on radio stations. How could someone become a millionaire through playing other people's records? Black suddenly felt the need to know. But the article had also said that Ewart 'remixed' records for people, for *artists*. This was how the people who made that trash referred to themselves. Presumably this meant that those 'recording artists' taped their offerings, their banal instrumentations, and the likes of Ewart reordered this material, adding those ghastly sound effects and horrendous drumbeats that you heard everywhere. In the magazine piece, Ewart had pompously spoken of his work as 'revolutionary'. That pounding, monotonous racket that had become so ubiquitous, even less palatable than the screeching guitar and vocal sounds that used to predominate. This, in essence, was the extent of Ewart's revolution: to take something vile and disgusting and then debase it even further. And Albert Black heard this ungodly racket everywhere here in Miami Beach, from the courtyards of the local boutique hotels and the expensive passing vehicles driven by exhibitionists, to his own grandson's bedroom. He would ask Billy about Carl Ewart when he got back. If nothing else, it might help to build some sort of dialogue between them.

And Ewart had been at the funeral of this Galloway character. Who had he been in attendance with? Birrell, the boxer, and that fool . . . what was his name? . . . Lawson: that idiot who had embarrassed the school by being arrested for football thuggery. Lawson. Dragged out of Easter Road stadium with that other simpleton, the so inappropriately named Martin Gentleman, then paraded around the perimeter track by the police for the benefit of TV stations across the country. The school's name had been sullied further through being mentioned in the newspapers. Albert Black had seen the incident. Fortunately, Lawson had already left the school by this time, but when Black had called Gentleman to account for himself at school assembly, the huge, simple youth had shouted some defiant curses from his sewer-like mouth before charging out of the school for good to join Lawson in a life of crime and debauchery. And good riddance.

Lawson and his blaspheming mouth. He had changed 'look ever to Jesus, he will follow you through' to 'look ever to Jesus, he will follow through' accompanied by loud noises simulating flatulence. It had spread like a moronic bush fire from that class to assembly, forcing Albert Black, although pretty much a psalm purist, to abandon one of his favourite hymns from the list.

The retired schoolmaster's knee clicked a habitual warning as he rose with youth's careless vigour, and returned to the News Cafe's shop, where he thumbed through some magazines until he found something called *Mixmag*. Inside a picture of Ewart, his milky-white hair now thinning a little. He was contemplative, and yes, intelligent-looking. Focused, thoughtful and reflecting on the forthcoming DJ conference in Miami.

Miami?

Surely not. But there were strange coincidences. Billy, his grandson, was a *fan* of Carl Ewart. This seemed so ridiculous to Black. His grandson, his *American* grandson – an acolyte of a disruptive clown from a west Edinburgh scheme! It was a strange world. Black checked the dates of this conference. Ewart was in Miami now!

Ewart. Here.

Black looked towards the heavens. The skies were still clear and he felt his old flesh tingle in a buzz of anticipation. The possibility of the guiding hand of divine forces could not be discounted. Indeed, there seemed no other reason for such an unlikely coincidence of circumstance. Almost at once Albert Black resolved to attend this conference and speak to Carl Ewart and ask, no, *demand* that he explain those offensive comments. Surely there must have been *something* that the school provided him with to equip him for this life of success, as degraded as it undoubtedly was. Black was suddenly desperate to find out where and when this conference was taking place. He supposed that Ewart would be delivering an address, as he himself had done several times on the subject of religious education (usually upon deaf ears and accompanied by sneering whispers) at the Educational Institute of Scotland's annual conference.

Returning to his seat, Albert Black finished his water and settled the bill, refusing to leave a tip. Who would bequeath a gratuity to be furnished with something that was provided by the bounty of the Lord? — Have a nice day, the server pouted in disgruntlement.

— Thank you for your wishes, Black said in cold piety, — though I would be more impressed if they were sincerely proffered.

The waiter shook indignantly and was about to retort when Black met his watering eyes, and said in kindly, almost pitying tones, — The forked tongue of American commerce doesn't impress me, my young friend.

The intense heat made Black recall his Scots Guards days, as he rose, turned away and marched stiffly down the street. He thought about the service he'd seen in the foot patrols in the strength-sapping jungles of Malaya, fighting the Communist terrorists. A soldier's world was founded on discipline and order. War had always been the spiritual salvation of the working classes. The compelling need for excitement that infects all young men with empty lives could be satisfied in this theatre, and the resulting *esprit de corps* could build nations. Black thought about his own service in Malaya's jungles, though sadly this took place after the war, and left him relatively untested in comparison to his own father, who had returned from World War II and that Japanese prison camp a failure as a soldier and a man; broken, morose, edgy, and prone to heavy drinking. How we so badly needed another *real* war, a ground war, where working men of different countries could see the whites of each other's eyes as they engaged in mortal combat. Even that was now nonsense, destroyed by the cold, satanic technology of the weapons industry. To be seared or incinerated by explosives or chemicals dropped on you from a height determined by computer programs, the death switch pulled by a coward miles away: it was no way for a man to die.

He headed across the street to the Miami Beach Tourist Information Centre, an art deco building on the beach side of Ocean Drive. Approaching the clerk, a middle-aged Latina woman, Black announced, — I wish to attend the Winter Music Conference.

The woman's large eyebrows went half an inch north as she regarded the old Scotsman. — It starts tomorrow, she confirmed.

— Where is it to be held?

The woman tightened her eyes in focus. Then something seemed to soothe within her and her voice dropped. — The WMC takes place across many different venues. I think the best thing for you to do is check the flyers that people are handing out.

— Thank you for your time, Albert Black said, leaving the building singularly unenlightened, and crossing the street as the busy traffic rumbled by. But walking on for a stretch he did indeed see a young man and woman issuing flyers, but only to the obviously youthful among the passers-by. About to steel himself past his reticence and approach them, he noticed fortuitously that some had been wantonly discarded on the ground. Black picked one up. There it was: N-SIGN. Ewart was delivering his address at the Cameo on Washington Avenue. Tonight. Ten till late. Albert Black resolved that he would attend. Oddly cheered, he headed home through Miami Beach, walking down those few art deco blocks of landfill that separated the Atlantic Ocean from the Biscayne Bay.

4

— Heh-low . . . the insistent toddler said again. And again. This time louder. His hapless mother now so preoccupied with the baby, she'd given up even trying to attend to him.

Children that age scared Helena. They made her think about the abortion. How could they have been so stupid? Only once, when her prescription had run out, and not long after her period. She thought it would be okay. It was self-torturing, and it was nonsense, yet it was impossible to see a child and not think about the parcel of tissue and liquid she'd had expelled from within her. What that one stupid, careless moment would have become. And she'd have to tell him that it was all taken care of; that she'd sorted it out. He had a right to know. He wasn't religious, and they'd never discussed having kids. They'd never discussed having anything other than fun. And never had fun felt so limiting, self-defeating and shallow than when she'd gone into that clinic. But she should have told him first.

Children made us all sinners, she reflected; whether we aborted, raised or ignored them. You picked up a newspaper and saw evidence of the fucked-up place you couldn't fix, couldn't make better, the place you'd brought them into. She looked at the kid again and felt sorry for the poor little bastard.

In a sudden seedy compassion, she grinned at him and whispered, — One day you are going to be so pissed off at your silly mother for bringing you here, mate. *All because she was too stupid and lazy to get a fucking job and take care of herself.*

The kid smiled slyly, seeming to understand. She decided she kind of liked him. — Hi, she said, louder, — what's your name, as the mother, with her cow-in-the-abattoir eyes, turned round and looked at Helena in stone-cold gratitude.

5

He wasn't even that close to the house, when Albert Black picked up the thumping beat of that music again. It was everywhere. Coming up from the basement, where the youth that called him Grandad resided like some cave dweller.

Billy.

Albert Black recalled when the boy was younger and visiting Scotland, how he'd taken him to Easter Road and Tynecastle stadiums. Black had always gone to see Hibs play one week, Hearts the next. Edinburgh was his adopted city and he supported both its clubs, an approach he knew many found queer in those partisan and tribal times. His pupils laughed at him, supporters of the rival maroon and green, but united in their derision.

But how could you expect classroom discipline? They had destroyed employment opportunities and flooded the scheme with drugs. That was bad enough, but then they had banned the tawse!

Black recalled that sleek, forked, leather strap, and the fear it inspired in many of the louder vagabonds. How their insolent faces would fall silent and flush as they were called out, knowing that soon their hands would be redder still, under its stinging lash. The implement was as essential to good teaching as chalk.

But Billy could tell him about this Winter Music Conference and N-Sign Ewart. It was something they could share. He descended the steps, before hesitating outside his grandson's bedroom door. He knew that smell coming from the room. It was marijuana. It had begun to get a foothold in the school, just as he was retiring. They smoked it by the annexe at the sports fields. Well, it wasn't getting a foothold here! Black pushed the door open. — Hey . . . you can't come in here, Gramps . . . Billy was lying back on the bed. He had one of those funny cigarettes in his hand. That young girl, the Mexican sort, was crouching between his legs, her head bobbing! She immediately ceased what she was doing, and

turned to him, her face flushed, her eyes primal, beastlike. —
What the fuck —

— Get out of here! Black shouted at her, pointing his finger
in scorn.

— Hey, hold on a minute, Billy protested, — *you* get out!
This is my freakin space! This ain't the Isle of Skye or shit!

Black stood his ground. — Shut up! He glared at the girl.
— You! Get out!

The young woman staggered to her feet, as Billy pulled up
his green canvas shorts and zipped himself up. — Valda, you
stay right there. You — he rounded on Black, — you sick old
bastard! Get the fuck outta my room!

— Me . . . *me*? Me sick! . . .

Black felt the anger of the righteous soldier rising inside
him, but then he suddenly saw Marion's face in their only
grandchild, and he'd been tricked, Satan was trying to control
him! The fight left him. Then, as his eyes stayed locked on
Billy, a darker, more shameful memory inserted itself like a
bolt of electricity through him, and he turned and marched
out of the room, squawking, — Your parents will hear
of this!

— Fuck you! Fuckin pervert!

His heart pounding, Black ran up the stairs and out of the
house, feeling the pain and the shame of this young man, this
stranger, laughing at him, like a snickering moron of a first
year. And how ridiculous he must have seemed to them, an
old man in glasses, Bible ever-present, talking in a strange,
almost incomprehensible tongue. He was a man out of place,
out of time. He always had been; but once it had seemed a
virtue. Now he was even subject to ridicule in the nest of
sinners that was his own family!

I was wrong . . . forgive me, Lord!

O turn unto me, and have mercy upon me; give Thy strength unto Thy servant, and save the son of Thine handmaid.

Shew me a token for good; that they which hate me may see it, and be ashamed: because Thou, LORD, hast holpen me, and comforted me.

His knee locking in protest at the swiftness of his departure, he hobbled down the driveway, out into the street. The temperature had risen and he found himself again the only pedestrian for miles as he made his way down the lush avenues, heading back through Miami Beach, thankful to mingle with the crowds on Lincoln. Thoughts of his family overwhelmed him. Who were they? William, here in Florida. His daughter, Christine, over in Australia. She had never married. Had always lived in apartments with other women. What sort of a woman was she? Who were they? What kind of a father had he been?

What am I? A tyrant. A bully. Marion was the one that had given them all the good things; the grace, the humility. All I ever contributed was, at best, my sullen piety. No wonder they couldn't get far enough away!

Neither could Albert Black. He was scarcely aware that he had retraced his steps back down to Ocean Drive. Composing himself, he found a cafe, sat down and ordered more water. As he sipped at the soothing cool liquid, he heard an accent, a voice from home. It froze him to his marrow.

6

— Lookit the fuckin tits oan that! ah goes, nudgin the Milky Bar Kid, cause this big fuckin pump's jist walked past. — Ah'd gie that fuckin biler a guid stoking, too right, ya cunt!

Ken whin ye git that hingower horn: aw they sleazy thoughts fae last night's peeve still in the system? Well, that's me, big time. Mind you, no that ah need a hingower fir that! But wi wir pished oan that plane yesterday, then straight oot oan the batter; cocktails, the fuckin lot, in they posh hotel bars. Ye cannae beat it.

— Where were you when political correctness was sweeping the world, Terry?

— Humpin dirty hoors, n avoidin fuckin Jambo cunts, ah tells um.

The Kid rolls ehs eyes. — Ye goat tae move wi the times, Terry. Stoap fightin these auld battles ay the past, eh smiles.

— Aye, right.

The fanny here's fuckin hotchin; it's like thaire's a top bird ootside every one ay they swanky joints oan that Ocean Drive, aw giein ye the eye n beckonin ye intae thir web ay sin. No thit the Milky Bar Kid's giein a fuck. Eh's goat Helena, ehs burd, or should ah say, ehs *fiancée*, comin in fae Australia the morn. Tae me that's aw the mair reason tae try n git baw-deep in some wee tart the night, git it oot the system before the nuptials git tied, cause eftir that it's the last time eh'll clap eyes oan another minge for a long time. Widnae be me, but, eh! Ah'm mair yir George Clooney type, the debonair, smoulderin-eyed playboy wi the suave air ay urbane sophistication, whae likes tae pit it aboot a bit. Well, yuv goat tae but, eh? Spice ay life. — Stall here a second, Carl, ah tells the Kid, — she's gantin oan it, ah say, eyein up this wee honey flashin a big smile n a laminate menu at ays.

— Terry, the Kid goes, — she's working. Emotional labour. Doesnae mean she fancies ye. Ye shouldnae personalise those things.

— Ah ken that, Ewart, but thaire's something in yon wee yin's look that *is* personal, ah explains tae the cunt. Naebody lectures me oan fanny; ah ken the score. So ah steams ower tae her. — Ah've hud plenty nosh the day, ah says tae her, — gittin the beef oan likes, n gies the belly a pat . . . Aye, this gut's coming back a bit, but she's no wantin tae hear aboot that, she wants tae hear what aw fit burds want tae hear aboot: her. — Youse Yanks can pit it away but, ah tells her. — No you though, you've got a great figure.

Ah goes n braces masel fir signs ay offence taken, but her hand flies tae the hair. — Why thank you . . . where are you from?

That wis game oan in ma fuckin book. — Edinburgh, Scotland. Ower here for the WMC but, eh, ah goes. She's gittin rode: baw-deep n rid raw. Ah turns tae the Milky Bar Kid. — Lit's pop in here fir yin then, ya cunt.

Eh shakes ehs heid wi thon serious look oan ehs coupon. — I need tae get back tae the hotel.

Wanker. Ye cannae tell thon cunt nowt whin ehs in that mood, n fair play, ehs peyed fir the trip, so ah turns back tae the bird, pittin oan a wee sad face. — Listen, doll, ah've got tae look eftir ma client here. That's management in the entertainment industry fir ye. We work when the rest ay youse play. But, ah adds, lookin deep intae the black bits ay hur eyes, — wi make up fir it n aw. What time dae ye finish the night? Ah'd like tae take ye oot fir a wee drink.

Ah'm gittin thon doubtful, measured look back. — I dunno, I kinda gotta a boyfriend –

— Hi! Never mind this boyfriend stuff, ah goes. — You speaka da foreign lingo. Ah'm jist in toon a few days fir the DJ conference.

— You really in the dance-music business?

— Too right. Some ay the biggest names in this game are oan ma books. N you're oan the VIP list for the Cameo the night, ah tells her, n goes, — Bet you're in the actin game. Yuv goat the looks fir it.

— Why thank you! I'm trying to break into modelling, but I wanna take acting lessons too.

— Knew it! Call it the sixth sense thit ye git in this business, but ye gied off that vibe. Well, loads ay film-industry punters'll be thaire, ah should ken, ah've goat the contacts. Stick wi me n the doors will open. Guaranteed. Kathryn Joyner, personal friend, ah sais, n she's lookin at me aw thon calculatin wey when ah turns tae Ewart n goes, — This is N-Sign, ken the DJ?

— Wow, are you really N-Sign?

Wir both pleasantly surprised by the bird's recognition. — Yeah. Ewart, aw embarrassed, squirms like a big poof.

Ah never thoat the day would come whin Juice Terry used the Milky Bar Kid's rep tae git a ride. — Aye! Ah'm ehs manager! Terry's the name: *Juice* Terry. N-Sign Ewart, ah points at the Milky Bar Kid. — We'll git her oan the list but, eh, Carl?

Ewart nods and smiles.

— Cool. I'm Brandi . . .

— Barry name, ah goes, thinking thit if this yin's ma wisnae a stripper, ah'll wear a Jambo's toap wi suzzies and stockins tae the East Stand at ER, *and* kiss the fuckin badge n aw, ya cunt!

Then ahm jist seein this huge fuckin shadow cast and ah looks up at this big poof, aw sculpted by steroids n years ay tedious denial in the gym. Strides forward like eh's fuckin Clint Eastwood. — Is there a problem, Brandi?

— No, it's okay, Gustave . . . she calls the boy, n ah'm nearly pishin masel, and Randy Brandi turns back tae me. — Yeah, tonight would be great. I'll meet you outside here at ten?

— Ten bells it is, ah sais, looking at this Gustave blatt-baws here wi a wicked wee smirk. — You can come along n aw . . . darlin.

Gustave pouts at ays like a big lassie, but he's no comin forward cause ah think eh kens that if eh does ehs baws'll be gittin tanned tae fuck by a size 11. Mind you, wi aw the steroids that cunt does, thaire willnae be much tae aim at so ah might huv tae go in wi the nut. So ah huds the stare till ehs eyes go watery n eh fucks off, before ah confirm ma appointment wi Brandi n head doon the road wi Carl. — She's gittin rode, that Brandi bird. Mark ma words.

The Milky Bar Kid looks at ays n goes, — Ah've got tae hand it tae you, Terry, you've no got any sense ay embarrassment at aw. You just steam in, and you sometimes come away with the baw.

— Goat tae, man, ah tells um, — it's the spice ay life.

— Brandi but, Lawson! Fuck sake: that is certainly Hibs class. Entertainment-industry management my erse. Cannae wait tae see her face when she finds oot you're a Hobo peg seller who makes muck movies with munters.

— Shut it, ya fuckin fud-faced Yam wankstain. Ah'd be drawin ma fuckin pension before you steamed in.

— I'm no interested in other lassies, eh goes, aw snooty.

— Aye, well, dinnae expect me tae be pinnin any fuckin medals tae yir chist, ah tells the cunt. Some high-n-mighty fuckers forget that one golden rule: a standing prick hath no conscience.

7

Albert Black, who from his seat at an adjacent table under a palm tree, was compelled to observe this scene, mirrored the bouncer's bemused rage. He had been moved to strategically pull the panama hat down over his eyes as Carl Ewart had scanned around in embarrassed response to Lawson's oafish behaviour. *Why was somebody famous and successful like Ewart still friends with this fool?*

Settling his bill with haste, Black stealthily followed Lawson and Ewart through the crowds to a smart-looking boutique hotel a couple of blocks up Ocean Drive. As they disappeared into the lobby, the retired teacher felt a surge of euphoria, a bizarre sense of purpose. He tried to tell himself that he was pathetically stalking two ne'er-do-wells from his old school: the troublemaking malcontent and the promiscuous thug. But still the charge of excitement wouldn't leave him.

Lawson was beyond redemption, he had nothing to offer anyone, except trouble. But Ewart, what had been the role of the school, of the Scottish education system, in his development?

Albert Black decided that he had to confront Carl Ewart, to call him to account for his comments in those trashy music magazines. *Comments that young people read and are influenced by!* In his mind, Black was tracing a mental line back from a classroom in a west Edinburgh comprehensive school, almost thirty years ago, to the performance of fellatio by a young Latina on his only grandchild in Miami Beach.

Tonight, Ewart is speaking at this Cameo place. Well, so too will Albert Black!

But now it was time to go and make his peace with his family. Thinking of the sin committed so casually by Billy and his slut of a girlfriend made his guts ache. Well, he could do nothing but pray for them both.

Hate the sin, love the sinner.

8

Ah could handle this fuckin heat aw year roond, eh. A lot ay cunts in Scotland would fuckin moan aboot aw this, n go: aw it's *too* hoat. They'd rather freeze thair fuckin baws oaf thin lap this up. Fuck that. So wir headin back tae the hotel n ah'm tellin the Kid aboot everything thit's wrong wi Scotland. Wi him kickin back n forward between London, Sydney n the likes ay here, eh nivir gits the chance tae keep up tae date wi what goes oan in the real world. Course, it brings it aw intae focus whin yir somewhaire like this: home thoughts fae abroad. — Scotland's too fuckin conservative, ah tells the cunt. That's the wey ower thaire; keep the movers n shakers doon, soas thi'll fuck off n leave the place tae the deadbeats. Ah've jist aboot hud it wi that doss masel, man.

— Seriously?

— Too right. A man ay ma talents wis meant fir the New World. Fuck Scotland.

— Aye, that's gaunny fuck things right up back hame; the production ay gonzo porn fae Wester Hailes'll grind tae a halt. Surprised Alec Salmond n Gordon Broon huvnae been compelled tae take action.

— Take action? In Scotland? That'll be the day.

— Stop badmouthin Scotland, Terry. Ah dinnae want tae hear it, eh goes. — Thaire's nowt wrong wi it, eh contends.

Aye, Scotland eywis looks better fae a Carribbean island or a boutique hotel in Miami or an apartment overlookin Sydney Harbour. — Thaire's fuckin plenty wrong wi it!

— Specifically?

— Well, take oor national industry, whisky. Ah wrote tae some ay the big boys, Grouse, Dewar's, Bell's, n goes: what aboot whisky alcopops? Yis jist gaunny sit back n lit the Russkis huv it thair ain wey wi the fuckin voddy? Ah mean, whisky n lemonade, whisky n Coke, guaranteed successes wi the alcopop generation. But naw, ah jist gits they snooty letters back gaun oan aboot 'tradition' n aw that shite. What aboot fuckin choice but? Ye dinnae see they Smirnoff cunts hudin back n whingin oan aboot tradition.

— So?

— So, ah'm tellin um as wi gits tae the hotel, n ah gie the doorman a wee wink, — they whisky industry cunts'll be fucked in twenty years' time. You jist wait till thair auld cunt market's six fit under. They think thit vision's what ye git fae Specsavers. Vision *isnae* what ye git fae Specsavers. Nae good huvin *these*, ah taps ma eyebaw, — if yir no usin *that*, ah taps ma nut.

Carl wanted tae git the heid doon cause ay the jet lag n wi us gaun right oot oan the pish yesterday, but ah clocks some ay they DJ boys fae Chicago through in the bar, the cunts thit eh introduced ays tae last night. — Thaire's yir buddies, ah tells um, — they black cunts. Lit's go ower n say hiya.

— Terry, ah need tae hit the hay fir a bit. Yesterday was mental, n ah'm oan the night, mind.

— Fuck that, ah sais tae the cunt, cause they boys look like thir huvin a good time. — Whatever happened tae N-Sign, the super caner? Pansy. Fuckin lightweight. That bunch ay black septics are huvin a proper perty. C'moan, one drink; nice tae be nice!

Ah ken that callin Ewart a lightweight is like a rid rag tae a bull, so pretty soon the peeve's flyin doon again, they margaritas n aw . . . ya cunt, ah could git used tae this . . . n ah'm arguing wi this tall gadge called Lucas aboot sport. — Yuv goat tae admit but, mate, basketbaw's a game fir faggots.

— Whaaat the fuck . . . the boy goes.

— That Michael Jordan's a big fuckin poof, aw they cunts that play that game must be –

— Bullshit, man, you are talkin outta your ass. That's the people's game in the ghetto, everybody shoots the hoops, every block in every 'hood has its courts, man . . .

— Awright, ah admits tae the cunt, — but that's the likes ay America, whaire they ken nowt aboot sport.

— What the fuck you talking about, Terry man?

— Awright, ah explains tae the cunt, — take that World Series basebaw. Two fuckin countries, youse cunts n Canada. Now compare that tae the people's game, fitba, played everywhere, right roond the globe; that's how it's called the *World* Cup. Cannae be denied.

Another gadge, a boy they call Royce, is pishing ehsel n shaking ehs heid. — Japan, Dominican Republic, Cuba . . .

Then the big Lucas cunt goes, — But basketball's played all over the world, man, and we kick ass at basketball.

— Cause it's a bufties' game, ah pits thum right, n turns tae Carl, but thaire's nae backup fae the Milky Bar Kid, the cunt's turned away n ehs resumed ehs discussion wi this DJ called Headstone, talking aboot thair old school influences, aw they DJs, whae wis the coolest motherfucker, the meanest dude, the fiercest honcho n aw this Americanied pish. So ah jist goes, — Ah'll tell ye the meanest mutherfucker fae the old school.

— You gotta be talking Frankie Knuckles, Headstone goes, n Lucas nods tae back um up.

— Naw, man, that's Chicago. In Edinburgh, the baddest fucker fae the old school was Blackie, eh, Carl?

— Aye. Carl plays it deadpan, but wi a wee smile creasin ays lips. — That boy was fierce.

Lucas goes aw thoughtful, then eh drops another couple ay DJ names. But ah'm gaun back tae ma main point here. — When we wir at school, whae played basketball? Carl? Eh's still no gittin intae this, no that it bothers me. Ah jist turns turns back tae big Lucas. — Wee fuckin lassies, only they called it netball. We *kicked* the fuckin baw, n only wee lassies picked it up and ran wi it n bounced it n threw it, ah explains, bendin muh wrist in a throwing motion. — Ooh, ducky, ah've flung ma wee baw intae the net, ah jist sortay lisps at the boy. — It's a game fir closet buftie boys, mate, cannae be denied.

Fair play tae they Chicago boys but, they jist took it aw in good hert, eh.

Then Carl, whae's been yawnin like a lightweight turns roond n goes, — I'm heading upstairs for a bit of kip. Before Helena gits here.

— Awight, me n aw, ah agrees, cause the late nights n the jet lag ur kickin in big time, n thaire's shaggin tae be done; a new bird tae be inducted intae Club Lawson. — Catch yis later, boys, n they gie ays they high fives, n ah jist go along wi it; nice tae be nice but, eh. So we heads up the stairs, and ah'm telling the Milky Bar Kid, — Sound gadgies. Ye can crack on wi they boys n they ken yir takin the pish, but they dinnae take the strop like some cunts.

— Probably cause they never understood a fuckin word ye said.

— How dae you ken they nivir understood a word? So you're the expert oan black Americans now, eh, Ewart? A Jambo tryin tae be fuckin cosmopolitan, that's a fuckin laugh n a half!

— Mibbe no, but mair thin you. Ah hing aboot wi they boys a lot. N it's got tae be said, Terry, that they came across as a lot mair dignified than you.

— Dignity? Fuck dignity! Dignity's for poofs, ah tells the cunt. — Ah'm intae huvin a good time, n tae dae that ye need tae git yir hands dirty. Take that shite elsewhere, Ewart. Another track if you please, Mr DJ, cause that yin disnae play doon at Club Lawson.

— Fair dos, Carl goes, yawnin n openin the door ay eh's fuckin suite, much bigger thin mine, by the way. Fair enough, he's peyed fir it n eh's goat ehs betrothed comin along, but ah've big shaggin plans ay ma ain, n ye kin fit mair fanny intae a king-sized bed thin a queen-sized yin. — See ye, Tez.

— Aye, lit's hook up again eftir forty wanks. Pleasant dreams, ah goes, cause the Kid is one sound cunt gittin ays oan the ticket n oot tae Miami. Aye, it'll be nice tae hit the hay. Mibbe even git some sweet dreams in aboot that Brandi ride thit's gittin the pummellin later oan! Ya fucker!

9

It could never really work out; they were kidding themselves on. Her constantly in flight from their Sydney apartment back to Wellington: just to be closer to her mum. Since her father's illness and death, she needed her, would need her, till she got over it. And would she ever really get over it?

Carl was off to London most of the time, then Edinburgh to see his own mother, in between travelling around the world with that box of records. How she'd grown to detest that gleaming metal box, to loathe watching him load it up, carefully selecting the tunes from his racks that took up a whole room in the apartment.

It had been so good with him, but it couldn't last. They weren't able to make the sacrifices they needed to, in order to be together; couldn't make that commitment and the compromises it entailed that would enable them to move beyond a long-distance relationship, which was therefore doomed to fail. The engagement had been an empty romantic gesture, a triumph of hope over expectation. Alternatives to the current impractical status quo had never been discussed or negotiated around. He would eventually meet somebody else on the road.

She owed telling him face to face that she wanted them to finish. Just like she owed telling him about her pregnancy and her termination of it. But could she really do either of these things? She looked at her engagement ring; thought about putting it in her purse. But she found that she couldn't bring herself to remove it.

10

As he walked home, Albert Black was moved to console himself by reminiscing about his life role as a Christian evangelist. But this was soured when he recalled his bitter conflict with the authorities at the Education Department. A scandal and a staff revolt against his discipline and methods. Under the hot, incessant sun, he considered his growing respect for Islam. How *they* didn't mess about with the satanists, how we'd lost the crusading zeal in the Christian world, and tolerated, even *indulged* blasphemers. He suddenly thought of Terry Lawson.

His mouth cursing, with fraud, deceit, is filled abundantly; and underneath his tongue there is mischief and vanity.

When Black arrived home he was surprised to find his grandson sitting with that shameless jezebel, and their sin apparently endorsed by his own parents! To all intents and purposes it was like a normal, cosy family scene!

— Hi, Dad, William Black greeted his father.

Albert nodded curtly at his son, who rose and beckoned him aside, guiding him through the conservatory and into the garden. — I understand there was a bit of embarrassment earlier.

— So you were informed of the sin that was taking place under your own roof. Well, at least there was some sense of contrition. Satan has —

William raised his hand to silence his father. Albert contemplated the indignant expression on his son's face. — Look, Dad, Billy and Valda are sensible and mature kids. They've been going out together for eighteen months, and they are in a committed relationship. They're doing what young people in love have always done and it isn't your or anybody else's business to interfere.

— I see.

— What exactly *do you* see, Dad? William challenged. — I really wonder.

Albert Black bristled and looked witheringly at his son. It was an old expression that had never failed to induce deference in William as a boy. But his son was no longer that, and he met his father's stare with an even gaze, and a slow, contemptuous shake of the head that acknowledged the sadness of the game. It humiliated Black, who could hear his voice rising in a recalcitrant squeak, — I see that you've wanted to make this sort of speech to me for a long time!

— Yes I have, and it was my mistake not doing so, William said. His voice jumped an octave and there was both wrath and scorn in the son's eyes. — And before you call me 'gutless' or 'yellow' like you used to when I lived at home, let me tell you now that I only kept quiet for Mum's sake. All your nonsense . . . he shook his head again, — . . . it was Victorian, fascist bullshit. It held me back, Dad, it embarrassed the crap outta me, he said, in an American voice.

Black stood watching his son, unable to respond. And he realised William wasn't lying. He had long since ceased to fear his father, and his deference had only been due to his respect for Marion's feelings. Now that she had gone, there was no need to continue this charade. His wife had protected Albert Black from William's contempt; the boy had held off and kept what was left of the family together, simply for her.

— Believe it or not, I still consider myself a Christian, and I think I must be a real one, as you did everything in your power to put me off it.

— I did my best, Black felt himself gasp, his voice soft, high and holy. — I put food on your plate, clothes on your back, paid for your education –

— Yes you did, and I'm grateful. But you never gave me a chance to be myself and make my own mistakes. You didn't want that. You wanted me to be a clone of yourself, and Chrissy one of Mum.

— What's so wrong with being like your mother?

— Nothing at all, but she isn't.

— If she found the right chap, and settled down –

— She's a lesbian, Dad! Open your eyes!

William walked away, head shaking, leaving his speechless father to ponder his words and stew as the sun went down behind the distant skyscrapers of downtown Miami.

Christine . . .

There followed a long spell where Black just stood, feeling a throb in his knee as he looked out onto the bay. Then he heard a conciliatory voice behind him say, — Come on in and eat, Granpa.

He turned to see Billy framed in the doorway of the conservatory. He was wearing the panama hat that Black had been using. He realised that the one he'd been given was not his son's, but his grandson's.

— I'd prefer not to, Black sniffed, painfully aware of an unedifying regression back into childhood, but unable to tear aside the shroud of pettiness that hung over him.

— I'm sure there's a stand-up guy in there somewhere, Billy said, — but you can sure be an asshole.

Rage welled inside Black and he moved with menace towards the youth, only to stop as William stepped outside onto the porch and stood between them. — You will never raise your hand to my son, Dad. I will not permit that.

Humbled to ignominy by this declaration, Albert Black pushed past two generations of his descendants and went to his room.

11

Cunt thit ye are, ah couldnae fuckin believe it when ah saw thon Brandi the Septic burd waitin fir ays at the Cleveland. Ah'd hud a good wank before ah came oot, well, ah huv tae, cause ah kin git a bit too frisky n make a cunt ay masel wi a burd, n it's nae use scarin oaf the fanny till the deal's fuckin signed, sealed and delievered. Mind you, when ah saw they pins in that pleated skirt, ah could feel the auld spunk tank fillin up again, big style. Too right; better game than tame, that's what ay eywis say.

So wi settle doon n huv a cocktail n wee blether. This burd kin fairly gab n it's aw borin shite aboot crappy modellin jobs, promotin aw sorts ay pony perfumes in malls n the like, but life's taught ays thit ye huv tae gie fanny a bit ay air time n pretend tae be interested in thair obsessions (them) if yir gaunny be drawin open they beef curtains later oan. Aye, yuv goat tae take a few tap-tappy jabs in order tae land the killer hook.

So eftir a bit ah suggests a wee stroll doon towards the club n wi head off but the first fucker wi sees oan the street is thon big Lucas gadge. — Juice T, my man! eh shouts, giein ays a big welcome. Sound cunt, that Lucas. Ah dinnae gie a fuck aboot the colour ay any cunt's skin, it's whether or no they

pit thair hand in thair poakit thit counts, n this fucker wisnae
shy aboot hittin the bar. The bird's well impressed n aw, ye kin
tell. Lucas must be quoted in the world ay hip hop; mind you,
aw that shite sounds the same tae me.

Ah like this Juice T tag but, eh. That's what the cunts doon
the Gauntlet, the Busy n the Silver Wing ur gaunny huv tae
git used tae. Ya cunt, wi the corkscrew hair, big tadger n natural
rhythm, ah'm mair ay a nigger thin any black cunt in this
fuckin toon!

As Lucas high-fives ays n gies Brandi a gentlemanly peck
oan the cheek before takin oaf, she goes, — Wow! Is that really
Lucas P?

— It certainly is. Great gadgie, one ay ma favourite homies.

Brandi's lookin at ays as if her ship has jist come in. It hus
n aw, but no the wey she thinks. As the lights ay the Cameo
come intae sight, she turns tae ays n goes, — Wanna do a hit
of X?

Ah'm wonderin what she's oan aboot for a bit, before ah
realise it's probably eckies. — Nae charlie? ah ask. Ah jist turn
intae a big touchy-feely poof oan that gear. Ah like tae see a
burd oan it but.

— No, but these are really great. We can score some coke
later.

So ah thoat, fuck it, ah'll take it, n ah necks the pill she slips
ays. Dinnae want tae be a party pooper, especially no wi game
fanny in tow. Besides, naebody here's gaunny walk intae the
Busy Bee or the Gauntlet or the Silver Wing n go, 'Aye, Lawson,
ah saw ye E'd oot ay yir nut in Miami Beach n actin the daft
twat instead ay daein ching wi the boys!'

When in Rome but, eh. That's me: as cosmopolitan as fuck,
ya cunt! Instead ay gaun straight intae the dance hall, we heads
tae this barry place called Mac's Club Deuce, fir a beer, jist tae
lit the pills kick in. Within half an ooir ah'm oaf ma fuckin

tits. Well, ya fucker, ah'm used tae eckies thit ye kin neck aw night like Smarties n still hate every cunt in the place, wi that crap, shite music still gittin oan yir tits. N coke where ye can dae a couple ay grams n still tackle a fish supper oan the wey hame n git the best fuckin kip ay yir life. So ah'm thinking, if the pills ur like this, how good's the fuckin ching gaunny be! Yuh cunt!

12

Emerging with stealth from his room a couple of hours later, Albert Black was intercepted by William and Darcy as he tried to sneak out the door. — Where are you going at this time of night, Dad? William asked.

— Out, said Black, feeling like a sullen teenager. They were standing so close to him, filling the narrow space between the marble pillar and the front door with their bodies.

— But you haven't eaten anything, Darcy said in a wide-eyed protest, which seemed to knock a decade off her.

— I'm fine, I'm just going out for a walk. Black felt his features condense to the point of concentrated insult.

William inched forward, his face pained and boyish, reminding Albert Black of the time his young son had stood on a jellyfish on that grim pebble beach near Thurso. He went to touch his sulking father's shoulder, then pulled back. — Dad . . . I lost the rag a wee bit earlier, and perhaps I was a bit . . . well, I know that things were different when you were growing up . . .

More's the pity!

— . . . and that you only wanted the best . . .

— Please, Albert Black tersely shook his head, — I think enough has already been said. I shall return later, and he looked at his son and daughter-in-law and swallowed down some humility. — You've both been very kind. It hasn't been easy for me . . . without your mother.

— But you've got us, Dad, William protested meekly.

Black forced a kindly smile and mumbled something in appreciation before departing.

It hasn't been easy.

But why, he considered, should it be easy? He was in the final phase of his life, and he was alone. Nobody, not even in the Good Book, told you it would be this hard, this frightening, to see out your mortal existence, to try and make sense of it all. God had never informed you that it was all over so quickly, or that your dreams turned to dust long before your body. His life's work; it had to mean something!

He walked down Alton, heading east on Lincoln, making his way towards the ocean. Albert Black now felt that he was on an island, a desert island full of people he was invisible to. A musky nightfall was thickening like smoke around him. As he pressed on towards the nightclub, the shops were still open and Lincoln remained busy. The urban exhibitionists, the street performers, skateboarders and bums strutted and surfed and ranted for the entertainment or irritation of the rest. Boys swaggered, girls giggled, couples laughed, people went in and out of stores.

On Washington, the red neon of the Cameo buzzed its invite, and a queue of youths were already lining up down the block. The name reminded him of the cinema in Edinburgh's Tolcross district. He found film a devious and corrupting medium, but had occasionally relented and accompanied Marion to the pictures as he knew how much she had loved them. She had always been inordinately impressed by William's employment. He tried to think of the last picture he had truly enjoyed: it would have been *Chariots of Fire*.

He looked ahead and there it was, in black letters against a lit background: N-SIGN. Black advanced to the door, disinclined to wait in the line of kids who regarded the old Scottish schoolmaster with a wary fascination. — No ticket, no can do, a well-built bouncer said in response to his enquiry about entrance. — Are you on anybody's guest list?

— No . . . but I know Carl Ewart, Black informed him. — N-Sign. Please tell him to put Mr Black from the old school onto the guest list.

The bouncer gazed quizzically at this old guy. Perhaps it was his age, or the strange accent, upright bearing and that authoritative demeanour, but there was something about Black that made the doorman feel duty-bound to at least try to comply. He pulled out his cell phone and punched a number.

13

The taxi Helena had taken at Miami International Airport cruised on a raised concrete freeway above the city, passing over the downtown area and onto the McArthur Causeway, bound for Miami Beach. The windows were shut, and cool air was blowing through the air-conditioning system.

— In town for the WMC? the driver asked. He wore the reflective shades of the psycho cop or killer.

— Sorta, yeah.

— Party time, he smiled into the mirror, exposing a row of crooked teeth. From the back seat, Helena could see her own face, drawn and tired, in the reflection. Then the driver's voice dropped into a zone of sleaze as he added, —You need anything, let me know. I give you a card.

— Thank you, Helena heard herself primly respond.

— I mean a ride, a taxi, or anything like that, the driver said, in more cautious tones, as her eyes scanned the sign in the cab that contained his number and who to call for official complaints.

I'm way too straight for Carl Ewart, she thought. He would have the guy cruising around town to some ghetto looking for drugs, or heading out to a racetrack. She wondered what her big bond was with him. Was it simply that they'd lost their fathers at roughly the same time? Surely there must be more to it than that? Surely. She couldn't think straight.

They stopped outside the hotel and she gave the driver two twenties and left him a decent tip from the change. — Remember my card, he smiled.

— Sure. *Don't fucking think so, mate.*

Normally she would have been pleased that no intrusive, tip-hustling bellboy descended on her, as was generally the American way, but with her fatigue after the long journey, she could have done with some help. She lugged her case up the short bank of front steps and into the cool, still foyer, where a camp desk clerk greeted her before issuing her with a key to the room.

14

Carl Ewart was chatting to Lester Wood, a local dance-music journalist, at their table under muted lights in a corner of the VIP lounge. He scanned the edgy ranks of the incoming cognoscenti and the usual liggers for signs of Terry, before remembering he had gone to meet the girl from the restaurant. He saw Max Mortensen, one of the promoters, making his way across the room towards him. — Hey, Carl. Had a guy trying to get in, says he knows you. A Mr Black from the old school.

A nefarious smile played across Carl Ewart's lips. *That'll be Terry fucking around.* They often took the pish out of Blackie, the tyrannical master back at their school, who was the religious education and modern studies teacher. Carl thought of the term 'housemaster', which the scheme comprehensive school had ridiculously borrowed from the English public-school system. — He's a very important character, Carl grinned, — and a huge influence on me. I'd be obliged if you could make sure that he, and whoever he's with, get the full VIP treatment.

— You got it, Max winked and clicked on his cell phone.

Lester sparked up a Havana, offering Carl one, who refused. He wasn't sure about Lester, but his grin seemed to be saying that he was a man of vices. You never knew with music journos. Many were closet wasters trying to get the business out the way before they partied, but others were total straight pegs playing the cool and hip angle though they'd obviously be happier working in corporate PR. He decided to take a gamble and cut to the chase. — Any pharmaceuticals kicking about?

The corrupting charm in Lester's grin could have had a Christian soccer mom turning tricks for ninety minutes. — Ask a silly question. What's your poison?

— Some pills and couple ay grams ay ching, eh, coke, Carl said gratefully. *Now I'm sure.*

— Done and dusted, Lester said, then asked thoughtfully, — Is that a Brit saying?

— Sounds generic, he mused, trying it on in cockney with a 'mate' tacked on the end, then in Glaswegian with a bonus 'big man', before concluding, — Maybe it is.

Lester inched forward in his seat. — And I have a little 'welcome to Florida' present for you.

— I'm all ears.

— You ever had angel's trumpet tree? *Brugmansia suaveolens.* It's part of the *Datura* family, a hallucinogenic *and* a narcotic. All grown locally.

— Heard of it, not tried it. It's supposed to be poisonous.

— For sure. You can't just pick that shit off the tree and cook it up and eat it without knowing what you're doing. You're pretty likely to drop down dead, or at least retch up. But if you get the right dose . . .

— How do you do that?

— A friend of mine picks it, dries it out and puts the measure into tea bags.

— I'd like to try it. I've always loved different teas. Count me in.

As they ironed out the details of the clandestine transaction, the news of his approved status was conveyed to Albert Black who, in spite of himself, basked in delighted vindication as he was wristbanded and issued with a VIP pass. — Any guests accompanying you, sir? the doorman politely asked.

At that point he heard a high screeching voice of disbelief coming from the crowd. — Granpa?

He turned to see Billy, accompanied by the ubiquitous harlot girlfriend. They were gaping at him in shock. Black instantly felt like he'd been spotted going into a strip club. But he fought the sense of mortification down, turning to the doorman and pointing over to them, gesturing at the youths to approach.

Billy Black and Valda Riaz tentatively made their way over. — This pair, said Black, forever the frugal Scot and gaining some satisfaction from thinking about what they would save in two admission fees.

— The VIP list at the Cameo? Awesome, Billy gasped. Black

couldn't help but be moved by the fact that he and his grandson wore identical panama hats. For a second or two he felt so close to the boy that he wanted to weep.

Black turned away in order not to let sentiment betray him, as they were signed up. Then he heard Billy asking him how he had this sort of clout.

— I know N-Sign, Black stammered, scarcely aware of what he was saying. *This clown represents everything I despise, and now I'm dropping his name.* — He's speaking at the conference . . .

The youthful couple were far too grateful with their passes and bands to take detailed note of Black's comments. — That's excellent, grandpa, Billy said, then struggled, — . . . thanks. Um, catch you later. Valda smiled and said, — Thank you so much, Mr Black, this is very kind of you.

She displayed such grace that Black, in spite of himself, felt shame gnaw at him. He thought of Alisdair Main, his old university friend, whom he heard had died some years ago. He felt himself profoundly wishing that he'd gone to the funeral, and fired off a quick prayer, attesting to the essential goodness of that particular sinner, and urging the Lord to err on the side of leniency.

— Thanks again, Grandfather, he heard his grandson say in formal, respectful tones, with no hint of mockery, before he and Valda vanished inside and into the crowd, both parties relieved to be free of the excruciating proximity of the other.

15

It wasn't a room; it was a suite. It had its own kitchen with all the mod cons, and a fridge and cupboard stocked full of luxury provisions. Eureka! A packet of Cuban coffee – that would help cut through some of the jet lag. She spooned it into the filter machine and the thick, tarry offering began to accumulate in the pot. The large four-poster bed showed evidence of having been recently occupied, and she pulled aside the covers and sniffed at the pillow. There was Carl's unmistakable male scent; it made her giddy and she felt her pulse rise and something soar within her. She wanted to wrap herself in it, but if she permitted her fatigued body and mind to succumb to it, she'd never move and she needed to see the real thing. Instead, she went back to the kitchen and poured herself a cup of the coffee. It tasted strong and bitter, and it felt like a line of speed.

Helena pulled an adaptor from her travel bag and charged up her cell phone. It took a while to click to AT&T, the US default service provider, but when it did, a series of texts from Carl buzzed into her device. The last one:

Had to go to club. Meet u there. Hope u got in ok. Luv u xxx

A kernel of relief and excitement buzzed in her chest. He was alive. No drug overdose, no plane crash, no stepping off the pavement stoned into the path of a truck. Sometimes she feared for him. Helena pulled off her clothes and stepped into the bathroom, looked at herself in the mirror and groaned. Then she brushed her teeth to remove the taste of aircraft and coffee, had a tepid shower, changed into fresh party clothes and applied some make-up. She went back to the full-length mirror, pleased at the results, till a wave of jet lag ripped through her. Something else was needed, but her state of mind was too fragile for drugs. Another Cuban coffee slammed head first into the jet lag.

It gave her focus as she left the hotel, walking up the street to the venue. Her jangly nerves (and here coffee and jet lag were in conspiracy) could have done without the whistles from a pumped-up group of young vacationing males, but she was granted easy and swift admission through the massing crowds via the guest list, and she prepared to go backstage. As she passed the VIP bar, the only other person present was an old guy in a straw hat, looking around like a rabbit surrounded by foxes as the punters started to file in. Already a DJ was in the booth, digging out the tunes for his warm-up set. Carl would be on soon, and she should go backstage to see him. But this old guy seemed so lonely and forlorn, miscast in this temple of youth; she was moved to speak to him. — Hi. You a DJ?

— No, I'm retired, said Black, somewhat surprised that this beautiful young woman with blazing brown eyes and short blonde hair had just started talking to him, and was now easing into a seat opposite. Black felt intimidated by the long legs she displayed; all that naked flesh suggested a wanton, reckless character, and she was showing cleavage in the way of the hussy. Yet this was offset by her easy manner; she had a soft voice and an accent that he took to be Australian. He thought of his own daughter; apart from the funeral, when they were briefly and awkwardly united, how many years had it been since he'd seen her? — I'm retired, Black repeated, stammered, as he sensed himself sliding into the fissure of his past as it cracked open beneath his feet. — Are you . . . are you involved in . . . he looked around at the growing crowd of youths who were pressing the bar staff for attention, — . . . all of this?

Helena was moved by the man's accent. It sounded Scottish! — No, my boyfriend, my fiancé, really, it's his thing, and she couldn't help displaying the engagement ring to him.

Black was taken aback. Surely this lovely, thoughtful and obviously intelligent girl, who had taken the time to speak to him, an old man washed up in this strange, fashion-conscious citadel of another age, surely she couldn't be Carl Ewart's girl-friend! No, surely not. There would be other DJs, club promoters, that sort of thing.

— Congratulations, Black said warily, — when is your happy day?

Yes, he was definitely a Scot. What were they like, those Scotsmen, as they grew old? Would Carl be like this man, a lost old codger in a nightclub full of young people? She'd often joked that he'd be the oldest DJ in the world. — I dunno, we're not too sure, she shrugged and made a pained face. Then with a gallows smile she conceded, — It hasn't been going too well recently.

— Sorry to hear it.

— Yeah. Helena Hulme looked at Albert Black. There was a kindness in the old man's sharp eyes that seemed to invite further disclosure. — Our careers are very different, and we come from different places. It's the long-distance thing, it really involves a lot of sacrifice from both parties to make it work. I dunno if we can hack it.

— Oh, Black said, thinking that the girl almost sounded South African now, the way she said 'hek eat'.

— Are you married?

— Yes, well, I was . . . Black struggled, unsure of how to respond. — I mean, my wife died recently.

Helena thought of her own father. Selling cars in a show-room for years so that she and her sister Ruthie could go to college. Then, on that otherwise unremarkable day, without prior warning, just dropping dead on the lot with a massive heart attack. Her hand lightly touched Albert Black's arm. — I'm so sorry . . .

Albert Black's head bowed. He looked as if something had crumpled inside him. He didn't resist when Helena reached out and took a hold of his hand. — I'm Helena.

— I'm Albert, he whispered, looking briefly up at her. He felt like a child. Tried to fuse himself with the contemptuous notion that he was being weak and stupid, but nothing happened, he was immobilised. He would have stayed in this moment for the rest of his life if he could. It was the closest to comfort and grace he had been since Marion's death.

— Please . . . how long has it been, Albert?

Black told her the story of his and Marion's love, and how it would never die, but how she was gone now and his world was empty. Helena told him about the terrible shock and crushing sense of loss she'd experienced since her father's death. The conversation grew metaphysical as Black explained his terror that his lifelong faith was now in question. How he feared that he would never see his wife again, that there was no spirit world in which they could be reunited.

Helena listened patiently, then asked the question that was fizzing in her fatigued brain throughout the old man's tale. — Do you ever regret making that commitment? I mean, how horrible must you feel when it ends in that way?

— Of course it's horrible, Black confirmed, seeing Marion's face in his mind's eye. Why had she stayed with him? *I can be a bit strident. Perhaps too domineering. Even tyrannical, some would say.* It went beyond duty; she really did love him. And by doing so, she'd made him much more than he alone could ever have been. A deep serenity filled his heart. — But I don't regret a second of being with her, though sometimes I lament how I was, he confessed, now downcast once again. — I was obsessed with the Church, with my Christian faith, and I wish I had done more for her . . . with her . . .

It was now Helena Hulme's turn to have a sudden revelation, as she thought about her fiancé, Carl Ewart. It was not new knowledge, but a powerful resurfacing of something she'd worried might be getting buried by the landslide of crap life could dump on you. It was that she loved him. God, she loved him so much. And he really loved her. — But she knew what you were like. She knew you had that great passion for something, and that didn't mean that you loved her the less for that. I'm sure she had things going on her life, things that she couldn't really get you involved in on a day-to-day basis. It didn't mean she loved you any less, did it?

— Yes . . . you're right. Black choked with emotion and said to her, — So I have absolutely no regrets at all. Her love was my salvation. So if you love this man, and he is a good man, then you must marry him.

— I do. Helena shook as she spoke. — I do love him. He's the best person I've ever met. The kindest, most generous, tender, loving, thoughtful and funny guy ever. You are so right, Albert, I have to marry Carl. He's from Scotland like you, she confirmed, and she squeezed his withered old hand.

This revelation, even though he had sensed its encroachment, was almost too much for Albert Black. He found his eyes scanning the room. — Yes . . . ehm, if you'll excuse me — he pulled his hand away, — I need to find a restroom.

— Sure. I'm gonna get a glass of wine. She nodded at the bar. — Would you like a drink?

— Water would be nice. Thank you, Black found himself shouting over the din.

— Still or fizzy?

— Still please. Thank you, said Black, rising and heading for the toilets. There was a queue snaking outside, and he was almost ready to depart, but was driven to return to the kind girl who was getting him a drink, and he really *did* need to relieve himself. Joining the line, to his abject horror, Albert

Black realised almost immediately that the person standing next to him, doing something unspeakable to that American waitress, was none other than Terence Lawson. And Lawson was looking right at him!

16

Ya cunt, ah've never broken oaf a snog wi a game, fit bird tae dae a double take in ma puff. But thaire's Blackie fae the school: fuckin *Blackie*! The cunt, aw auld, bit jist like eh eywis wis, standin thaire next tae us in the queue for the fuckin bogs! Ah'm comin up oan this fuckin pill this Brandi bird gied ays, n now ah'm pushin her tae the side and starin at him n eh's lookin at ays, so ah jist goes: — Mr Black! Ah dinnae believe it!

— Terence Lawson . . . Blackie gasps; the cunt's as shocked tae see me as ah ahm him. Fucker even minded ay ma name! Nae wonder but: the bastard belted ays every fuckin morning in reggie!

Ya cunt, ah'd spent half ma life fantasisin about the fuckin kicking ah'd gie the 'Black Bastard' if oor paths ever crossed in civvy street. But now, wi this fuckin Ecstasy pill tinglin ays fae the back ay ma skull tae the bottom ay ma scrotum, aw ah kin think ay daein is stepping forward n giein the auld cunt a big hug. Ah wraps muh airms roond the frail auld fucker; the cunt's a fuckin bag ay bones! Wis eh eywis like that? Surely no! Ah'm wishin ah'd been oan the fuckin ching, then ah would've rammed the nut oan the auld cunt. But then ah'm thinking that ah did see um once in civvy street . . . at perr wee Gally's funeral.

17

Albert Black inhaled with force, parade-soldier stiff, in the arms of Terence Lawson. *Lawson!* Then the fool, now a hulking brute of a man, swung him round, while locking his other arm around the pretty young waitress. — This is an auld teacher ay mine fae Edinburgh, Juice Terry announced, — Mr Albert Black. This is Brandi. Merican, likes.

— Hi, Albert, Brandi said, and stepped forward kissing Black on the lips.

No woman other than Marion had ever touched him in this way. At first Albert Black felt a surge of rage at this betrayal, but it quickly morphed into a deep longing for his departed wife.

Marion . . . why did You *take her!*

Terry seemed to catch his old teacher's distress. Rubbed his bony back. He could feel every one of the vertebrae. — What are ye daein here, Mr Black . . .

— I'm . . . I'm lost . . . was all Black could stammer, eviscerated by events and, to his great surprise and discomfort, horribly aware that he was glad to be with Lawson.

— See this gadge, Terry smiled at Brandi, then at Albert Black, — me and him fought like cat n dug back at the school. We never got on. But see, when ma mate died, mind Gally, Mr Black?

— Yes, said Black, thinking first of the Galloway boy's funeral, then Marion's. — Andrew Galloway.

— This gadge . . . eh, chap, Terry explained to Brandi, — he was the only one fae the school, oot ay aw the teachers n that, that went along tae Gally's funeral. This man here. Juice Terry turned back to Albert Black. — Ah dinnae ken what yir daein here but ah'm glad that ye are, cause ah never hud the chance tae tell ye how much that meant tae us aw, you showin up at the funeral like that. Me, his mates, and his ma and famely n that. Terry felt his eyes well up in recollection. — Especially as we never goat oan wi ye at the school.

Albert Black was gobsmacked. As a Christian, he'd done his duty by attending the funeral. However difficult, the Good Book was adamant that it was essential to love the sinner. Nobody had given him any indication that this unsavoury penance had meant anything to them. But he thought of everyone who had come to Marion's funeral, and how much he had valued that simple display of human solidarity.

— It's funny, it goat me thinking aboot how even wi us eywis fightin aw the time, how ye wir still ma favourite teacher.

Black couldn't believe his ears. He had belted Lawson as a boy every other day. And now the man actually seemed sincere in this bizarre contention. And there was something about Lawson, something spiritual, almost angelic, with his gentle bonhomie, and his large, expressive eyes. It seemed as if they were full of the love of . . . the love of Jesus himself! — Wha-why . . . ehm, why do you say that?

— Cause you *wanted* us tae learn. The rest ay them wrote the likes ay me off. Just let us run riot. But *you* never. You kept us in line and forced us tae work. Ye never gave up tryin tae teach us. Tell ye what, ah wish ah hud listened tae ye. He turned to Brandi, whose eyes blazed like saucers. — See, if ah'd listened tae this boy –

— Wow . . . it must be great when you meet somebody you really looked up to as a kid, Brandi said to Terry Lawson, and then turned to Albert Black, — and it must be fantastic to learn what a great influence you've been on somebody's life.

Fuckin good pills, Terry was thinking. *Ah'm as likely tae be shaggin fuckin Blackie by the end ay the night as this Brandi bird . . . need tae git some ching intae the mix . . .*

— But I wasn't — Black protested.

— Listen, mate, if ah fucked up, n ah did, then it wis aw doon tae me. Terry's index finger drummed his chest. — If ah hudnae met the likes ay yourself n Ewart — he's playin here the night by the way — ah'd huv been ten times worse. Ah wis jist scum, right . . .

Black stared blankly at Terry Lawson. *Does he really expect me to refute this contention?*

— . . . but see, when ye meet guys whae've goat a sense ay right fae wrong, like you, guys whae've got the goods, that steys wi ye, surein it does.

As the restroom line divided by gender, they drifted off from Brandi and moved steadily down the men's queue into the urinals, before breaking off the conversation to pee. Black's head spun as he watched his pish splash into the trough. It seemed almost symbolic that it was merging with Lawson's, who stood further up, a power jet hammering the metal at force from what Black couldn't help noticing looked like a fireman's hose.

Lawson seemed repentant. Genuinely repentant!

When they were done, Terry only washing his hands after noting Albert Black fastidiously cleaning his, they waited outside for Brandi and went back into the dance hall together, where Helena greeted them. — Kiwi burd! Terry shouted, hugging her. — So yuv met Blackie . . . eh, Mr Black . . .

— Yes, but I didn't know you were friends of Albert's . . .

— Too right, we go way back, Carl n aw.

— You know Carl, Albert?

— Yes, Black said sheepishly, — but I didn't really connect you with him until I saw Law — eh Terry, in the restroom queue. I taught them both . . .

— Great! Jesus Christ, it's a small world!

— Let's get in and see the Milky Bar Kid, Terry said,

introducing Brandi, while informing her and Helena of Black's status as one of their most memorable teachers.

— Carl will be so excited, Helena said, as Albert Black allowed himself to be led, in a shock of trance, over to the back stage door.

— Aye, the Milky Bar Kid's gaunny git a wee surprise, that's fir sure, Terry laughed. When they got inside there was no sign of Carl – he had gone sidestage to prepare his set – but Terry introduced Black to a tall Negro man, who looked down at him. — This is Lucas. Lucas, this is the old school boy ah wis telling ye aboot.

Lucas pulled Black aside, and said with some reverence in his voice, — So I hear you're old school.

— Yes, Black replied, looking nervously across to Terry, who was kissing Brandi, with an arm around Helena.

— I heard that you guys pulled a whole heap of shit, back in the day.

Unable to understand what the man was driving at, Black was moved to simply agree. — Yes.

— Tell you some shit, man, Lucas said, — and you folks wanna be takin note: we owe the old school big time.

Albert Black regarded this tall, dark-skinned man. There were no Negro children at the school. He would have remembered. — You . . . you weren't old school . . .

— No, man, no way, but I heard all about the good shit you guys did. The kinda influence you was, back in the UK, jus like we had over here. Without guys like you we wouldn't be here today. In the South Side of Chicago, there are brothers who wouldn't have done jack, without the likes of you guys inspiring them and kicking their asses. We had them too, man. Guys who steered us right, otherwise it would have been all guns and powder. Believe it, brother.

It meant that there were teachers like him, here in America;

true Christians, driven by the gospel of Jesus to save, to educate, the deserving poor. They had been the salvation of this tall Negro, in his lawless Chicago ghetto. Yes, there were virtuous men and women who had rescued this wayward soul: just as surely as he had the likes of Ewart, and even Lawson, back in that ugly Edinburgh council scheme. — Ewart . . . Carl Ewart and, er, Terence said this?

— Sure as shit, bro. What they call you, man?

— Mr Black . . . He considered the reality of the situation. — . . . Blackie, I suppose.

— Black E. Right . . . Lucas scratched his chin. — I'm sure I heard about you, he said charitably. — You were one fierce motherfucker! Right?

— Yes . . . Black looked guilty and sheepish as the image of the tawse snapped into his mind. But how else was he meant to enforce discipline? To get them to shut up, stop messing around and do their work? But suddenly Terry Lawson was back over and was steering him into a boxed-off zone with a huge mixing desk presided over by a technician. It looked out from the VIP area onto the dangerously crowded dance floor. Helena and Brandi were hanging out there, in conversation. Black looked across to the small booth as Carl Ewart came on to a rapturous cheer, high-fiving the outgoing DJ. He was dressed in leisurewear, stick-thin, with that white hair shaved to a stubble. Black still recognised those clever, slightly sly and knowing eyes, and his old nemesis exacted an amazing reaction from the crowd, simply by putting on a record which sounded *exactly* like the last one to Black's ears. Albert turned to Juice Terry who caught his puzzlement.

— He's only put a record on. Why are they so excited?

— Aye, it isnae fuckin rocket science, Terry scoffed. — This ravey housey shite's garbage, ah jist hing aboot fir the fanny but, eh. It's ey hotchin at things like this. Spice ay life, eh. He winked at his old teacher, while Black sensed that he had now descended into Sodom. Lewd and obscene behaviour abounded. Some girls were barely dressed. Yet, there seemed no sense of threat, as he'd sometimes experienced in the football crowds back home. Black stood in the area by the mixing desk as Ewart played record after record. He noticed that something was happening. The beat was building up with the crowd becoming increasingly frenzied and hysterical. They were raising their hands in the air, some of them saluting Ewart like he was the messiah! Perhaps that was what it was really about; seize control of their minds and thus render them vulnerable to the messages of satanism! At the same time, he realised that there would be no speeches from Ewart or anyone else. This supposed 'conference' was actually about people gyrating to this noise in a zombie-like trance.

Once we travelled to strange lands to spread the gospel, and now Western youth had adopted those primitive, tribal dances and beats from people who were little more than savages!

A sinful nation, a people laden with iniquity, a seed of evildoers, children that are corrupters: they have forsaken the LORD, they have provoked the Holy One of Israel into anger, they are gone away backward!

Black wanted to leave again, but Helena had returned with more water. No, he had come this far; he had to confront Ewart. At one stage he saw Billy and Valda, conducting a lewd and exhibitionist dance. *In public, like dogs on heat!* He stepped back into the shadows, out of their range of vision. How could their ugly promiscuity be a shock when they were trapped in the brainwashing frenzy of that devil music? Black's torment continued until Ewart stepped off the stage, soaked in sweat, as he fell into the arms of Helena. Black watched them devour each other's faces before Ewart broke off to ask his fiancée, — Good flight?

— A nightmare, honey, but I'm here now. And we got a surprise for ya! Your friend from Edinburgh, Mr Black, from the old school, is here!

Carl laughed. One of Terry's daft fuckin games, he thought, before he turned to face Albert Black, MA (Hons), who was looking at him from under a panama hat with those small rodent-like eyes, dark and intense as ever.

— What the fuck . . . He looked at a grinning Juice Terry in disbelief. — What's fuckin Blackie daein here!

— Eh wis in toon, so eh swung by the gig, eh, Mr Black? Terry said, surprising himself with his protective feelings towards his old oppressor.

— Who the fuck brought him back here? Carl glared at Terry.

— Nice tae be nice, eh, Terry said.

— I did, Helena snapped at Carl. — You behave!

— Behave! That fucking sociopath belted me for not saying 'sir' when I addressed him! Carl hissed under his breath.

Helena stood her ground. — He's had a bad time, Carl. Leave it!

Carl looked at his New Zealander fiancée. It was so good to see her again. Helena Hulme. His favourite phrase: *Don't be so sceptical, Ms Hulme.* He'd entertained a romantic notion of her as a lost daughter of Caledonia, exiled to the other side of the world, only for them to be reunited under a mirrorball with a throbbing 4–4 beat in the background. He smiled at her and then Albert Black, forcing himself to extend a hand. His old teacher looked at him for a couple of beats, then at Helena, and shook it.

The claw-like grip of the old man was strong, and belied his thin frame. — Eh, what brings you to Miami Beach? Carl asked.

Albert Black faltered on answering the question. He didn't know. Helena intervened. — His family live over here. We just met up, and we've been having a good chat.

— Aw aye? Aboot me? Carl pouted, before he could stop himself.

— It's not always about *you*, Carl, Helena hissed. — There *are* other topics of conversation, believe it or not.

You and your fucking acid-house music, it's dying out all around you. It was just another fad, not a great revolution. Grow up, for fuck's sakes.

— I didnae mean that, it's just that me and him –

Terry cut in, unhappy, in his harmonious Ecstasy trip, at the discord between Helena and Carl. He rubbed Brandi's back for reassurance. — He wis talking tae me n aw, eh, Mr Black?

Black shifted uncomfortably. — Yes . . . look, I really should go.

— No, Albert, please stay for a while, Helena pleaded, then urgently turned to Carl. — Tell him!

Carl Ewart managed to keep some grace in his tones. — I'm playing another gig, out in the Everglades. Please come along.

— But I can't . . . Black protested meekly. — It's very late and I –

— Yes you can. Helena smiled sweetly at him, and took him by the arm. Brandi flanked him, and Black allowed them to lead him outside. He felt as if his very self had melted away, that nothing was holding him up, there were no faculties left that would enable him to make even the most mundane of decisions.

Watching them depart, Carl grabbed Terry by the sleeve of his shirt. — Since when did that sadistic cunt Blackie become 'Mr Black'? He looked at Terry's saucer-like pupils. — Awright, I get it. Well, it'll take mair than a strong ecky tae make that fucker anything other than an evil bastard in ma book!

Terry's grin expanded gleefully. — Ye goat tae lit go ay the past, Carl, stoap fightin the auld battles. Is that no what ye eywis say tae me?

Carl Ewart handed a box of records to Terry Lawson. — Jist git a hud ay these.

— Want ays tae clean the fuckin bogs before we go? Terry pulled a face, but complied with the instruction and they headed outside, following Albert Black and the girls.

18

The air was dense and dark as the revellers exited the Cameo on Miami Beach's Washington Avenue, dissolving into a vapid South Florida night. Billy Black couldn't quite believe it as he and Valda Riaz witnessed his grandad being fussed over by some hot pussy, climbing into an SUV followed by the DJ, N-Sign, and some other people in his entourage! Billy and Valda gaped at each other.

Are those hookers Grandpa's going with? Where are they taking him?

Lester sat in the driver's seat and greeted Albert Black, Helena Hulme, Brandi, Carl, and took the box from Terry Lawson, sticking it on the front seat. — Where are we going? Albert Black asked.

— Perty in the Glades. Thaire's a wee sound system gaun oot n Ewart's keeping it real, daein the back-tae-ehs-roots thing.

— I really should go home, Black said, even as he settled

into the vehicle, somehow not wanting to leave, now really desperate for the company of the others.

— No you shouldn't. You're one of the gang now; the main man in the posse, Helena smiled.

— If I'm not being a nuisance . . .

— No way. Carl, tell him.

Black looked in front of him to where Carl Ewart was seated. Helena was massaging his neck and shoulders. The DJ shot a look back at his old nemesis, making it clear that he didn't want Black here. — Mr Black can do what he likes. It makes no odds to me.

Helena raised her eyebrows as Lester started up the SUV and Terry groaned, — Lighten up, Ewart! Ye'd think eh'd jist gie'd ye the fuckin web yesterday. Git ower it fir fuck's sake! Ah goat lashed mair times thin you, n ye dinnae see me gaun aw moosey-faced aboot it. Mind you, he turned to Black, — ye did gie it sair.

Black was disconcerted to feel himself puffing up with this ratification.

— Aye, when you gied the web, ye *gied* the web, if ye ken what ah mean, Terry stressed.

— You were top three, Carl conceded with a rueful smile, — level mibbe wi Masterton, but still behind Bruce by a fair old distance.

— Aye, Bruce in tecky. Terry grimaced at the memory. — That bastard!

Black was deflated. *Bruce. That drunken peasant scumbag: without the ability to string two sentences together.* It was a travesty that such a man was teaching in a secondary school. Bruce would enjoy inflicting punishment for its own sake. But then again, had he, Albert Black, not obtained some sort of stress release from that same violent exercise?

No . . . surely not . . . it was the sin I hated, not the sinner. I always followed the righteous path and loved the sinner . . . but . . . but . . . to smite an enemy, with the vengeful taint of wrath in one's mouth, to watch them crumble before your power, surely that was the device installed in us by the Creator in order that good men could execute just retribution . . .

Or was it Satan, with his cunning wiles, insinuating himself into us, even under the cloak of righteousness? Could it be possible, that even as the Christian soldier wielded his sword in his crusade of right, that he was, at the point of victory, being seduced and subverted by the devil himself?

— Stop here, Carl barked, — I'll just be a minute.

Black noted that they had pulled up outside the hotel he had followed them to the previous day. Ewart got out and quickly vanished through its doors.

Helena was talking to that Lester character, and Black couldn't help but hear Lawson making the same lewd and shameless propositions to this American woman that he did back at the school to the giggling, vacuous girls, almost thirty years ago.

— So we're gaunny be lovers then?

— Maybe.

— Is that a maybe, a definitely maybe, or a maybe definitely, baby?

— You never stop, do you?

— Nup.

Black saw the seedy driver pass back a packet of white powder to Lawson and his companion. It was obviously a drug of some sort. He noted that Helena had the sense to decline this poison. She was truly a lovely young woman. It would have been too much to hope that Lawson and this American slut would have shown the same restraint, and they were soon inhaling little piles of this powder up their noses, from the back of what looked like a house key. Albert Black turned away to the window.

Terry went to offer his old teacher some, then thought better of it. He passed it back to Lester. — Nice one, buddy, game on, he said.

Lawson seemed to become excited as Carl Ewart returned, carrying an electric kettle, a teapot, a jar of honey and some styrofoam beakers.

— Git some ay that ching intae ye, Ewart! Terry Lawson roared.

— No way. Tea's my thing, Carl Ewart smiled.

Black felt the enriching balm of his own magnanimity render him heady, as he exonerated Carl Ewart, while the vehicle pulled off, and powered across the causeway towards central Miami. He had underestimated Ewart, or, more likely, the effect of this Helena girl's influence. *Maybe he was worthy of such love, and maybe I was worthy of Marion's.*

The SUV, with bass-heavy sounds pounding on its stereo, seemed to form part of a night convoy that meandered through Miami. Black looked outside, as the lights of the city suddenly dissolved. He realised that Lawson, obviously intoxicated, was ranting obscenities into his ear.

To his surprise, Albert Black wasn't annoyed, he just felt so tired and confused. And there was a strange, grim comfort in the rhythm, if not the content, of the Edinburgh scheme man's speech. — Ah hud an idea for a new product, so ah wrote tae Guinness in Dublin. Cunts never even got back tae ays: nae fuckin vision. The idea wis fir fizzy Guinness, tae satisfy the new alcopop generation, ken, cause they lap up the fizz. Eftir aw, ye git black velvet: Guinness and champagne. Stout's jist an auld cunt's drink, so it's aw aboot rebrandin. Aye, ye heard it here first, Lawson nodded in conspiracy. — Rebrandin is impor-tant. He dropped his voice. — Ah've even rebranded masel. Tae be honest, ah'd lit masel go. Ah'd pit oan the beef n ah wis happy jist cowpin the same muck-buckets fae the scheme.

Black recalled his wedding, Marion in her white dress. His father, drunk, asking his son where his friend Allister Main was. Vice was always around us. Everywhere. But Lawson was unceasing in his depravity. Black suddenly thought about the Bard; how his verse always comforted in times of stress.

> And sic a night he taks the road in,
> As ne'er poor sinner was abroad in.

— Then ah hud this thought, sort ay one ay they road-tae-Damascus-type moments as you might say, Lawson raved on, — that if ah shed some timber n sterted moisturisin n workin oot, ah could be chasin the premium young minge again. Too fuckin right. A middle-aged gadge has goat assets a young cunt'll never huv. Thaire's plenty young birds whae want an aulder boy that kens ehs wey aroond a lassie's boady. Some burds cannae be daein wi the wham-bam-thank-you-ma'am mentality ay the young cunts. Ah've the Milky Bar Kid tae thank fir that enlightened approach, ah mean, tae tell ye truth, ah wis eywis a sweaty humper, eywis hud the young cunt's approach tae shagging. Jist git a hud ay thum n pound thum intae submission wi auld faithful here. He rubbed at his crotch and licked his lips, one brow tilting skyward. Black gritted his teeth.

Why boastest thou thyself in mischief, O mighty man? the goodness of God endureth continually.

The tongue deviseth mischiefs; like a sharp razor, working deceitfully.

Thou lovest evil more than good; and lying rather than to speak righteousness.

— Aye, whin this boy's batterin intae thum they ken it's aw hands oan fuckin deck awright! Nae chance ay a burd zonin oot n thinkin ay ehr shoapin list, no whin auld faithful here's screwin her erse intae the mattress! But Carl once sais tae ays:

ah make it a golden rule that a lassie needs tae huv at least two clitoral and two vaginal orgasms apiece before ah goes n spills the beans, so tae speak. So ah took that advice oan board n Lean Lawson wis reborn: nae fry-ups n pints ay lager, that shite's a thing ay the past. So the auld Coral Reef flies oaf. Well, ah starts gittin the eye fae the young things, n there ah ah'm, aw they lassies ah'm ridin now, jist like ah wis cowpin thair mas back in the eighties when ah wis oan the juice lorries! Goat a few ay thum intae the auld stag-movie rumpy-pumpy n aw. Cannae beat it. That's what *really* makes ye want tae watch they love handles but, eh. Ken how actors say that the camera adds on pounds? Thir no jokin. But whin ye start the Ian McLagan oan screen, that fairly gies ye the incentive tae keep thum oaf. Cannae knock it: spice ay life.

The girl, the American waitress: Lawson eyed and pawed at her in lewd obscenity as he havered on. It was as well she probably couldn't understand a word he was saying. Or more likely she was as depraved as him. That trickle of sweat that dribbled from the honey skin from her slender neck down to her cleavage. Sin. It was everywhere. *Must not give in. Never give in. Do not let Satan enbeast you!*

They turned off the freeway, down a slip road, surrounded on all sides by darkness. After a while they pulled into a roadside car park, the vehicles lining up around a truck, which opened up at the back to reveal a sound system with a DJ booth. Black assumed it also contained a generator, for as they got out of the car, harsh, throbbing strobe lights, placed around the edges of the truck, pulsed into action, then speakers rumbled like the pipes of an old plumbing system, and sinister trance music gushed into the night. It seemed that it was shaking the large palms and eucalyptus trees around them, but that was probably down to the building wind, as some young men were struggling to erect two mildewed green tents on

aluminium poles onto a patch of impacted ground. The vege-
tation that grew around it buffeted the site, which had obviously
enjoyed past use for this purpose, and Black could see the lights
of the freeway shivering in the distance behind them. The party
was soon in full swing. Swaggering young men, with feminine
reptilian grins, danced with uniformly beautiful girls. — We
party till sunup! a deranged young woman screamed at Black,
her face contorted, doubtlessly due to the same corrupting bounty
of Satan that Lawson had been so keen to ingest.

Black looked around in the swampy darkness. This was the
Everglades. The place seemed wild and dangerous. There was
a looming cadence in the air, as if the night was stalking them,
closing in on this band of dancing, gyrating devil-worshippers.
It was hot and rich with corruption.

*Your country is desolate, your cities are burned with fire: your land,
strangers devour it in your presence . . .*

At the SUV he saw that Carl Ewart was doing something
with an electric kettle, seemingly preparing tea or coffee. The
two men caught each other's eye and exchanged curt, tense nods.
Black looked around and saw Helena standing alone, leaning
against a car bonnet, and moved across to her.

— Are you okay? she asked.

— Yes. It's not the sort of thing I've experienced.

— Don't worry about it, talk to me. I don't have my party
hat on, the jet lag's kicking in, she yawned.

Black again found himself telling her how much he was
missing his wife. It was making Helena think of the life that
she and Carl were hoping to share, but giving her a terrible
sadness that it would all end up in pain and heartbreak. But
then an epiphany gripped her; it wasn't right to feel this way.
She realised that she wasn't just down; she was suffering from
depression. Since her dad's death she'd been dwelling too much
on negative scenarios, and not getting on with her life. It was

for living, not for passing away in obsessive and self-defeating morbid and banal thoughts. She resolved that she would see a doctor. Perhaps do some bereavement counselling.

As the emotions rose in him, Albert Black felt self-indulgent and weak. He must be boring this girl, although she was gracious enough not to show it. Excusing himself, he went to explore.

Passing the SUV, Black noticed that Ewart, who had gone off to the truck, had been making some tea in that pot he'd gone out of his way to procure from the hotel. Perhaps he'd misjudged him. While everyone else seemed to be ingesting all sorts of terrible chemicals, Carl Ewart was doing something respectable. It looked a little like camomile when Black poured it into one of the styrofoam beakers. There was no milk but there was sugar and honey, which he stirred into it, as the elixir was like all herbal teas to his palate, exceedingly nasty, though Marion swore by them. Black headed back to the edge of the dancing crowd, sipping his infusion.

He watched Ewart and Lawson, now dancing with the girls: Helena, looking tired but going through the motions, and the American whose name he kept forgetting. But they were also dancing and having as much fun with each other as they were with their girlfriends. (Though it was surely stretching it to refer to the casual congress between Lawson and the waitress in such terms!) It forcibly struck Black, a lonely outsider, that he had never known a friendship like the one Ewart had with Lawson.

Allister. At the university.

This dredged up an unpleasant memory, but the resulting nausea went beyond that. It dawned on Black that he was feeling sick and his head was spinning. There was an urgent pressing on his bladder. He turned away from the revellers, who seemed to be contorting into unnatural shapes in silhouette, and moved tentatively into dense foliage, in order to find a private spot to urinate. Pushing through some eucalyptus bushes to a clearing, he felt the wet sawgrass under his feet, seeping into his shoes.

It was so dark; he looked back and he could no longer see the strobe, although the sound still followed him. But he could no longer be sure that it was the dance music, it seemed to coming from somewhere inside his head. He felt his throat dry out as his knee clicked and his heartbeat rose. Parting his legs to stabilise himself, he kept most of his weight on the one with the stronger knee, and unzipped himself and started to pee. He had never urinated so much; it wouldn't stop. A convulsion bubbled up from his chest and shook him. He retched, but it was dry, as he'd eaten nothing. He could feel the queasy tea in his guts, but it wouldn't come up. He tried to steady his breathing. His nostrils flared. He wasn't even sure he'd finished pishing, but he put his penis away and felt a gust of wind, which seemed to come from nowhere; it was going through his body like an X-ray.

> *The wind blew as 'twad blawn its last;*
> *The rattling showers rose on the blast;*
> *The speedy gleams the darkness swallow'd;*
> *Loud, deep, and lang the thunder bellow'd:*
> *That night, a child might understand,*
> *The Deil had business on his hand.*

He used to scare William and Christine as children, with a dramatic recitation of this poem. It seemed so long ago, and now they were barely in his life. Like so many, they had become strangers. Why had Allister Main followed him everywhere, like a stupid dog, back at the university? Was it any wonder he had been driven to sin by the unremitting attentions of this sick fool? It had been the whisky; that very first time he'd been drunk. At first some joking around (frivolous laughter, the Trojan Horse of the devil) then indulging in foolish horseplay, then Allister's face on him, their clothes somehow loosened and strewn, then . . . fellating him with his girl's mouth! Albert Black, the young Christian student, even as he screamed in pain and rage, still kept a firm grip of the other boy's head, clasping it to his needy crotch as the seed exploded from him in the grateful cavern of his fellow divinity scholar's throat.

And I'd never asked Marion to do the same, to offer me that terrible pleasure.

Since that horrible evening in the Marchmont student flat, Albert Black seldom drank. One glass of whisky on Burns Night sufficed, the same measure on Hogmanay, and, very occasionally, on his own birthday. But even the unsavoury and long-repressed thoughts couldn't root him, because he was prisoner to an ascending nausea, thick and uncompromising, creeping through him like a dark poison. He retched dry again, raising a faltering hand to his sweating, pounding brow. He could hear no music now, could not turn to get back to the others, surely only a few yards through the patch of eucalyptus bushes, as his legs seemed stuck fast.

What is happening to me?

Why should ye be stricken any more? Ye will revolt more and more: the whole head is sick, and the whole heart faint.

Black didn't know where he was. The bushes, trees, creeping vines and tall grasses were bending into strange shapes, it was as if the swamp was coming to life around him. But there was something else, out here with him, in this terrible wilderness.

At first he could only see the glowing eyes, a burning sulphurous yellow, staring out of the blurry, oily darkness ahead, watching him. Then the low growl of the satanic beast erupted, inhumane, monstrous. The rumble of what might have thunder followed, or perhaps it came from the sound system.

> *There sat auld Nick, in shape o' beast;*
> *A towzie tyke, black, grim, and large,*
> *To gie them music was his charge:*
> *He screw'd the pipes and gart them skirl,*
> *Till roof and rafters a' did dirl.*

Then the beast let out a low hiss. Even as Black felt the skin being stripped from him, he looked into its heinous eyes and, thinking of Marion, began to recite in a calm, even voice as a lightning bolt jabbed in the sky, briefly illuminating the macabre, slouching figure ahead. — It was said that when the cool voice of truth falls into the burning vortex of falsehood there would always be hissing! Perfect love casts off all fear! Innocence rusheth into the sunlight, and asks to be tried, Black declared, almost in song as the tears ripped from his eyes. The retired schoolteacher and old soldier wrenched his heavy legs and stepped forward, fists bunched, and roared into the night, — IT DOES NOT SLINK AWAY AND HIDE!

The creature sank back as if on hunkers, growled, then twisted round and headed off. It looked back once, hissing again, and departed into the bush.

— BEGONE! Black thundered into the darkness as the sound system battered out a steady beat. Then he felt himself sink and fall forward as his knee gave way and he tumbled down into what felt like a dark, wet abyss. There was stillness for a while, before he opened his eyes. Thunder roared and lightning crackled in a mottled sky above him. Rain fell on his face. He struggled and tried to pull himself free from the swampy ground that seemed to be holding him to it by suction. It was claiming him for its own; it was as if he was bleeding into it. With great effort, his hands reached out and pulled on the branches of a bush and he struggled and hoisted himself upright.

He could see lights ahead, but not bring himself to move towards them. Locked onto the bush, he'd stay here. Now it was time to succumb to the dark. To unite with her. He shouted her name, or perhaps thought it loudly.

And Albert Black must have been screaming for a long time or no time at all, he would never know, as Terry, Carl, Brandi and Helena found him, demented, soaked, and holding onto a eucalyptus bush for grim life.

— Albert! Helena shouted.

— Fuck sake . . . wir soaked here. Terry Lawson tried to grab his old teacher, to pull him from the bush and the water he stood in up to his mid-shins. — C'moan tae fuck, ya radge, thaire's alligators n panthers n black bears n aw that oot here!

Black pushed his hand away, and screamed into the night as the rain hammered down on them. — Inspiring bold *John Barleycorn!* What dangers thou canst make us scorn! Wi' tippenny, we fear nae evil; wi' usquabae, we'll face the devil!

There was no way he was going anywhere. He held on in mortal desperation, his crazed eyes bulging.

— He's off his fuckin tits, Carl Ewart said. — Bla – Mis – Albert, did you take that tea? Carl scrambled down beside him. Felt the water rise up his legs. Black saw Ewart's face distort, into that mocking sneer he knew of old. He needed a weapon, something to smite this monster. But there was nothing to hand, and Ewart was no longer a boy. No longer a bad boy. There was a kindness and concern in those eyes of this white-haired man, a glow around him, like the golden halo of sainthood, and a soft voice was urging him. — C'mon, Albert, give me your hand. Let's go and get you dried off, mate.

Then Black saw a frightened young boy, cowering away from him in his office as he produced his tawse. His own son, as a boy, running tearfully out the door. Marion rising, standing in front of him, in order to stop him from pursuing the child. His eyes burned. He miserably reached out and Carl Ewart gripped him under the arm.

— I never meant to hurt you . . . I never meant to hurt anyone . . . Black moaned.

— Never mind that, did you drink that tea? Ewart asked, as Terry assisted them out of the ditch.

— The tea . . . Black puffed, feeling his slimy soaked feet setting down onto firmer ground.

— It's not proper tea, Albert. It'll make you sick. You drank too much of it, Carl said, and put his arm around the old man's frail shoulders, and led him through the bushes, back to the motorcade and into the SUV as torrential rain thrashed on them. Consoled in the back of the car by Helena, Black drifted into some kind of fevered sleep. He woke briefly as they hit the outskirts of Miami, as the slow surge of dawn danced in the eastern sky. Then sleep took him again.

19

One narcotic, the other narcoleptic, the two lovers had talked, tried to sleep, then argued through their exhaustion. Helena Hulme sipped at the cup of Cuban coffee as she reclined on the chaise longue, looking from her feet to Carl Ewart, who sat on the bed, rocked by her disclosure, his head in his hands.

— I feel terrible, he moaned.

— I should have told you, Helena conceded. — I just didn't know how you'd feel about it. I didn't want to be pregnant, Carl. I thought you might try and talk me into having it.

— No way . . . you don't get it, Carl gasped, then fell onto his knees and collapsed in front of her, placing his head on her lap, looking up at her with a sad smile, — I don't feel bad about *that*; you did the right thing. I just feel awful that you had to go to that place alone, go through it all alone.

— I should have told you.

— How could you? I was never there. By email or text? he said sadly, then, suddenly animated, sat up alongside her. — I've been thinking about us. I cannae face another summer in Ibiza, another round of playing records to kids who'll listen to anything if they're fucked up enough. Ah'm no vibing on that shit any more, Helena.

Helena stroked his hair. It was so fine and soft. She idly traced patterns on his scalp.

— Jake's asked me to score his film. I said I would. The money isn't great up front, but if it does well I'll get royalties on the back end. So I'm going to move the studio over to Sydney. If it works out, I'd like to do more of that sort of thing. It means that you'll be close enough to your mum to see her regularly and have her come over.

— But what about your mum? She's older, and our Ruthie lives close by mine . . .

— We have to accept that, for whatever reason, your mum needs you right now, more than mine needs me. Let's try it for a couple of years. If your mother settles down and adjusts we can think about London after, or even LA if I make it big, he smiled.

Helena wrapped her arms around his thin torso. — I love you, Carl.

— I love you . . . and I want to be with you. I don't want to be away all the time and just get fucked up cause you're not around. I'm too old for that; it's boring me. I'm forty now; dance music is a young punter's game. It's time for me to phase it out.

— Okay, she said in gratitude, as they felt the tension between them lanced like a boil, — let's talk about it later. We should go to bed.

— I'll never sleep.

Helena felt the hit of the coffee. The jet lag had tricked her. Exhausted a few minutes previously, she was now buzzing again.

— Me neither. Let's go out and lie in the sun, maybe force down some breakfast.

— Okay. I'll take the factor twenty, in case we fall asleep doon there.

20

Albert Black woke up in a strange hotel room. He was fully dressed and lying on top of the bed. The bottom of his trousers felt damp. The room still reverberated in the light, but the pulsing was milder now. He sensed it was over. Satan had gone from his body, though it was still in shock from his infiltration. The tea. *Why had the garden of God always been littered with Satan's bitter fruits?*

He removed his spectacles and rubbed his eyes. Replaced them. Standing up shakily, deferential to his apostate knee, he headed downstairs. Passing by the back of the hotel, he looked out and could see Carl and Helena lying by the pool: him in shorts, her in a two-piece blue bikini. He was about to slip away but they saw him and beckoned him over.

— Are you okay? Carl asked, sitting up on his lilo, as Helena smiled and waved as if nothing untoward had happened.

— I was intoxicated . . . that tea . . . I fear I made a fool of myself.

Carl rose, and sat at a table, inviting Black to do the same. — We all did, but who cares? There are more important things to worry about than somebody getting off their faces, Albert.

Black slumped miserably into the seat, and shook his head in a rueful manner. — I don't know what to do . . .

Carl nodded to an approaching waiter carrying a silver tray. — Stay here and have some breakfast with us.

— I can't take any more of other people's hospitality . . . someone gave up their room for me last night.

— That was Terry.

— Law – Terry. How charitable of him. I feel terrible depriving him. Where did he . . . ? Black faltered as he saw Ewart's smile widen.

— I think he was alright. In fact, you probably helped him out.

— I don't know . . . Black said, shaking his head, but Carl Ewart had poured him some orange juice and was putting in a request for the waiter to bring food. Above, the pale cloudless sky seemed to invite serenity, and he allowed himself to succumb to the growing lassitude in his bones.

— You have to go and see your family in a bit, Helena said, joining them at the table, a sarong wrapped around her shoulders, — they'll be worried about you.

— Yes. It's just been so difficult. We don't really get on, my son and I.

— You should try and sort that one out, Carl Ewart said sadly, suddenly thinking of his own deceased father. — Or you'll miss the things you never said to each other. So will he.

— Yes, Black conceded. There wasn't much time.

— So say them. You've lived a life together. Whether you believe in an afterlife or you don't, the life you shared has got to mean something, he said, feeling Helena's eyes on him.

— I'll drink to that, she said, raising her glass of orange juice.

Black regarded his former pupil. — You are all being so kind to me, Carl. I mean, back at the school . . . I'm sorry if I –

Carl Ewart raised his hand to silence his old teacher. — Albert, I could have gone to Eton or Rugby and I'd probably have been just the same. Some of us will never be happy unless we've got something straight to kick against. Thank you for being that force, that influence, and I mean it. But you might want to try being a wee bit kinder to yourself, and the people around you.

Black smiled in terse recognition. It was true. Marion would want him to have a relationship with William. And Christine. He knew she lived with another woman, and that unnatural act of sin wasn't something he could ever endorse, but you had to love the sinner. As for the sin itself, it was up to the Lord to pass judgement. He would go to Sydney and see her. What else would he possibly do with his savings? There *was* a purpose to life. Those fences had to be mended.

They ate tentatively. The strips of bacon with eggs over easy, the fruit and croissants with jam and butter, all seemed too vast for constricted stomachs. The orange juice and the water was much more welcome. Black regarded the happy couple, a now middle-aged man with his more youthful girl-friend. — Did you get the name N-Sign from the pub up by the castle?

— No. Carl Ewart looked at Albert Black as if he was crazy.
— *You* told me, at the school. First day at reggie, I told you my name and you told me the story of Charles Ewart.

— Yes . . . you remembered that?

— Of course. How he took the standard of the Eagle from the French at Waterloo. It was a great story and you told it really well. I walked out of that class feeling ten feet tall, because

I had the same name as this big, heroic Scottish warrior. Later on I looked him up in the library. He became my hero. He was born in Kilmarnock, that's where my dad's family came from.

— So you might be a direct descendant, Black said, unable to keep the excitement from his voice.

— It would be nice to think so, but it's a very common name down there. But whether it's the case or not, it was an inspiring tale and it made me feel very special. It gave me a good stage name with a story behind it. So thanks for that.

Black nodded thoughtfully, gave a slight but appreciative smile, and nibbled on a croissant.

They sat chatting in the morning sun, struggling with the food, though all managing to get something into their stomachs. When they had finished, Albert Black rose and said, — I shall return to my family now. But I would really like to invite you both to dinner, or lunch, at their home. My grandson is a fan of your music and he'd love to meet you.

Carl looked at Helena. — We'd be delighted.

— For sure.

— Tomorrow night at seven? Black suggested.

— Sound by us, Helena said. — Carl?

— Aye, great. I've nothing on then.

— Good. And thank you again for looking after me.

— No worries. We're old school, Carl Ewart smiled, and he watched his former schoolteacher smile in wan appreciation before turning and walking, a little shakily for the first few steps, then, like the old soldier he was, striding through the tropical garden, round the pool. As he got to the hotel back door, Black turned round and called out, gravely, pointing the finger, — Remember, Ewart, seven o'clock means precisely that! You know what I'm like for punctuality! And for the first time in a long while, something approaching a grin came over the old man's face.

— Receiving you loud and clear, Carl Ewart smiled and stiffly saluted his former teacher. He couldn't quite bring himself to say 'sir' but this time the old boy didn't seem to mind.